Mary and the Bear

Published by Phaze Books
Also by Zena Wynn

The Contract

A Matter of Trust

Illicit Attraction

Cincinnati, Ohio

www.Phaze.com

Mary and the Bear

A novel of erotic romance by

ZENA WYNN

Cincinnati, Ohio

A Phaze Production
Phaze Books
6470A Glenway Avenue, #109
Cincinnati, OH 45211-5222
Phaze is an imprint of Mundania Press, LLC.

To order additional copies of this book, contact:
books@phaze.com
www.Phaze.com

Cover art © 2008, Skyla Dawn Cameron
Edited by Shell Dowdey

ISBN-13: 978-1-60659-137-6
First Print Edition – March, 2009
Printed in the United States of America

10 9 8 7 6 5 4 3 2 1

Chapter One

Mary Elizabeth Brown sat in the crowded church, numb with grief and an assortment of other complicated emotions she just didn't have the energy to examine closely. The last few days had been a hellish whirlwind of activity, culminating today as they gathered to pay their last respects to the woman laying in the casket—her twin sister, Barbara Ann Brown-Remington, more affectionately known as Babs.

Every now and then, stray comments drifted to Mary Elizabeth's ears above the softly playing music.

"Oh, no."

"What a shame, she was so young."

"She was such a beautiful person. An angel, really."

That last comment almost pierced through the numbness and brought a smile to her face. *An angel? If only they knew*, she thought. Babs thrived on being wicked, on pushing the limits. Unfortunately, it was Mary Elizabeth who usually ended up suffering because of her schemes.

Mary Elizabeth allowed her gaze to drift around the church. The first two pews on the right were reserved for family. Her sister's husband of seven years, Charles A. Remington, III, sat the end of the pew, near the center aisle and closest to the casket. Seated next to him were her mother, Susan Brown, and then her father, Richard. From where Mary Elizabeth was seated, at the opposite end of the pew, huddled in the corner, she could see that the knuckles of her mother's hand were white from the grip she had on her father's hand. Her other hand, which was placed on Charles's knee in a silent show of support, was also clenched. There was no other family present.

Lying in the casket, Babs looked like the angel she'd been compared to—long, naturally blonde hair, a porcelain complexion, and stunning blue eyes hid behind closed eyelids framed with long eyelashes. With her figure, she could have been a swimsuit model. She'd loved showing off her long, toned body and large breasts. She'd played the role of the naive, beautiful blonde so well that even now not many realized that behind that china-doll appearance was a very, shrewd mind.

Only two people knew the true nature behind the angelic look, Babs and herself. Mary Elizabeth would be taking that truth with her to her own grave. No one would believe her stories any way. Babs had perfected her angelic act while still in the cradle. Her parents had certainly been fooled. They'd worshipped the ground she'd walked on. And her husband? Totally clueless as to the true nature of the woman he'd married.

As far as Charles was concerned, his marriage was the stuff of fairytales, with him in the role of the rich, handsome prince who rescued the beautiful yet poor princess from her life of drudgery, giving her a life of luxury. In return, the grateful princess had dedicated her every moment to showering the love she felt for the handsome prince by seeing to his every need.

If only that were true. The reality was that the princess died while sneaking away to meet her likewise married boss for an illicit weekend affair. There were only two people left alive in this world who knew where she'd really been heading, and neither one of them were talking. One of them, because he had too much to lose. As for herself, Babs had sworn her to secrecy. Just another one of the hundreds she'd kept for Babs over their thirty-two years of life.

Though they were twins, Mary Elizabeth was the exact opposite of her sister in appearance and nature. While Babs was tall, standing five-eleven in her stocking feet; Mary Elizabeth was short, only five-four. Babs had long flowing hair that was so fine it resembled a baby's, while Mary Elizabeth's hair was thick, coarse, and perpetually frizzy. So opposite were they in appearance that most people had to be told they were sisters, never mind twins. She couldn't count the number of times she'd heard, "*This* is your sister?"

The service had started while she reminisced. Mary Elizabeth came to attention only to realize they were at the part of the service she dreaded most. It was time to walk around for one last view of the body. Time to say her final goodbyes. Charles was against having a graveside ceremony, for which she would be eternally grateful. First, the family would be escorted past the casket. Afterwards, they were to line up in the vestibule to greet the mourners and accept their condolences. Then, she would finally be able to go home, and hopefully get some rest.

She hadn't had a moment to herself since she'd received the phone call informing her of Babs' death. Charles called her first, leaving it to Mary Elizabeth to break the news to her parents. Upon hearing the news, her mother had to be tranquillized. Her father just sat there, gazing at nothing. She'd spent the last week at her parents' house, running interference, answering the phones and taking care of her parents, scared to leave them alone for any length of time. When she wasn't busy with them, she was helping Charles.

Charles went first. He stood stoically by the casket, the blank expression on his face masking his feelings as he took one final look at his wife. Mary Elizabeth's heart hurt for him. If the last week had been hard on anyone, it was Charles. He'd been a rock throughout this whole ordeal, but Mary Elizabeth knew he had to be hurting, losing his wife so suddenly. When he'd stood there longer than seemed warranted, the funeral director discreetly urged him to move on. They were on a timed schedule and there were still a lot of people waiting for their turn.

Next came her mother, supported on one side by her father and on the other by a funeral attendant. During the service, she'd held it together surprisingly well until she stood next to the casket. With a loud cry, she threw herself across the open casket, sobbing. "God, why? Why did it have to be my baby? If one of them had to die, why couldn't it have been Mary Elizabeth?"

Her father and the attendant pulled on the distraught woman, struggling to get her to release the casket and move on. Her father whispered something into her mother's ear that Mary Elizabeth couldn't quite hear over all of the wailing her mother was doing. This continued for some time until her mother finally nodded at whatever he was saying and released her hold, allowing them to lead her away.

Mary Elizabeth went rigid as pain and embarrassment pierced through the shield around her emotions, making her want to crawl into a hole and hide. She was grateful for the veil she wore that partially covered her face. She could feel sympathetic glances sliding her way in the heavy silence of the church. She knew that she wasn't her mother's favorite, but it was something entirely different to hear her mother's declaration, and to have everyone else there hear it as well. It was beyond humiliating.

With the ease of years of practice, Mary Elizabeth shoved the hurt deep down inside. Then, wrapping her dignity around her like a cloak, she stepped up to the casket. She looked impassively at the body lying there. She didn't think of it as her sister. Her sister had been vibrantly alive, not this wooden thing. A stray thought crossed her mind. *Maybe now I can have my own life.* She pushed the disturbing thought aside, ashamed to be having thoughts like that when her sister was dead. She walked away from the casket before she could be prompted and joined her family in the vestibule.

Standing in the receiving line with the others, she greeted mourners as they left the sanctuary. There were long-time family friends, friends of Babs and Charles, neighbors, co-workers, and country club members all wishing to express their sorrow at the family's loss. There were so many people that they all began to blur. She shook hands by rote, with whichever person was standing before her.

That is, until she heard a familiar voice and looked into the face of the one person she was happy to see. Kiesha Morgan stood before her. Standing protectively at her side was an amazing specimen of manhood, clearly devoted to her. Kiesha was more than her boss. She was her friend. Kiesha owned a chain of consignment stores where Mary Elizabeth was employed as one of the assistance sales managers.

"Mary Elizabeth, I'm so sorry for your loss. I wish I could have been here sooner." Kiesha was in the middle of relocating to a small town in North Carolina and was only back in Pirate's Cove tying up a few loose ends.

"Thank you. Just you being here means more than you realize." Of all the people here, Kiesha was the only person to whom she really felt close.

"I know this is neither the time nor the place, but when you get the chance, give me a call. I have some business I want to discuss with you."

"Okay." She wanted to know more but like Kiesha said, this was neither the time nor the place. Already the line was backing up and people were getting impatient. After giving Kiesha a final hug, she allowed her to move on. After about an hour, the church was finally empty and the family was free to go home. She was glad to see the last of them go. Her feet were killing her.

"Are you coming by the house to get something to eat, or going to your parents? There's plenty and you need to eat," Charles said. Though they weren't close, Charles took his role as brother-in-law seriously.

"Neither. I'm heading home. Tomorrow's a work day and I have a lot to do between now and then." Besides, if she didn't get some time alone soon she was going to scream.

"How can you go to work as if nothing has happened?" her mother asked in a shrill voice. "My Babs is dead," her mother wailed, bringing her handkerchief to her eyes again to mop up the fresh flood of tears.

"Susan, leave the girl alone. She's got to earn a living. There's nothing she can do for Babs now." Mary Elizabeth was stunned that her dad came to her defense, something he'd never done before in her life.

Taking advantage of her mother's shock, she gave her father and Charles a hug, and squeezed her mom's hand before quickly walking out the door. God, she was glad that was over. These last few days had been trying. Maybe now things could get back to normal. Well, as normal as possible with Babs gone. It was still hard to believe. There was a hole in her heart where her sister used to be.

Unlike most twins, she and Babs hadn't had the most loving of relationships. She'd loved her sister but couldn't always say that she'd liked her. Mary Elizabeth never imagined Babs would die. Babs had always been there, and Mary Elizabeth assumed she always would. She got in her car and headed home. Like her father said, there was nothing she could do for Babs now. It was time to pick up the dangling pieces of her life.

* * * *

Glad to be home, she changed out of her dress into a comfortable pair of old, ripped jeans and a baggy, faded t-shirt. She looked in the mirror and sighed. As usual, she looked like a cleaning lady. Mother and Babs were always complaining about her distinct lack of style.

Mary Elizabeth desperately wanted to lie down and get some sleep, but she was too wired and her apartment was a mess. Cleaning would keep her hands busy and her mind quiet, she hoped. Starting with the kitchen, she loaded the dishwasher and then wiped down the countertops. From there, she worked her way through the rest of the apartment, cleaning everything in sight and as she cleaned, she did her laundry.

Her apartment was so small; it didn't take long to finish. Casting about for something else to do, she remembered Kiesha and gave her a call.

"Mary Elizabeth, I didn't expect to hear from you this soon."

"I came straight home after the funeral and cleaned. I know I need to rest but I'm too wired. I go back to work tomorrow." Even now Mary Elizabeth was pacing around in her living room, unable to sit still.

"You know you don't have to return to work now if you don't want to. Feel free to take all the time you need."

"I'm ready to go back. Sitting around thinking about what happened will only make it worse."

"Well, I offered. If you change your mind later, the offer still stands. I know what you're going through." She sure did, Mary Elizabeth thought. It was only a few years ago that Kiesha lost her mom. "But that's not why I asked you to call. You know that I'm opening another store in North Carolina, right?"

"Yes." She heard about it from one of the other managers at the store where she worked.

"I want you to be the manager. It would mean relocating, but I'd be willing to pay all of your moving expenses. I have to warn you, this store is located in a really small town up in the mountains."

"I don't know what to say. It sounds wonderful, but the timing ... With Babs gone, I'm going to be needed at home now more than ever."

"Mary Elizabeth, that's exactly why you should leave. You need to get away from your family. It's the only way you'll ever have a life of your own. Your mom doesn't depend on you, she uses you, and you allow it. Remember how you hated being compared to Babs? If you come to Refuge, you'll be somewhere no one has ever heard of her. You'll be out from under her shadow and finally be able to be yourself, without interference from your family."

"I'll think about it. I promise." It really sounded appealing and at any other time, she'd have jumped on the opportunity.

"Take all the time you need, but don't take *too* long. I haven't told the other managers what I'm about to tell you. The guy with me at the funeral? His name is Alex. We're getting married soon and already expecting our first child. I'm going to need a lot of help getting the new store up and running, and of course, I really want my best friend with me."

"Kiesha, that's great! I'm so happy for you. I didn't even know you were seeing anyone."

"I wasn't. It's happening extremely fast, but we're very happy. Anyway, that's what's behind the promotion. I really need help and you're perfect for the job. Also, the timing is perfect for you. I don't want to push, so I'll stop talking now. Think about it and let me know."

"Okay, I'll let you know real soon what my answer is." Her other line beeped and Mary Elizabeth looked at the caller's ID. "Kiesha, got to go. I have to take this call."

"Talk to you later. Bye."

"Bye." She clicked over. "Mother?"

"Mary Elizabeth, your father and I have been talking. Now that Babs is gone, we think it's time for you to move back home. Neither one of us are getting any younger. It won't be long before we'll need someone to take care of us."

"Mother, you're only fifty-three and Dad's not even sixty. Both of you are in perfect health. It could be another twenty years before you need someone looking after you, possibly longer."

"We're healthy *now*, but that could change overnight. You're not getting any younger yourself. If you had managed to get a husband and have children, I wouldn't ask this of you. I'd understand that your family needed you, but you don't, and at your age it's doubtful you ever will."

"*Mother*! I'm only thirty-two. I have plenty of time to get married and have kids."

"If you were as beautiful as my Babs, I'd say that was true, but you're not. In fact, you're rather plain looking, bless your heart. You take after your father's side. Then, there's your size. How many times have I told you if you'd just lose weight, you might be able to attract a man's attention? No, it's time to be reasonable and realize that you'll never find a man to marry you. Whatever small chance you had of attracting a husband is gone."

A knock sounded at the door. "Mother, there's someone at the door. I need to go. I'll speak with you later." Thank God for whoever was at the door. She just didn't have the energy to deal with her mother right now.

"Don't forget what I said. We'll expect you here soon. Just throw out your furniture. Most of it's trash anyway. Where you got your taste in furniture from, I swear I don't know."

Another knock sounded at the door. "I've got to go now, Mother. *Goodbye*."

"Yes, yes, fine. See you later."

Mary Elizabeth heaved a sigh of relief as she disconnected the call and walked to the door. Looking through the peephole, she was surprised to see Charles standing there. She opened the door and stepped back, allowing him to enter. "What are you doing here?"

Charles indicated the box in his hands. "Since you didn't come to the house and eat, I brought you some food. I have way more than I can eat by myself. I offered to take some around to your parents, but they have just as much food there."

Mary Elizabeth led the way into the kitchen. "Put it down here on the countertop. If your kitchen looks anything like my parents, you have enough food to last a month, if not longer."

"This wasn't the only reason I came. I couldn't take another moment in that house. It's so empty, the memories are getting to me." He'd changed out of his suit into a pair of snug fitting jeans and white Polo shirt that showed off his lean athletic build. Charles was an extremely attractive man, with his golden blond hair and baby blue eyes.

"I'm sorry, Charles. It's rough for all of us right now, but eventually, it will get better. Let's go into the living room and sit down. Have you eaten? Would you like anything to drink?" Mary Elizabeth put away the food. She'd eat later when she had more of an appetite.

"I don't suppose you have any beer?"

If the smell of his breath was any indicator, Charles had already had enough to drink. "No, sorry. I rarely drink. Your choices are juice, water, milk, or soda."

"I'll take a soda." She grabbed two sodas out of the fridge and joined him in the living room; glad she'd cleaned up. She definitely wasn't expecting company. She searched for something to say. "The service turned out really nice."

"Yeah, it was more than that bitch deserved."

"Um, excuse me?" Mary Elizabeth's gaze stopped bouncing around the room and locked onto Charles. She couldn't have heard correctly.

"I said it was more than she deserved. The bitch was

14

cheating on me with her boss."

Mary Elizabeth said nothing, though inside, she was shocked. Charles knew about the affair?

When she didn't respond or act surprised, he said, "You knew about it, didn't you? You knew she was cheating on me with that scumbag boss of hers."

Mary Elizabeth debated over what to say. She could admit to knowing the truth, but she'd promised Babs and it would go against every principle she had.

"Don't bother trying to lie. I can see the truth on your face. I should have known she would tell you about it. She's used you for years to cover for her."

"I don't know what to say." There was a part of Mary Elizabeth that felt guilty. If she'd tried a little harder, would she have been able to talk Babs out of what she was planning? If she had, maybe Babs would be alive today.

Charles left the window he was standing by and sat beside her on the couch, picking up her hands and holding them in his own. "Just tell me, why did she do it? I have to know. What did he have that I didn't? What did I do to make her turn to another man?"

"Charles, Babs didn't give me a reason. She wasn't big on explaining herself or her actions." Why did Babs do any of the things she did? That was one thing Mary Elizabeth had never been able to figure out.

"I can't believe I wasted so much time with that faithless bitch. You know, she was the reason we never had kids. She didn't want to ruin her figure. Never mind what I wanted. I made a big mistake when I didn't marry you. I should have known what she was like the night she seduced me, her own sister's fiancé. Instead, I was flattered that she wanted me so much. What a fool! I fell right into her hands."

"Charles, if you'd really loved me, Babs wouldn't have been able to seduce you. We were never more than good friends who happened to become engaged. Didn't it seem strange to you that we never had sex, yet we were planning on getting married? No, you didn't make a mistake. You and Babs were meant to be together. She was a much better wife for you than I would have been." Mary Elizabeth thought back to a recent conversation she and Babs had concerning kids. Babs had been scared that if she'd given Charles the children he wanted, it would have taken his attention away from her. No sense explaining that to Charles now.

While she was speaking, Charles moved closer, placed his arm around her shoulders and pulled her against his chest. "I don't know what I would do without you, Mary Elizabeth. You've always been good to me, even after all that's happened between us. I can always count on your support. Why the hell didn't I marry you? You would have never cheated on me. We could have been happily married with our two-point-five children if it hadn't been for Babs." Before she could respond, he lowered his head and kissed her. Held securely in his arms, she froze, not knowing what to do. In truth, she was shocked.

When she didn't respond to his kiss, he moved from her mouth and placed kisses all over her face. Turning her head to the side, she tried to get her hands up between them to push him away, but they were trapped by her sides. "Charles, stop."

He began kissing her neck. She wiggled, trying to get away from him. "Charles, stop it! You're not yourself right now. Don't do anything we'll both regret."

He tried to kiss his way down to her chest, but they were pressed too close together. What a time for her not to be wearing a bra! Moving more forcefully, she threw herself back, attempting to break his hold on her. At the same time, he unexpectedly loosed his grip. As a result, all she succeeded in doing was landing flat on her back on the couch. Charles quickly alighted on top of her.

She could feel his erection against her thigh. This

couldn't be happening. She was not sitting in her living room fighting off a drunken pass from her sister's husband. Damn, she was getting angry. She didn't need this crap on top of everything else. Granted, the man had just buried his wife and probably wasn't thinking straight, but she was his sister-in-law, not some floozy from a bar.

"Charles," she said sharply, "let me go! You're drunk. You need to go home."

"I'm not drunk. I know what I'm doing. Let me show you how good it can be between us." He latched his mouth onto her t-shirt covered breast while trying to pry her legs open with his thigh. Enough was enough. She lifted her leg up, kneeing him in the groin. Not hard enough damage, but definitely hard enough to get his attention.

"I said, NO!" She shoved him and jumped to her feet as he rolled off of her onto the floor, clasping his balls. "You need to go. Now!"

Slowly he got to his feet and hobbled to the door, still clutching himself. When he drew even with her, he stopped. "This isn't over between us. I know you think this is the grief and alcohol talking, but it's not. I've known for a long time now that I made a mistake. Now that Babs is no longer a concern, I intend to have you like I would've if I hadn't been so stupid."

"Goodbye, Charles." She opened the door wide, a hint for him to leave. Giving her one last look to show how determined he was, he slowly walked out. Closing the door with a thump behind him, she leaned her back against it and closed her eyes, tired beyond belief.

Damn, what a day. First there was the funeral, then the call from mother, and now Charles. She could only hope this Charles thing was temporary. But her mother? That was a different story. Mary Elizabeth always found it difficult to tell her mother no. It was a habit she'd developed as a child when she'd been willing to do anything to gain her mother's attention and approval.

What was she going to do? The picture of herself old and gray, at the beck and call of her demanding mother flashed through her mind, causing her to shudder in fear. Whatever it took, she had to keep that from happening. Like a light bulb going off in her head, she remembered Kiesha's offer. What a godsend! Someone upstairs was looking out for her. Picking up the phone, Mary Elizabeth dialed her number. "Kiesha, it's me. I accept. When do I leave?"

Chapter Two

The scenery in the mountains was just amazing. Too bad she was too tired to enjoy it. Mary Elizabeth was mentally and physically exhausted. She'd broken the news to the family the next day, during their weekly, Sunday dinner get-together. In hindsight, maybe she should have waited, but there was no time to delay. The longer she waited, the more time her mother had to wear her down.

Her mother didn't take the news of her moving well. To say her reaction was unpleasant was putting it mild. She went ballistic. "Mary Elizabeth Brown, I can't believe you would do something like this. How can you be so selfish? You know with your sister gone, we need you now more than ever. Who's going to cook Sunday dinner? Who's going to drive me to my hair appointments and bridge games? Who's supposed to take our clothing to the dry cleaner? You know we depend on you."

"Mother, you and Daddy don't need me. You have a brand new car that you're perfectly capable of driving. You'll be just fine and don't forget about Charles. You know you can call him if you need anything. North Carolina isn't that far. I'll still come home for visits. Between phone calls and emails, it will be like I'm still here."

Nothing Mary Elizabeth said pacified her.

Her mother was dead set against her leaving and did everything in her power to talk her out of it. She got her friends involved. Mary Elizabeth's phone rang off of the hook with people calling to talk her out of it. She couldn't go anywhere in town without someone stopping her to express their opinion of her actions. Her mother even complained to their pastor and then he was on her case as well.

If it hadn't been for her father, Mary Elizabeth would have caved under all of the pressure. Just when she was ready to give in, call Kiesha and tell her she wouldn't be coming after all, her father had a little talk with her.

"Mary Elizabeth, I know I haven't been the best father to you girls. I let your mother have her way because it was easier to give in than to fight for what I wanted. I should have stood up to her more often, especially about her treatment of you. I realized that when Babs died. Don't be like me. Fight for what you want. Take advantage of this opportunity. Do whatever you have to do to get away from here and experience life. You've spent enough of your life catering to the whims of this family. It's time you did something for yourself."

Mary Elizabeth pulled her thoughts from the past and consulted the map. She was getting close and needed to pay attention if she didn't want to get lost. Kiesha said Refuge was tucked out of the way and hard to find, and this hazy twilight that made it seem later than it was didn't help. She tried to leave early so it would still be light when she reached her destination, but Charles showed up at her apartment this morning in one last determined bid to get her to stay, delaying her departure.

Finally, she spotted the last turnoff. From here it was a straight shot into town. Alex, Kiesha's fiancé, made arrangements for her to rent the only available apartment in town. It was located above Refuge's only eating establishment, which was probably why it was sitting empty. Not many people would want to live above a place that was noisy and always smelt like food. She was too happy to have a place of her own to care.

An hour later she pulled into a parking space in front

of the crowded diner. The sign above it read, "Eat at Moe's." Someone had a really strange sense of humor. Hugh Mosely, the owner of the apartment, was expecting her. She'd been instructed to ask for him in the diner.

After locking the truck, she walked inside. Several people stopped what they were doing to gawk at her. Spotting the waitress, she walked over to her. Her nametag read Cyndi. "Excuse me. Can you tell me where I can find Hugh?"

Cyndi arched one eyebrow, looked her up and down and then turned away, dismissing her as unimportant. "Hugh! Someone to see you," she hollered, then went back to flirting with the male customers at the counter.

"I'll be there in a sec." A deep voice that sent shivers down her spine came from the kitchen area. Around her, she could hear customers speculating what her business with Hugh might be.

"Who wants me?" She turned at the sound of the voice behind her. Holy moly! A great big mountain of a man was coming toward her. He was tall, very tall and built like a linebacker. The closer he came, the bigger he grew and the more her head tipped back to take him all in. Good Lord, and she'd thought Alex was big. He must have been in the kitchen for he was wearing a white apron and wiping his hand on a towel. His jet-black hair was pulled back into a queue. From this angle, she couldn't tell how long it was.

He was an attractive man, despite or perhaps because of his size. He had high cheekbones and a dusky complexion that betrayed his Native American ancestry. His nose was long and sharp and his lips were sensuously full.

She attempted to pull her sluggish mind together. His mammoth size had briefly shocked her out of her weariness, but now it was all rushing back. "Me," she croaked. Clearing her throat, she tried again. "I mean, I was told to see you about the apartment upstairs?"

"Are you Mary Elizabeth?"

God, she loved his voice. It was deep like Barry White's and made her feel all shivery inside. "Yes."

"Bring your vehicle around back. There's a stairway to the apartment. I'll meet you with the keys." That said, he turned and walked away.

Okay, obviously a man of few words. Ready to get settled in after the long drive, she trudged back out to the truck to do as he instructed. She backed out of the parking space, drove around to the back of the diner, and parked near the bottom of the stairs. According to Alex, the apartment was furnished, which was a big plus. Less stuff she needed to transport. Her truck was loaded with clothes and personal items that she couldn't bear to part with, and of course, her expensive cookware. The rest of her things she'd placed on consignment at the store back home.

Hugh was waiting at the bottom of the stairs as promised. Turning off the engine, she grabbed her purse and jump out of the truck. He led the way up the stairs, talking as he went. "It's a two bedroom apartment, fully furnished. The furniture is old and the place needs a new coat of paint, but the heat and air work just fine. Brand new appliances and water heater. Anything don't work, you let me know."

He opened the door and motioned her inside. "I'm downstairs in the diner most of the time. Rent is due on the first, no later than the fifth. You need an extension, you talk to me and we'll work something out. Rent is three hundred a month plus a hundred dollar deposit. Feel free to fix the place up any way you like. God knows it needs it. Any questions?"

"You have a lease for me to sign?" He didn't have any paperwork in his hands. She wanted to get everything settled tonight.

"No lease needed. Alex says you're good people and

that's enough for me. Here are your keys. If you lock yourself out, I keep a spare set downstairs in the office. If you'd like to eat in the diner, tenants get a fifty percent discount. Come down tonight when you finish unloading and eat, on the house. By the way, utilities are included in the rent. Can't separate them from the diner below so you won't be getting a bill. Stove's gas. Hope that won't be a problem. Phone's already on. Number's listed beside it."

With that, he dropped the keys in her hand, took one last look around and headed out the door. For such a big man, he moved quickly and quietly. She couldn't even hear him on the stairs as he descended.

Looking around at what was to be her new home, she realized she had a lot of work to do. The place was definitely a fixer-upper. A few coats of paint would go a long way toward sprucing it up. You could tell it had been several years since anyone had lived there.

Under the tiredness, there was a tiny spark of excitement growing. She'd always liked do-it-yourself projects and now she could indulge. She'd done it. She'd moved, and now she had two weeks to get settled into her new place before reporting to work.

A brief look at her watch showed it was almost six PM. She made herself get moving. There was the truck to unload, the bed to make and some cleaning to be done before she could call it a night. Groceries would have to wait until tomorrow. Good thing she'd packed a few things and stored them in a cooler for the trip. They should suffice until she could get to the store.

Trudging down the stairs, she made the first of many trips to the truck. She doubted she'd get everything unloaded tonight, but at least she'd have the essentials. One thing for sure, after all of this, she shouldn't have any problems sleeping.

It was close to eight o'clock when she finished. She was deeply satisfied with all she'd accomplished today. It had been a long day. She was exhausted, but there were still a few things to do before she could call it a night. She cleaned the bathroom, made the bed and unpacked the few essentials that she'd need in the morning.

That done, Mary Elizabeth gave a sigh of relief. She considered going down to the dinner for some real food, but was too tired. She fixed a sandwich and ate it standing up at the kitchen counter. Now that she wasn't moving as much, she realized it was cold in the apartment. After searching for a few minutes, she managed to find the thermostat and turn on the heat. She made sure everything was locked up tight, turned off the lights and went into the bedroom.

She grabbed her nightclothes and headed into the bathroom for a quick shower. She really wanted to soak in the surprisingly large tub, but was afraid she'd fall asleep and drown. Rushing through her shower, she dressed for bed and turned in for the night.

Normally she had problems sleeping in unfamiliar beds and strange surroundings. She prayed that tonight it wouldn't be an issue. She needed sleep. In the last few weeks since Babs died, she'd only napped. If she didn't get any rest tonight, she'd break down and buy some sleeping pills.

As she was falling asleep, her thoughts drifted back to her new landlord. What a strange man. He was appealing, but not handsome in the traditional sense. Grandma Pete would have said that his face had character. Her last thought would have shocked her if she'd been more alert. She wondered if it were true what they said about men with big hands and feet.

* * * *

Hugh glanced through the open window of the kitchen into the dining room every time the door opened.

He wondered when his new tenant would show up. It didn't sit well with him that he'd left her to unload all of the boxes he'd seen piled on the back of her truck by herself. Unfortunately, he had a diner to run and the food wouldn't cook itself.

For a human, she did an admirable job of hiding her reaction to his size. People quivered with fear upon first seeing him. They equated his largeness with violence. Then, there were the women. The ones whose eyes would measure the size of his body before falling to his crotch like they had x-ray vision. Those wanted to see if his penis was a match for the rest of him. It was, but they'd never know. Aggressive women were not attractive to him.

He knew his size was intimidating. It was something he used to his advantage when needed, like while he served in the military. Like all were-bears, he was very large and very strong. In bear form, he was over five hundred pounds of pure muscle. Despite his appearance, he was a gentle man until riled. Fortunately, it took a lot to spark his temper.

One more hour and he could pack up and go home. Again his thoughts wondered back to his tenant. She was a little bitty thing. He admitted to himself that she probably didn't appear small to anyone else, but it was all comparatively speaking. He was six-seven and weighed in at over three hundred pounds of solid muscle. To him, most women were small, especially this one that barely managed to come up to his sternum.

This one managed to bring out his protective instincts. There was a sadness in her eyes that punched him right in the gut. He didn't know what her story was, but could tell she'd recently been through the wringer. If her eyes hadn't given her away, the dark circles under them and her pallor would have. He made his spiel about the apartment as short as possible because she was so tired,

25

she'd swayed on her feet. It made him want to gather her close and tell her everything would be alright.

He would have to pick her up to kiss her. The thought stopped him in his tracks. *Where had that come from?* He couldn't remember the last time a woman managed to catch his interest sexually. The hours he put in at the diner were long. He had neither the time nor the energy for a relationship. Yes, he had needs but he was past the age where he needed sex just for the sake of sex. He was at a time in his life where he was looking for a long-term relationship, something that would lead to marriage and kids. He was looking for a mate.

His tenant was off limits, for several reasons. First and foremost, Alex requested that he watch out for her. That meant she was under Hugh's protection. Also, she was living in his building and it was bad business to start something sexual with someone he was in a business relationship with. Lawsuits had been won over less. Besides, she didn't need any attention from him. Soon, she'd have men coming out of the woods to take a good sniff at her, literally. Young, single women were in short supply in Refuge. The human men in town would be checking her out to see if she was a potential conquest. The male shifters would be sniffing her to determine if she was their One—their true mate. He would not be one of them.

Finding a true mate among humans was rare. True mates were humans whose DNA was compatible with the shifter to whom they destined to be mated. The odds of his finding a human female match was between slim and none. The lack of compatible mates was one of the reasons shifters as a whole were dying out. There'd be no true mate for him. He didn't have one. As far as he knew, the true mates discovered to date had all been for wolf shifters.

The thought saddened him because his species was nearly extinct. Their birth rates were extremely low. In his lifetime, he'd only run across three other were-bears, and those were all male. Breeding with a female of another species was not an option. Just as in nature bears didn't breed with wolves, the same was true for shifters. While he could and did occasionally have sex with females of other species, he couldn't procreate with them. If he took a woman from another species—including humans—as mate, there would be no children, and he wanted a family.

He was proud of who and what he was. He was determined to do all that he could to continue his species. To that end, he'd been hunting for a female were-bear. He'd managed to find an on-line dating service that matched shape-shifters with others of their species. The service was a well-kept and closely guarded secret. Many of his kind used it in an effort to find compatible mates. So far, the service managed to find two promising prospects.

He'd been meeting with the two ladies in a supervised chat room, trying to get a feel for them. He had no idea what they looked like or where they were located. He was hoping one of them would accept him as mate, but competition was stiff. There were several males for them to choose from. They could afford to be picky and take their time.

Almost closing time. Mary Elizabeth must be too tired to take him up on his offer. He wasn't exactly sure what made him do it. It wasn't like him to offer free or discounted meals—to anyone. He never discounted a tenant's meal. She got to him, and that wasn't good. He'd have to be careful. He was determined to have offspring and she was a threat to all of his carefully laid plans.

* * * *

It was the sun shining directly in her face that woke Mary Elizabeth the next morning. Squinting, she raised a

27

hand to shield her eyes and looked at the time. Ten AM. Boy, it felt like she'd just closed her eyes. More sleep sounded like a good idea, but she had too much to do. She got out of bed, and began making plans for the day.

A trip to the grocery store to stock her kitchen was first on her agenda. Then, the apartment needed cleaning from top to bottom. She also needed to see what was available in the way of paint and supplies around town. She was glad Hugh gave her permission to fix the place up any way she liked.

There was nothing she wanted to eat in the kitchen. She picked up her purse and headed to the diner. The heavenly aroma of cooking food hit her nostrils as soon as she opened the door, making her stomach rumble. She sat at the counter and studied the menu to see what her choices were.

"What can I get for you?" There was a different waitress on duty this morning.

"A ham and cheese omelet with toast on the side. A cup of coffee to drink."

The waitress's name was Anne. After placing her order in the window, she came back and poured Mary Elizabeth's coffee. "You must be the new tenant Hugh told me about. You're the friend of Alex's mate, Kiesha?"

"Yes, that's me. I arrived last night."

"That's what Hugh said. Well, welcome to Refuge. There's not much to it, but the folks here are friendly. You need anything, you let me know, ya hear? I can give you directions and help you find your way around until you get settled."

"Thanks. I appreciate the offer. I need to buy groceries and paint. I saw the grocery store on the way in. Is there anyone around here that sells paint?"

"The hardware store closed down a few years back, but there's a Home Depot about forty-five minutes away in the next town over. You might want to get your groceries there, too. The store here is fine for some things, but for a major stocking job like what you're needing, I would do my shopping at one of the stores there. Bigger selection, greater variety and better prices. I can give you directions on how to get there so that you don't get lost."

"Thank you. I appreciate the help and the advice."

"Oops, got to go. There's your food. I'll have the directions wrote down for you before you go." She walked off to see about her other customers.

Anne was really nice, a true example of small town friendliness. She was an older woman, in her late forties maybe? Her ash blonde hair was liberally streaked with gray. She had a kind face, and the lines around her mouth and eyes suggested that she spent a lot of time smiling. There was a motherly look about her, and her manner enforced Mary Elizabeth's opinion that this woman was the nurturing type. She was looking forward to getting to know her better.

Polishing off her plate, she allowed herself one more cup of coffee before going to the register to pay. Anne handed her the directions as promised. Mary Elizabeth gave her a hefty tip then collected her truck and went to do her shopping.

Chapter Three

The week flew by pretty fast. She saw little of her landlord or anyone else as she spent her days unpacking and decorating, turning her apartment into a comfortable home. When she wasn't painting or shopping, she was sleeping. She got plenty of rest and felt much better.

On her second day in Refuge, she reluctantly called home to let her parents know she arrived safely. Her reward for being considerate was another thirty-minute lecture from her mother on what a big disappointment she was as a daughter and how Babs would have never gone off and left right when she was needed most. Her dad earned her undying gratitude when he got her mother off of the phone.

A couple of days later, Charles called. Mary Elizabeth was covered in paint at the time. "Hello?"

"How's the new job?"

She sat down on the floor. "I haven't started yet. Kiesha is giving me time to settle first."

"You know, I never realized how big a part of my life you were until you left. I miss you. I wish you'd come home."

"Charles, I just arrived. It's only been a few days since I left. Besides, it's not like we spent a lot of time together before Babs died." After her death, Charles was constantly at her apartment. Mary Elizabeth understood how difficult things were for him and hadn't complained. He was a welcome addition when he chipped in and helped her prepare to move.

"But I knew you were there, and now you're not. Why didn't you call and tell me you were okay?" He sounded hurt.

"I honestly didn't think of it. I called and spoke with Mother. Didn't she tell you?"

"Yes, that's how I got this number. But it should have come from you. Don't I mean anything to you?"

"Ummm..."

"I'm still family, aren't I? Even more than that, I thought we were friends."

Damn, now she felt guilty. "You're right. I should have called. It didn't cross my mind that you would worry. I'm sorry."

"I forgive you. Have you given any more thought to what I said?"

"About...?"

"About us. I told you, that wasn't the alcohol speaking. Lately, I've been giving it a lot of thought."

"Charles, we can't recreate the past. You're my brother-in-law and my friend. Let's leave it at that."

"You give it some thought. I know you're busy, so I'll go and let you get back to what you were doing."

"Charles...Charles!" He hung up. She didn't understand this need of his to revisit the past. When the split first happened, she was so hurt, she would have been happy to hear that he'd made a mistake, but that was almost eight years ago. It was too late to change things now.

She hadn't told her mother about the incident with Charles. She would just accuse Mary Elizabeth of being jealous, a scheming seductress out to steal Babs' life now that she was gone. She hoped Charles didn't go to her mother with this nonsense.

It was funny really. While she'd never been jealous of Babs a day in her life, at times she'd wondered if her twin could say the same. Babs had convinced people that Mary

Elizabeth couldn't bear to be separated from her. In truth, it had been just the opposite. Babs needed Mary Elizabeth because she made Babs shine. She'd refused to enhance her own natural beauty because it intimidated Babs and left her feeling insecure. Babs needed to be the focus of attention and, with the exception of their mother, Mary Elizabeth could have cared less who noticed her.

Growing up, their mother focused so much attention on Babs' looks that her life had revolved around her image. Babs needed to believe in her beauty because she was convinced it was all she had. Her mother had taught Babs to use her beauty to get what she wanted in life, and Babs had learned her lessons well. That was how she nabbed Charles.

After the fiasco with Charles, Mary Elizabeth turned her attention to earning her degree and becoming financially stable. She was saving money to purchase her own home. She'd been saving for her dream house since high school. One day, she would have it. It would be hers, on her land, built to her specifications. She had enough money now to purchase the land and put a good down payment on the house. She was looking for property when the call came about Babs.

Now that she was in Refuge? Well, time would tell. Life was short and she wasn't getting any younger. One day, she'd have children and give them all the attention, love and acceptance she never received as a child, with or without a husband. There were a lot of children in this world that needed a loving home. She was more than willing to adopt and remove some poor child from the system.

Enough introspecting. She'd been cooped up in this apartment long enough. It was time to get out and meet some of the locals. She'd start by eating dinner at the diner. From there, she'd find out what Refuge had to offer in the way of entertainment. If nothing else, there had to be a local watering hole. She didn't drink, but even the bar scene would be better than spending another night at home.

* * * *

It was about five when Mary Elizabeth entered the diner. To her surprise, Anne was still working.

Anne called out to her as she rushed by with a platter full of food. "Grab a seat, hon. Be right with you."

"What are you still doing here? I thought you got off at three?" She grabbed her usual seat at the counter. She and Anne had become friends over the last week. Mary Elizabeth came down for breakfast every morning, more for the company than for any other reason. She usually stayed for an hour before going back to the apartment to finish whatever project was slated for that day.

"Cyndi called in—again. Hugh didn't have anyone else so I'm working a double." She distributed the food and rushed back to the window to pick up an order that was ready.

Ouch, that had to be rough. Business was picking up as the dinner crowd streamed in. Coming to a sudden decision, Mary Elizabeth grabbed Anne on one of her passes by. "Point me to an apron and an order pad and I'll help."

"Oh, that's sweet honey, but you don't have to. I can handle it. This is not the first time this has happened."

"Let me help. I don't mind. I was tired of being upstairs. This will give me something to do and let me meet some of the locals. Besides, I know what I'm doing. This is how I supported myself in college."

"Okay, hon. If you're sure you want to help, the aprons are over there and the pads are under the counter. You handle the counter and I'll handle the tables. Is that okay with you?"

"Sure. Whatever you say."

Finding the items right where Anne said, she donned the apron right as the first dinner rush began. Behind the counter she took orders, greeted customers, and basically handled herself like a pro. She could see Anne watching her closely, but once she saw that Mary Elizabeth knew what she was doing, she stopped and concentrated on her own customers.

The next few hours went by quickly. Many of the male customers chose to sit at the counter where the pretty new waitress was serving. It had been a long time since men flirted with her. She actually found herself enjoying it, not taking any of the things they said seriously. She was a lot more mature and self-confident then she'd been in college when she'd last done this.

Finally business slowed down and even the men lingering at the counter ran out of excuses and were forced to leave or appear foolish. When business trickled down to just a few customers, she made Anne sit down and take a breather while she took their orders. She knew Anne had to be tired. She was slightly tired herself and she hadn't been on her feet for twelve hours. She placed a ticket in the window and then sat at the counter beside Anne while she waited for the order to come up.

"Thanks, hon. You're a life saver."

"Is it like this every night?"

"Most nights, yes. I think we had a few more tonight than usual. There were folks coming in to check you out, but for the most part, this was normal."

"And there's only the two of you? I mean, doesn't Hugh have more waitresses?"

"Actually there are five of us, two for each shift and one relief. Candy is out on maternity leave and won't be back for another two weeks. Misty had to go out of town unexpectedly to see about a sick relative and we aren't sure when she'll be back. The other girl quit. Hugh is going to have to hire some more help. I can't keep doing this, and that Cyndi's getting more and more unreliable."

When the bell rang, Mary Elizabeth got up and took the food to her waiting customers, checking to see if they needed anything else before coming to sit back down. "Will he have any problems finding help?"

"Lord, no. Jobs in Refuge are hard to come by and Hugh pays good. The tips are decent, too."

"Speaking of tips, where do you want me to put yours?"

Anne looked at her in astonishment and then shook her head. "Hon, you keep the tips. They're yours. I appreciate the thought but you've more than earned them."

Prepared to argue, Mary Elizabeth let it go when she saw how adamant Anne was. The longer she sat, the more she realized how hungry she was. It was close to nine. It was a little later than she liked to eat, but she was hungry. She wrote out an order for a burger without the fries and stuck it in the window. Anne took advantage of the quiet spell to eat as well.

Instead of placing the food in the window, Hugh brought it out of the kitchen and sat it on the counter. He usually came in to help with the lunch and dinner crowds before disappearing into his office to handle the paperwork. He was surprised to see his new tenant helping out in the diner, and doing such a capable job of it, too. He hadn't seen her since the night she arrived. Hugh set the plate down in front of her, grabbed a cup of coffee for himself, and then sat on a stool next to them.

"Dinner's on the house. It's the least I can do for all your help. You handled yourself well. Where'd you learn to waitress like that?"

Anne spoke up, beaming like a proud parent. "She used to waitress in college and I was glad for the help. Hugh, you have to do something. I'm too old to keep working these kind of hours."

He smiled at the idea of Anne being old before responding. "You're not old, and I'm working on the problem. When I get into the office, I'll pull some applications and see if any of the applicants are still interested. Thanks again for staying over. I know it's not easy."

He finished his coffee and moved to get up. He still had paperwork to do in the office. Before he could rise, Mary Elizabeth placed her hand on his arm. Her action caused him to stop and stare at her hand, which she snatched back. "I need to give you my rent and deposit, but I left it upstairs. When do you want it?"

"If you have it ready and you're done eating, I'll come up and get it now."

"Now is fine." She finished her drink and said goodbye to Anne before leaving. He was right behind her. He waited while she stopped to take a deep breath of fresh air before continuing up the stairs to her apartment.

Mary Elizabeth opened the door and stood aside to allow him to enter before crossing over to the table where she'd left the check. He stopped right in the doorway. The difference in the place was amazing.

"You said I could fix it up. I took you at your word. I hope you don't mind?"

Her words snapped him out of the daze he was in and he looked around. He closed his eyes, and then looked again. The change was incredible. "*This* is what you've been doing up here all week?"

"Yes, I only have two weeks to get settled in before I report to work. I wanted to get everything situated."

"You mind if I look around?"

"No, help yourself. It's your place after all."

He walked into the kitchen and took in all the changes. He liked what she'd done with the hooks, displaying the pots while at the same time placing them within easy reach. On the counter was a mouth-watering, chocolate cake, a favorite of his.

"You made this?"

"Yes. Would you like a piece? I like baking but haven't learned the art of making smaller portions yet."

Rubbing his hands in anticipation, he sat at the kitchen table while she served him a slice. He moaned in pleasure as the rich chocolate flavor exploded in his mouth. Man, this was good. It was so moist that it was melting in his mouth. All he needed was a glass of milk and he'd be set. He wondered how he could get more without appearing greedy. "This is really good. My customers would love this."

"You want to take it down to the diner? If it sits here I'm just going to eat it and I certainly don't need the extra calories."

Her comment drew his attention to her body. He gave it a slow once over from head-to-toe, smiling when she blushed and started fidgeting. "If you're sure you don't want it, I'll be happy to take it with me."

He rose and placed his dirty dishes in the sink. Then he turned and looked the place over again. "Did you do anything to the bedrooms?"

"Just mine. I haven't decided what to do with the other one, yet. I'm thing about making it into an office, but I really don't work much from home. Of course, that may change with this new position. I'll just have to wait and see. You can see it if you'd like."

He headed for the bedroom, curious to see what it looked like now. The rest of the place looked great. The blue/green color scheme she'd chosen was very relaxing, creating a homey feel to the place that wasn't frilly. It was a place a man could kick back and relax in. He could easily picture himself spending time here.

When he stepped through the doorway of the bedroom, her scent permeated the room, almost driving him to his knees as his beast stirred, its interest roused.

His cock hardened and lengthened, and like a homing beacon, sought the source of that amazing smell. Lust hit him hard, and his eyes began to shift as his beast rose to the surface, demanding he take action. He backed out of her room quickly, holding his breath until he was back in the living room where the strong scent of paint, chocolate, and the perfume she wore lingered, covering her natural fragrance.

She stared at him like she was questioning his sanity, but he couldn't be concerned with her impression of him. Let her think he was a lunatic. He had to get out of here before he threw her down on the floor and fucked her.

From his beast's reaction, one would think she was his mate, but that just wasn't possible. There was no way that she could be his One. He didn't know what to make of it. He'd never had that strong of a reaction to a woman's scent before. All he knew was that he had to get out of here and do it now before he did something criminally stupid.

He snatched the cake off the counter. "The place looks great. Thanks for the cake. Gotta get back to work." With those words, he rushed out the door, slamming it shut behind him.

He hurried down the stairs and into the diner, not stopping until he was closed in his office. His breathing was labored and his hands shook. He'd fought for every step he'd taken away from her, his beast fighting against him to remain and take what it wanted. He leaned against his office door and stared at the cake in his hands, sweat pouring down his face. He didn't know what it was about her that triggered this reaction, but it couldn't be allowed to happen again.

* * * *

Brrringg! Brrringg! Brrringg!

What the hell was that sound? She shoved the pillow over her head to drown it out.

Brrinngg! Brrinnggg! Brrinnggg!

The phone! She flipped over and jumped out of bed. Her feet got tangled in the covers and she fell to one knee. Pushing up off the floor, she raced into the living room to catch it before whoever it was hung up.

"Hello?" She panted, out of breath and slightly lightheaded from the adrenaline rush.

"Mary Elizabeth, it's Kiesha. I'm sorry. Did I wake you?"

"Yes, but it's alright. What's up?"

"We haven't spent any time together since you've been here. I've been busy with finalizing the purchase of the building and getting permits, but today is for you. I thought we could get together and catch up. What do you think?"

Mary Elizabeth sat on the arm of the couch. "I think it's a great idea. What do you have in mind?"

"Well, since you can cook and I can't, how about I come over to your place for lunch? Your food's better than anything around here."

She laughed in delight. "Come on over. You can see what I did with the place. I'm sure I can whip up something for us. What time?"

"I have a meeting with a contractor at ten. What about noon? I should be finished by then."

"Works for me. See you then."

Hours later, Kiesha arrived just as she was taking the last item out of the oven. "Come in. Door's open."

"Wow, it smells great in here. What are you cooking?" Kiesha placed her things on the couch and came into the kitchen. "This is really nice. When Alex first told me about this place, I wasn't too sure. But this is great."

"Thanks. It looks a lot better now than when I first

39

arrived. I've been working on it for the last week. I hope you're hungry. I made lasagna, heavy on meat and cheese—the way you like it—and homemade garlic bread. Food's on the table. Help yourself."

Mary Elizabeth knew the moment Kiesha spotted the brownies because she squealed. "Oh, you doll. You made brownies. I love brownies, especially now. I can't get enough chocolate."

"I know, you dope. Why do you think I made them?" *Plates, forks, serving utensils, glasses and napkins. What was missing? The tea!* She got the pitcher out the refrigerator and placed it on the table. Now they could eat.

Mary Elizabeth took a seat at the table facing Kiesha. "So, tell me what's going on? The last time we talked, you weren't seeing anyone and then bamm! A new man and a baby on the way. Talk about moving fast. What happened?"

Kiesha got this look on her face that Mary Elizabeth couldn't decipher. "You wouldn't believe me if I told you. Yes, it's all happening really fast, but you know? I'm happier than I've ever been. He really completes me."

She paused with her fork in the air. "I'm happy to hear that. Really, I am. Just be careful, okay. Know what you're doing. You're making a lot of changes for this man. I hope it works out for you."

"It will. There are things going on of which you're unaware. Things we need to discuss, but let's eat first and then we'll talk. It's kind of complicated. In the meantime, tell me what's been going on with you. How you holdin' up since Babs' death? And what made you decide to come? Don't get me wrong. I'm totally glad you did. I just wasn't sure you would."

Mary Elizabeth brought her up to speed on all that happened while she was gone. She told her about Babs' affair, the visit from Charles and the phone call from her mother. "You know how Mother is. She pulled out all the stops this time, and got everyone in town involved. If it wasn't for Dad, I'm sure I would have caved." Then she told Kiesha what her father said.

"Wow! Your dad stuck up for you? You must have been floored. And that Charles! Is he crazy? After seven years, he thought he could just show up and say he made a mistake and you were supposed to just fall into his arms?"

"No, just a little lost. I think he's taking Babs' death worse than he's letting on and he's using me as a crutch. I just hope he doesn't go to my mother with this foolishness."

Kiesha's hand hovered over the bread as her mouth dropped open. "You think he would do that? Your mother would go ballistic."

"Don't I know it. Yet another reason that it was time for me to leave. I don't need the drama that he would bring into my life. I've finally got a chance to be free of my family. Don't get me wrong. I'm not happy Babs died. She was a big part of my life. That was the problem. She and Mother took up so much of my time and energy that there was barely any left for my own life. I never realized it until Dad and I had that heart-to-heart talk. Now I have a chance to do what I want, when I want and how I want without worrying about what mother will think or how it will affect the family. I intend to enjoy every moment of it."

Kiesha gave her a huge grin. "Good for you. You know I told you a long time ago that you needed to cut them loose, especially Babs. She was entirely too dependent upon you."

Mary Elizabeth shrugged. "I know you did and I agreed totally, but it was something that was easier said than done. It's hard to turn loose someone that doesn't want to let go. As much as I resented her at times, I understood her too well. She was my sister, my twin. That's a bond that's not easily broken."

"Not having a twin of my own, I'll have to take your word for it. Well, this is your opportunity. Have you thought about what you're going to do?"

"Not really. I'll let things settle for a while. Give myself time to adjust to these changes before deciding where I want to go from here. After all, I just had two major life changes—a new home and a new job. Let's save something for next month, okay?"

Laughing, Kiesha agreed with her. They spoke of more mundane topics until they finished eating, then they carried the brownies into the living room with them. Once they were seated comfortably, Kiesha turned to Mary Elizabeth and began.

"I'm going to tell you some things that will be hard for you to believe, but I want you to know that it's the absolute truth."

After that introduction, she began telling Mary Elizabeth all that happened to her, beginning with Alex finding her hanging bound in the woods, right up through the funeral three week ago. She explained about true mates and the effects of the bonding process. Mary Elizabeth sat there listening quietly as she spoke, saying not a word until Kiesha was finished.

"So you're telling me that Alex is a werewolf, and you're slowly changing into one as well?" Mary Elizabeth found it difficult to believe what she was hearing.

"Don't let Alex hear you say werewolf. They prefer the term shape-shifter, but yes, that's exactly what I'm saying. Do you believe me?"

"It's a lot to take in. It's evident that you believe what you're telling me. I'll need some time to think about it. What made you decide to share? Why not keep it to yourself?" *If it was me it happened to, I wouldn't have told a soul,* she thought.

Kiesha shrugged, then grinned. "Because you're my best friend and I desperately need someone like me I can talk with about this. It's all new to me, too. But more importantly, because this affects you as well."

"In what way?" Try as she might, Mary Elizabeth couldn't see what Alex being a werewolf had to do with her.

"Well, Alex is the Raven pack's alpha. That means he's their leader. When I became his mate, that made me alpha as well."

"That's very generous and forward thinking of them, but I'm still not getting the connection. How does this affect me?"

"Because you are my friend, Alex extended the pack's protection to you, making you an honorary pack member. Remember what I said about true mates and the logic behind them?"

"Yes. True mates are the one person that can speak to both the nature of the human and beast. They are recognizable by scent and taste. In human mates, the human has a gene or something in their DNA that makes them compatible and allows them to mate and have offspring together." Mary Elizabeth spoke by rote.

She'd listened to every word Kiesha said. The jury was still out on whether she believed any of it. But for right now, she was willing to give her friend the benefit of the doubt.

"Good, you were listening. What I didn't tell you is that most of the males in the Raven pack are looking for mates. All of them are anxious to meet you to see if you could be their One. That's why Alex put you under the protection of the pack. This way he'll have control and you won't have all of the unmated shifter males bombarding you at the same time."

Mary Elizabeth drew back in surprise. "Wait a minute. There are more men like Alex around here? And they all want to meet me? Just how many men are we talking about here?" Maybe she hadn't been listening as well as she thought.

"Well, Alex said there were about seventy men in his pack. Of that seventy, about half are unmated."

Quickly doing the math in her head, she looked at Kiesha in shock. "Thirty-five! We're talking about thirty-five men sniffing me to see if I could be the future mother of their children?" Even if she didn't believe this shifter nonsense, that was still a lot of men. Maybe coming here hadn't been such a good idea after all.

Kiesha waved away her concern. "Don't worry. Alex is taking care of it. That number may be slightly exaggerated. I don't know how many are too young or too old for a mate, and some of them who are of age may not even want a mate. Alex is having a party to introduce me to them. All of the members are required to be there. He wants you to come as well so that you can be introduced. I think it's a good idea. The men can get a sniff of you without being obvious about it and you can meet some of the locals."

"What if one of them decides I'm his mate? What happens then? I have enough going on in my life right now without a man trying to complicate things." She shook her head forcefully. Not going to happen. Not if she could help it.

Kiesha smiled at her in sympathetic understanding. "No one will force you to do anything. But if it's anything like what happened to me, no one will have to. The attraction will be mutually overwhelming. Alex and I could barely keep our hands off of each other."

She must have saw that Mary Elizabeth needed further convincing. Kiesha laid her hand on her arm. "Look, you won't be the only single female there. We just had a new young female join our pack. She'll be introduced at the party as well. Her name is Shannon McFelan. She's the CPA I hired to handle all of the store accounts. You two will be seeing a lot of each other at the store, so it'll be a good time for you to meet."

"When's the party?"

"Friday night at our place. I'll give you directions to the house. Go out and get yourself something stunning for the party. Consider it your 'coming out.' Just think, these people don't know Babs. You can be you without anyone making comparisons."

Mary Elizabeth liked the sound of that. A 'coming out party' to introduce the new her, only no one there would know it was a new and improved version of herself. She'd have to think about the other part—the part about the men. She didn't have a lot of experience and she wasn't sure she was ready to be the object of so much attention.

Kiesha rose to leave, but not before making one final remark. "See you Friday. Wear something sexy and let them see how attractive you really are. Stop hiding. Be the attractive woman God created you to be."

"I'll think about it." She gave Kiesha a hug and closed the door behind her. As she cleaned the kitchen, she thought about Kiesha's tale. It was hard to believe, but what did she know. There were a lot of things in this world that couldn't be explained. Believing that humans were the only intelligent species on earth was as arrogant as believing that humans were the only intelligent beings in the universe. Humans came in all sizes, shapes, and colors. She shouldn't be so surprised that there were other species, as well.

She thought again about the attraction Kiesha spoke of between mates. For some reason, Hugh came to mind. It was a foolish thought. He was as human as she, and as far as she knew, wasn't even attracted to her. As for her, well, she liked his size and how small and feminine it made her feel, but that was as far as it went. Like she'd said to Kiesha, she didn't want a man in her life right now. Maybe later, when things settled down somewhat and she'd adjusted to all the changes in her life. Even if she were interested, her taciturn landlord would not be a consideration.

Chapter Four

Mary Elizabeth was ready to scream. The walls were closing in on her. She needed to get out of this apartment. This sitting around with nothing to do was driving her crazy. As she looked around frantically for something—anything—to do, her eyes fell on the leftover brownies. The sooner she got them out of the house, the better. As bored as she was, she'd eat the whole pan and with her the saying was true—"Once on the lips, forever on the hips."

It was almost four. Anne should be getting off soon. Maybe Anne would take them home with her. She put on her shoes, grabbed the keys and the brownies, and walked quickly out the door before she changed her mind. These things couldn't stay in the house another moment. She had to catch Anne before she left.

As soon as she walked into the diner, she could see that she needn't have rushed. From the looks of things, Anne was going nowhere. Cyndi must have called in again. She took a seat at the counter until she could get Anne's attention. On her way to the window with an order, she stopped to speak with Mary Elizabeth. "What can I get you, hon?"

"Nothing for me. I came down to snag you before you left. I wanted to give you these brownies to take home, but you don't appear to be leaving. What happened? Cyndi call in again?"

"Yes, selfish bitch. Oh, I'm sorry, hon. Pardon my French. It's just that it makes me so mad. She knows Saturdays are our busiest nights. That's why she called. I can't believe the laziness of that heifer. She knows I won't leave Hugh by himself."

"Doesn't he have help in the kitchen?"

"He does, but it takes the two of them to keep up. Listen, I got to go, hon. Orders are coming up. I appreciate the thought, but I'm allergic to chocolate. Maybe one of the customers will take them." With that she hurried off, greeting a customer that walked in the door even as she set a plate in front of another.

Well, I was looking for something to do. This is as good as anything else. Mary Elizabeth grabbed an apron and went to work. She manned the ten seats at the counter, leaving the tables to Anne. It wasn't much, but even the little that she did would help. The jukebox in the corner was blaring out a country tune, making it difficult to hear. The place was packed and the conversations loud, as people got in an early meal before continuing on with the rest of their Saturday night plans.

It got busy and stayed busy until well after nine. Mary Elizabeth had no idea this many people lived in the area. Just when she thought things were slowing down, the after movie crowd came in wanting dessert and coffee. In all her running around, she hadn't seen a movie theatre in Refuge. She didn't know until this moment that there was one.

They chased the last customer out of the door at eleven. Hugh locked the doors, turned the sign to *Closed*, and turned off the outside lights. To the ladies, he said, "Thanks for all your help. You go on home. The guys and I will get this place cleaned up."

Not needing to be told twice, Anne grabbed her purse, said goodbye and left. Hugh locked the door behind her and then turned to Mary Elizabeth, who was still wiping down the counter.

"Leave the counter alone. We'll get it. You've done enough for one night. You keep helping out like this and

I'm going to have to add you to the payroll."

"I'm almost done. I'll go home in a minute. As far as payment goes, you can deduct it from my rent." She winked at him and laughed, showing she was only kidding with him.

Hugh gave it serious consideration. "Deal. I'll deduct a day's wages from your next month's rent. Give me the receipts for the paint and supplies you purchased and I'll deduct those as well."

"I was joking." Her eyes rounded in shock, a look of sheer disbelief crossed her face. The rag hung limply from her hand.

"I'm not. For what you did, you deserve to be paid. Since I can't legally pay you without adding you to the payroll, this is the next best thing. I'll knock sixty-five dollars off of the rent for your work tonight and another thirty-five for all the painting you did. Give me the receipts and I'll knock off even more."

"That's too much. You can't do this," she complained.

"Who says? I pay my waitresses six dollars an hour plus tips. You worked seven hours tonight. You can't tell me you paid less than thirty-five for the paint, and that doesn't included labor. You increased the value of my property, therefore, you deserve compensation."

She was steadily shaking her head while he spoke. *Stubborn little thing.*

"I was bored and you needed help. It's a win-win situation for us both." She threw the rag back into the sanitizing water. "It's not like I was doing anything else. The apartment I fixed up for me. I'm the one living there and I enjoyed being able to decorate any way that I wanted. That's all the compensation I need." She grabbed her stuff and the envelope with her tips and turned to go out the front door.

"Go out the back. It's closer to your apartment." He

guided her to the other exit. "I'm knocking a hundred off of your rent. I don't see what the big deal is. It's the least I can do."

"I don't want your discount. I made over fifty in tips tonight. That's more than enough money if that was my goal, but it wasn't. I pitched in to help out my friend. If I were after money, I would have asked for payment that first night."

"Thanks for reminding me. I'll knock another fifty off. Next month, you only pay me half of the rent due." He opened the door for her.

"Aaargh! Are you big *and* stupid? You're getting the full three hundred next month. The rent is ridiculously low as it is. How do you keep this diner running, giving away money like you do?"

At her words, he spun her around and slammed the door shut before she could walk out. Hugh crowded her until she was backed against the door, bent down and planted his hands on either side of her, boxing her in. He lowered him face until they were eye-to-eye. "I'm not stupid, and quit being so stubborn. If I want to reduce your rent, that's my prerogative."

"No."

"You're taking the markdown. I won't accept payment from you until you do." His bear stirred in response to his rising anger.

"No."

"Do you realize how childish you're being? How stupid this argument is? Quit fighting me and accept the price cut." It was all he could do not to yell.

"I won't and you can't make me." Then she stuck out her tongue at him.

Hugh let out a snarl of frustration just as her scent hit his nose. Already on edge, he didn't have the control necessary to resist the urge to kiss her into submission. Angling his head, he pressed his mouth to hers. His kiss was dominant and forceful, an expression of the frustration he was feeling. Her taste went to his head like wine, intoxicating him with her flavor.

He growled deep in his chest as he deepened the kiss, thrusting his tongue into her mouth, wanting and needing more. He pressed forward and tried to ground his erection against her. She was too short. He lifted her by her hips until he fit perfectly in the notch between her thighs. There he pressed against her, rubbing his cock against her mound. He wanted inside and he wanted in now.

Hugh gathered the material of her sweatpants in his fists and began pulling them off of her body until he'd bared her hips. To take them the rest of the way off, he would have to move back, something he wasn't about to do. He stroked his fingers against the crotch of her panties, zeroing in on her opening. Her panties were damp, but he wanted them wet. He slid his fingers under the edge of her panties and worked her folds open. He would stroke her pussy until her cream filled his hand. Once she was wet enough, he'd rip the panties off her body and take her. He had two fingers poised at her entrance, ready to thrust inside when she whimpered. It shocked him back to his senses. *What the hell was he doing?*

He snatched his hand out of her pants and dropped her on her feet, pulling her pants up at the same time. Then he jumped back out of reach. She fell against the door, panting, a dazed look on her face. The beast in him scented her arousal and roared, *Take her! Take her now!* Before he lost control again, he pulled her away from the door, opened it, and hurriedly pushed her outside. "I'm sorry. Lost my head. Promise it won't happen again. Hurry upstairs. We'll talk about the rent later." Then he slammed the door in her face.

Once she was safely on the other side, he bolted the door, breathed a sigh of relief and leaned back against it. Whew, that was close! A few more minutes and he'd have taken her, and then there would be hell to pay. Alex would have killed him. He was supposed to be protecting her, not raping her. And he hadn't given any thought to the men working in the diner. They could have come back at any time. What was happening to his control?

On the other side of the door, Mary Elizabeth stood looking around blankly. What happened? She remembered being angry and arguing with Hugh, something she rarely did with anyone. Then he'd kissed her. Actually, it was more than a kiss. It was a claiming, like something out of a romance novel.

Before her mind could wrap around the fact that this was taciturn Hugh kissing her, he'd literally shoved her out of the door and slammed it in her face. He'd said something at the time. She caught an apology but not much else. His words ran together, not making any sense. She leaned against the door with her lips tingling and her body throbbing. Why had he stopped? Things were just getting interesting.

Climbing the stairs on legs that shook, she told herself to be grateful that he'd come to his senses when he had. Hugh was a complication she didn't need in her life right now. It didn't matter how intense the attraction was between them, or how much she enjoyed arguing with him. The man was her landlord. Nothing good could come of it. Yes, it was a good thing he'd stopped when he did. Now if she could only convince her body.

* * * *

The rest of the week passed quickly. Mary Elizabeth avoided Hugh, only going into the diner in the mornings when she knew he wouldn't be there. She smiled as she remembered her conversation with Anne that next morning.

"I gave those brownies to the customers and they

were a big hit. You should make more and sell them in the diner. It'd be a nice little side income for you. The guys are already asking for them. Good thing I didn't tell them who made them or they'd be knocking on your door, day and night, begging you to make extra."

"I like baking, but it's just a hobby of mine; something I do to relax. I'm not interested in turning it into a business venture."

"You should really think about it. If the rest of the stuff you make is good as those brownies must have been, you could make a killing."

Mary Elizabeth just laughed it off and there was nothing Anne could say to convince her otherwise.

On Tuesday, Mary Elizabeth shopped for an outfit for Friday's party. Since she was shopping, she purchased a lot of new outfits in colors and styles that flattered her full-figure. She thought about what Kiesha said and realized that this was the perfect time to create her new look. She also had her hair cut and styled. It now fell in a silky waterfall to her shoulders in a style that suited her heart-shaped face. The perfect outfit in hand, she was ready for Friday.

On Wednesday, she walked to the store to see how things were progressing and met Shannon. They immediately clicked. She had no doubt that they were going to be great friends.

Finally, Friday arrived and it was time to prepare for the party. She dressed carefully, paying particular attention to her makeup. Finished, she took one final look in the mirror. Completely satisfied with her appearance, she picked up her things and headed for the door. Kiesha hadn't asked her to bring anything but her mother taught her to bring a gift for the host, especially if this was your first visiting their home.

Her hand was on the doorknob when the phone rang. She groaned. Not Kiesha *again*. She'd swear that woman was more nervous about tonight than she was. "Yes, ma'am?"

"Miss me, darling? I've missed you."

Damn, I mean darn! I have got to get caller I.D. "How are you, Charles?" She forced herself to be polite.

"You didn't answer my question. Do you miss me? Aren't you lonely, ready to come back home?"

"Charles, I spoke to you yesterday, and the day before that. In fact, you call every day, and I tell you the same thing. This is my home now. We've discussed this before and I'll tell you the same thing I told mother when she asked. I like it here." She tried not to sigh with impatience.

"She doesn't understand this foolishness any more than I do. Your mother and I spoke today and I explained to her about us. She understands and has given her approval."

"You did what? What is wrong with you? Why did you do that? You know how mother is. Please, get this through your head. There is no us, and hasn't been for a long, long time. You were married, remember? You got married and I moved on. We're friends, Charles. That's it. That's all it will ever be. *Now, you go back and tell her the truth!"*

"Darling, I'm so sorry I upset you by telling your mother about us before you were ready for her to know. You're right. I should have waited, but your parents need to know that your sister tricked me. That conniving bitch, she hid her true personality from all of us."

"That 'conniving bitch' was my twin, and for seven years you were happily married to her."

"She made a fool of me. You would never have done that. You loved me."

"That's right, Charles. Loved, as in past tense. Look, I know you're hurting and your ego is bruised. I'm sorry, but this is the way it is. You made your choice a long time ago and I'm content with it. You're my brother-in-law.

We're family, and that's all we'll ever be. Now, I have to go. You caught me on my way out the door. Goodbye, Charles." She placed the receiver back in its cradle and stood there for a moment, just staring at it, her mind elsewhere. It immediately started ringing again, but she ignored it. She knew grief did strange things to people, but Charles had some serious issues he needed to deal with. *Not your problem*, she told herself and walked out the door.

Kiesha lived up the mountain in an area known as Raven's Peak. She drove slowly and followed the directions carefully. The road was dark and heavily forested. A half an hour later, she was in front of Kiesha's house, looking for a place to park her truck. The front yard was huge and packed with the vehicles. She climbed out of the truck, tugged her skirt back into place, reached inside and grabbed her things before approaching the house.

When the door opened, she exclaimed, "Wow, what a great house. Looks like it belongs in one of those designer home magazines labeled as the perfect mountain retreat." She handed Kiesha the homemade chocolate cake she'd brought as a gift.

"I know," she laughed, "Isn't it great. Alex had it built. It's a toss-up as to which I love more, the house or the man?"

"Hey! I heard that. There's no doubt about it woman. It's me you love, then the house." He spoke confidently as he extended his hand to Mary Elizabeth in welcome. "There's something I've been dying to know. Does everyone call you Mary Elizabeth? No one's ever given you a nickname or tried to shorten your name, maybe to just one of them?"

"And ruin a fine southern tradition?" She sounded properly horrified. Seeing the uncomfortable look on his face, she burst out laughing. Kiesha joined in. "Sorry

Alex. I couldn't resist. Actually, people have tried, but nothing seemed to stick. My mother was a stickler for propriety. She corrected anyone that tried to shorten my name, until people quit trying. I'm used to it now."

"Come on, let's put this cake in the kitchen and then I'll introduce you to our guests. By the way, you look great. Love your hair," Kiesha told her.

Mary Elizabeth looked around as Kiesha led the way to the kitchen. The living room was dominated by a massive fireplace on one side and a staircase leading to an upper level on the other. The ceiling in the living room was vaulted, directing one's attention to the skylights in the roof. Someone wrapped Christmas lights around the stair rail, giving the room a festive glow. The house was packed. There were people everywhere, on the stairs and the landing above, as well as scattered throughout the living room.

Kiesha deposited the cake in the kitchen before backtracking back to the living room where the majority of the people were gathered, and led her over to one of the couches near the fireplace. Once there, she introduced her to Carol Johnson, an extremely pregnant African-American woman who looked as though she would pop any day now.

Mary Elizabeth's gaze traveled from Carol's swollen belly to her face. "I don't mean to be rude, but should you be here? You look like you're going to blow any second now."

"That's exactly what I said and why I was against her coming, but what do I know? I'm just her husband and the father of her unborn child," said the very attractive, bald male sitting by her side. Kiesha introduced him as Mark, Carol's husband and Refuge's only pharmacist. "Welcome to Refuge and to the Raven pack."

"Thank you," she said as she reached out to shake the hand he extended toward her.

Rolling her eyes, Carol shifted in her seat. "Please! Don't get him started. I'm a nurse. I know what I can and can't handle. I'm sitting, aren't I? Besides, I'm the pack's beta and this is an official gathering. It's mandatory that I be here."

Alex walked up in time to hear the last comment. "I don't want to add fuel to the fire, but you know that's not true. The health and welfare of an individual comes before any social gathering. I would have understood if you didn't come. And having said my bit, I am once more backing out of this discussion."

Carol stuck her tongue out at him. "Coward. Be that way. Really, I'm fine," she said to Mary Elizabeth. "Alex is my doctor. If anything happens, he's right here."

Kiesha and Alex took Mary Elizabeth around, introducing her to the rest of the pack and the neighbors. Though primarily a pack function, close friends of Alex were also in attendance so that Alex could show off his new mate. Those that Kiesha knew, she introduced. Alex performed the rest of the introductions.

Finally, she saw a familiar face. "This one I've already met. Hi, Shannon. I'm so glad I'm not the only newbie here. I feel like I'm wearing a sign that reads, 'Fresh Meat, come and get it!'"

Shannon laughed. "I know what you mean. It's been a long time since I've been sniffed and sized up the way I've been tonight."

"Is this normal? I know Kiesha told me what to expect, but even with her warning, I didn't expect this."

Alex answered before the women could. "You're very observant. Most people wouldn't notice. The males are sniffing to see if you're mated. Some are testing for compatibility and some just like the way you smell. By the way, you do smell nice."

Both Kiesha and Shannon had explained about shifters highly advance sense of smell. Because of it,

Mary Elizabeth did without the scented body lotion and perfume she usually wore and only used the scented body wash, which gave just a hint of fragrance. She hoped it would be much easier on the sensitive noses present.

She stood conversing with the three of them until some of the bolder men of the pack approached the alphas to ask the ladies to dance. Giving each other a 'what the heck' look, Mary Elizabeth and Shannon agreed and joined the people line-dancing on the makeshift dance floor.

This was so much fun. She wasn't a great dancer, but here it didn't matter. Fast songs. Slow songs. She danced them all, mostly due to the steady stream of partners who refused to let her sit down. Quickly heating, she took off the long-sleeved, red shrug she'd been wearing, revealing the black, leather and lace corset she wore beneath. The corset proudly lifted and displayed her generous breast while emphasizing her tiny waist. The skirt lovingly cupped her generous behind, displaying her figure to its best advantage. She wasn't a small woman, but she was an extremely curvy one. Curves she'd hid in the past were proudly displayed tonight. She couldn't help but notice that they were noted and appreciated by the men present. High on the attention and desire in the gazes of the men around her, she threw herself whole-heartedly into the party, enjoying being the center of attention for once.

Hugh arrived late. He'd waited until things slowed down at the diner before coming. Then he went home, showered and changed into a pair of fitted, black jeans and a close fitted black pullover that displayed his powerful body to advantage. When he walked through the door, he was instantly the center of female attention, not that he noticed. He slapped Alex on the back and bent down to give Kiesha a hug, congratulating them on the coming of their cub.

As he walked around, greetings were called out to

him, since he knew everyone present. He spotted Mary Elizabeth on the dance floor, surrounded by wolves and she looked hot! She'd done something to her hair, something that made him want to run his hands through its silky length. His gaze slid down her body, taking in the outfit she wore and felt his pants get tight. He reached down and adjusted his cock to a more comfortable position.

She wore leather the way he liked it, figure hugging, short and black. Man, he loved leather on a woman. The way the leather cupped her body should be outlawed. It was clear from the smile on her face that she was having a great time.

His gaze switched to the cub she was dancing with and he took a step forward before he could catch himself. He could smell the wolf's lust from here. Reigning himself in, he reminded himself of the bigger picture. He had a plan for his life that included a mate and little baby bear cubs. Mary Elizabeth was not part of that plan. No deviating from the plan, he warned himself.

While he was giving himself a stern talking to, another wolf came up close behind Mary Elizabeth and placed his hands on her hips, rubbing his body against hers in a semblance of sex. His move pushed her closer to the man she was dancing with, sandwiching her between the two of them. The men were so close to her he doubted he could squeeze a sheet of paper between them. When the man in front slid his hands up the side of her body to rest just below her breast, Hugh lost it. A growl broke loose as he stalked toward the dancing trio. Screw the plan!

* * * *

Alex was in the kitchen refilling the ice buckets when Shannon approached him. "Alex, you got a minute?"

"Sure, Shannon. What do you need?"

"I want to make an appointment to see you."

"As alpha or as your physician?"

"As my physician."

Concerned, he put the ice bucket down and crossed over to where she stood leaning against the center island. "Is there a problem? You seemed to be healing just fine. Are you in pain?" About three weeks ago, some wolves from her former pack attacked Shannon. One of them was her brother, Rory McFelan, the Sparrowhawk's pack alpha. He tried forcing her to mate and breed to keep their race from dying out. He'd picked two of the strongest males in his pack, hoping one of them would prove strong enough to subdue her. Regrettably for the men involved, neither were.

It was a dominance fight, pure and simple, and as such had been fought in wolf form. Shannon defeated both men in combat before taking on her brother. Wounded and tired, he easily defeated her before leaving her wounded and alone out by the ridge overlooking the river. Shannon was found and brought to him for medical treatment by their resident vampire, Nikolai Taranosky. She'd sustained a lot of damage and was too weak to shift back to human form, so Nikolai carried her to them after placing her under compulsion to keep her from attacking him. While she had perfect recall of the fights, she had no memory of the rescue, which, in his opinion, was a good thing. Nikolai had shown a little too much interest in Shannon for his comfort. She'd healed amazingly fast, even for a shifter. Carol was concerned that the healing was too rapid, but Alex hadn't thought anything of it. Maybe he should have checked into it like Carol requested.

"No, I'm not hurting anywhere. I mean, my stitches are all healed and everything's working just fine. It's just that, well, this is going to sound really strange. I think something is going on with me, inside my body. I don't hurt or anything. I just feel off. I can't put my finger on it or pinpoint anything in particular. I just know that something is wrong."

Alex tried not to show how concerned he was. "I don't think it's strange. You know your body better than anyone else. If you think something is wrong, we definitely need to check it out. Call the office on Monday and tell the receptionist I said to fit you in as soon as possible. I'll examine you, possibly run some tests and see if we can determine what's going on inside."

When Shannon's face fell and her shoulders slumped in disappointment, he became suspicious. "What aren't you telling me?"

After a quick look around, she lowered her voice and leaned close. "I can't sleep at night. I've only been getting about three to four hours of sleep a day. I'm restless, moody and irritable. My body is so sensitive that sometimes I can't stand anything against it. If I didn't know better, I'd swear I was going into heat, but that's crazy. I've already had my season this year."

Alex felt his pulse racing. "Forget Monday. You come into the office tomorrow morning. The practice doesn't open until noon. You be there at nine."

While Alex was waiting for Shannon's agreement, Mark rushed into the kitchen, interrupting them. "Alex, we have a situation. Carol's water broke. Kiesha just took her into the guest room to lie down. The fool woman's been in labor all day and just now decided to tell me."

Sharing a sympathetic look with Shannon, he placed his hand on Mark's shoulder in a calming gesture. "I'll be right there. Let me go and get my bag."

"Carol's already got it. The woman's in nurse mode. She's already got the room set up for delivery. Would you mind telling her to lie down like a normal woman? The only reason she went into the room is because I threatened to carry her. She wanted to avoid making a scene."

Laughing because he knew his beta, Alex refused to make any promises. "I'll see what I can do. Shannon, tomorrow morning at nine. Don't be late."

"I'll be there. Go see about Carol." She could tell Mark was about at the end of his rope. She watched them walk off. She hoped Alex could discover what was wrong with her. The stress of not knowing was getting to her. The last thing any of them needed was a stressed out wolf, especially when that wolf was an alpha like herself.

Chapter Five

Mary Elizabeth danced with a man named Eric. He was tall, built on the lean side, and handsome in that preppy, college-boy kind of way. He was a too young for her taste, but he was a really good dancer. He held her close, but not too close. From the way he was looking at her, she could tell he really liked the outfit she had on, or more specifically, the cleavage she was revealing since his gaze rarely traveled above her chest.

She didn't really pay much attention when she felt someone come up behind her. It was a house party after all, and space was limited. Then someone placed their hands on her hips and a very aroused male body pressed against hers. His action pushed her against Erik, whose hands were already on her waist. Erik took advantage of the situation by pulling her in even closer, until with each movement, her chest brushed against his and his erection rubbed against her stomach.

She'd never been sandwiched between two horny males before, but she was handling it fine until she felt Erik's hands began to inch toward her breast. At the same time, the hands on her hips glided toward the hem of her skirt. Oh, boy! Things were getting out of hand. What to do now? Babs would know what to do, she thought sadly. She was so out of her element. Sliding her hands from around Erik's neck, she brought her elbows down in an attempt to force some space between their bodies. She'd barely finished when the male body plastered to her back vanished.

She heard a low, menacing snarl behind her that raised the hairs on the back of her neck. At the sound, Erik turned sickly pale and jerked his eyes from her chest and his hands from her body. He held his hands up in the universal symbol of surrender to show he was harmless while backing slowly away. Once he had enough room, he turned and disappeared quickly into the dancers crowded on the floor.

Not really wanting to know who or what could cause that kind of reaction in a grown man, Mary Elizabeth took a step forward only to be pulled up short by the big, heavy hand that landed on her shoulder. Really not wanting to know who was behind her, but recognizing that she didn't have a choice in the matter, she slowly turned.

Hugh was standing behind her, but it was Hugh she'd never seen before. He was larger, more aggressive, almost scary looking in his anger. And what was with the growls rumbling from his chest? The hand on her shoulder slid to her upper arm and spun her the rest of the way around. His other hand dropped to her hip and jerked her forward into his body. "What the hell are you thinking?"

Any gratitude she might have been feeling toward him for getting her out of an awkward situation disappeared when he yelled at her. "Excuse you?" The ice in her tone should have given him frostbite. No one spoke to her this way, except maybe her mother.

"And what the hell are you wearing? Where are the rest of your clothes? What, you advertising now? How much for an hour? Maybe we can deal."

She sucked in her breath sharply, his words shocking her. "Are you implying that I look like a *hooker*?" She put both hands against his chest and shoved hard, while at the same time twisting her body out of his grasp. The combination of actions caused his hold to loosen enough for her to get away. "Screw you!" She turned and stalked off, not noticing the attention they were drawing.

Cursing violently, Hugh came after her. Reaching out, he grabbed her hand and pulled, using her momentum to swing her body around and into his arms. He locked an arm around her waist and slid his hand into her hair, using it to pull her head back. Then he kissed her. Well, some might call a kiss. She called it a macho, he-man stamp of ownership. She hung there limply in his arms while he pressed his mouth against hers.

When he tried to force his tongue into her mouth, she got violent. She pulled back foot, and kicked him in the shin – hard. She was really glad she'd let the sales lady talk her into these boots. These bad boys were capable of doing some serious damage.

Hugh jerked his mouth from hers. "Ow! What was that for?"

"For manhandling me. I'm surprised you didn't just whip out your penis and pee on me. Put me down. Now!" What was it with men? First she had to deal with Charles, and now this.

He loosened his hold and she slid down the front of his body before her feet touch the floor. He allowed her to take a step away from him but his arm around her waist kept her from getting too far away, and he still had his hand in her hair. "Manhandle? All I did was kiss you. I was trying to apologize."

"No, that wasn't a kiss. A kiss is what happened between us last week. This was you pissing on me like a dog marking its territory. You men are driving me crazy! First Charles went off the deep end, and now you!"

"Charles! Who the hell is Charles?" He was shocked into releasing her.

"None of your business." She turned on her heel to stalk off, but that was as far as she got before Hugh grabbed her again.

"Who is Charles?" He all but roared the words at her, his grip on her arms tight enough to prevent her from walking away before he had an answer to his question.

"What business is it of yours? It's not like we're involved or anything. Now let me go. You're causing a scene." This last part was hissed at him as she noticed all of the stares directed toward them.

Noticing that they were the center of attention, he let her go and stalked off. He wasn't exactly sure what happened. One moment he'd been minding his own business. The next, he'd lost it. What was it about her that affected him this way? He never lost control, especially over a female. He stalked out of the house, the expression on his face fierce. A path cleared before him as though by magic. No one wanted to tangle with an angry bear. He walked around outside, hoping the cold air would clear his mind and help him see reason. The whole time he wandered around, one question ran through his mind. *Who was Charles*?

* * * *

As far as Mary Elizabeth was concerned, the incident with Hugh was over and done with. The man had issues, serious issues. She just didn't understand his whole 'I don't want you but I don't want anyone else to have you either' attitude. He kissed her senseless, apologized and then spent the next week avoiding her. Well, to be fair, she'd been the one avoiding him. Then tonight, because someone else was paying attention to her, he went into a rage and pulled some jealous, he-man stunt. He couldn't have sent a clearer message if he'd hit her over the head with a club and dragged her off by her hair.

No man owned her. This macho crap had to stop. *You liked the way he handled you and you know it. You love knowing he's jealous*. She told the voice in her head to shut up.

Her life was finally her own and she was going to

enjoy every bit of it. For once, she didn't have to worry about anyone but herself, and it was lovely. She walked out on to the deck at the back of the house to see what was happening out here. It was chilly, but not unbearable. Alex had strategically placed fires that provided heat and light. The bar was located out on the deck where there was more space. Once outside, she could see that what she thought was a deck was actually a porch that wrapped around three sides of the house. Nice. Very nice.

Her wanderings took her close to the bar. The bartender smiled and spoke to her. "Hey, pretty lady. What would you like to drink?"

She shook her head and laughed. "I'm not a drinker."

"Come on, it's a party. Live a little. I'll make you anything you want."

She spotted several people sporting cute glasses with umbrellas in them. "What are they drinking?"

He looked in the direction she gestured. "Oh, that's a Shifter Surprise. You don't want that. It's really strong. Let me get you something else." He proceeded to rattle off a list of drinks that she might prefer.

She interrupted him, more interested in the drink he didn't want her to have than any of the ones he was listing. "What's in it?"

"What, a strawberry daiquiri?"

"No, I know what's in a daiquiri. I'm talking about the Shifter Surprise. How do you make it?"

He reluctantly told her. "It's a mixture of fruit juices and liquors, giving it a sweet and sour taste. But if you're not a drinker, it's going to be too strong for you. Let me make you a daiquiri."

His attitude was really starting to bother her. "I don't want a daiquiri. I want a Shifter Surprise. If it's too strong then I'll just eat some food with it."

Actually, that wasn't a bad idea. She hadn't eaten and drinking on an empty stomach was always a bad idea.

Food would keep the alcohol from going straight to her head. Besides, with the kind of night she was having, a drink sounded really good.

The bartender made the drink and gave it to her. "The alpha's not going to be happy about this."

"You tell him that I insisted."

"Yes, ma'am. I surely will," the young bartender told her.

As she walked back into the house to go get some food, Mary Elizabeth tasted her drink. Normally she didn't like the taste of alcohol, which was one of the reasons why she didn't drink. "Oh, this is *good*." She took another sip, a larger one this time as she went into the dining area to fix a plate.

She had to hand it to Kiesha; this was quite a spread. There were cheeses, all kinds of meats, crackers, chips and dip, the makings for nachos, and of course, desserts. She loaded her plate with a variety of foods, heavy on the meat and cheeses, and found a quiet corner to sit and eat.

While eating, she people watched. It was hard to believe that the majority of them were shape-shifters. By just looking at them, she couldn't tell human from the non-human. They all appeared the same to her, except for that nose thing she'd caught some of them doing. They just seemed so normal. She wasn't sure when she made the decision to believe Kiesha's tale, or if she'd actually made one. She just trusted that her friend was telling her the truth, strange though it may seem.

She didn't know what time it was, but she noticed the crowd was thinning. A lot of the older people had already left. She watched as families herded their children toward the door. Now that there were less people, she realized she hadn't seen Kiesha for some time.

She finished eating and had drained her drink when she noticed something strange. When she arrived, men were swarming all around her. Now, although a few cast looks her way, none of them approached. Shrugging her shoulders, she pushed the thought out of her mind as her head bobbed to the music. The mood of the party changed. Someone dimmed the lights and hung a disco ball, creating a strobe effect. The music was hipper, and the beat more driving. Her toe was tapping as she swayed from side to side. The beat got into her soul, compelling her to move. She allowed the pulsing music to drive her onto the dance floor, joining the other gyrating bodies already there.

* * * *

Hugh leaned his shoulder against a wall in a corner that gave him a good view of the room. He pinned his gaze on Mary Elizabeth, watching her every move. Whenever any man approached her, he growled possessively, knowing that the sound would carry. The wolves, recognizing the sound for what it was, steered clear of her, not wanting to risk antagonizing off an already angry bear.

He groaned as she danced her way onto the dance floor. He straightened, his posture aggressive as he physically dared any man to dance with her. Hugh watched as she strutted her stuff, mesmerized by the swaying of her hips. Her body called to his like a siren, and he was helpless to resist. He pushed his way through the crowd until he was directly behind her. Not wanting her to stop, he matched his movements to hers, easing closer a little bit at a time. He wanted her to become accustomed to the feel of his body against hers.

* * * *

In some small portion of her mind, Mary Elizabeth was aware that it was Hugh she was dancing with. She could tell by the way that her body responded. She didn't react this way with any other male. She eased back into him, enjoying the feel of his body against hers. She made no complaint when he claimed her hips with his hands, pulling her firmly into his aroused body. Instead, she lifted her arms up and back until she could lock her hands around his neck.

This position thrust out her chest, causing a dangerous amount of cleavage to be exposed. She didn't care. She wanted him to see, wanted him to feel what she was feeling. The rhythm was pulsing, driving, sexual in nature. She closed her eyes and gave herself up to the music, letting her inhibitions melt away. She wanted this man, needed him to assuage the ache building in her body. She spread her legs and arched her back, changing the movement of her body so that it rubbed sensuously against his.

* * * *

Hugh swore under his breath as her action caused brown of her areoles to be revealed. A little bit more and he'd be able to see her nipples. He wanted to see them. He wanted to touch them and squeeze them, to put his mouth on them and see how sensitive they were. He wanted to know if he could make her come just from sucking on her breasts.

The woman was driving him crazy. The smell of her arousal was making him dizzy. She undulated against him, making his cock swell even more. Sweat broke out on his body as he fought back the urge to come. Hugh allowed his hand to move from her hips to rest low on her belly, the tips of his fingers mere inches from the hem of her skirt, which rose several inches as a result of her movements. The other hand he slid up her body until it rested just below her breast. Giving into the urge, he allowed his thumb to stroke her nipple through the soft leather. He wanted to pull the material down and stroke her bare breast. He was hanging onto his sanity by a mere thread.

Mary Elizabeth felt her panties drench, thinking of all the marvelous things he could do with those fingers, if he would just slide his hand down a few inches. Hugh laid his nose against her neck, rubbing it against her throat. Then he played with her ear, nibbling and licking on it until goose bumps broke out all over her body. The hand on her stomach pressed harder, teasing her with its closeness to her mound.

Grabbing him by the hair, she pulled his mouth to hers for one of his bone melting kisses. Then she slid her hand down his arm until it rested over the hand laying on her stomach. Linking their fingers together, she moved his hand and positioned it over her clit, and pressed down hard, demonstrating what she wanted him to do. *Touch me*, she thought as she rubbed body against their hands.

Hugh tore his mouth away from hers, groaning deeply. This was getting out of control. If he weren't careful, he'd fuck her where she stood, unmindful of the people all around them. Just then Mary Elizabeth let out a sexy little whimper of need, and gave an extra roll of her hips. Oh hell, he needed privacy and he needed it quick. If she came here on the dance floor, his control would snap. He'd throw her to the floor and bury his dick in her. They had to get out of here. He looked around desperately, trying to determine his best course of action, a very difficult thing to do when he was almost blind with the need pulsing through his body.

People were everywhere, out on the patio, outside by the vehicles, and seated on the stairs. *The kitchen!* He wrapped an arm around her waist and half-carried her toward the kitchen. Mary Elizabeth cupped his cock through his jeans and squeezed. Hugh picked up the pace. There were people in the kitchen. Ditto, on the den. Finally, he thought of the one room where no one would be.

Doing an about face, he took her through the kitchen, down a hall and into a side room, shutting the door against intruders. It was dark, but light shined into the room from the gap beneath the door. He spun her around until her back was pressed against the door, in a position reminiscent of their first kiss. With one hand cupping the back of her head, he jerked her up to meet his mouth. Then he plundered and took what was his.

He shoved his knee between her legs, opening her for his touch. His hand glided up her inner thigh until he was cupping her pussy. Feeling how wet she was, a shudder rippled though his body. He hooked his fingers into her thong and pulled, ripping out the crouch. He wanted nothing preventing him from touching her as he desired. He slid one finger, and then another one into her wet, hungry sheath.

Too low, he needed her higher. He snatched his mouth from hers and bent, hooked a hand beneath her knee and lifted, sliding her body up the door. "Wrap your legs around my waist and hold on."

She gripped him tightly with her thighs, her back braced against the door for balance. "Please," she begged.

"Just a minute. Open your top. I want to suck on those luscious breasts."

She fumbled with the hooks. When they wouldn't give, she reached inside and lifted her breasts until they rested on top.

"Perfect. Cup 'em, baby. Lift them up for my mouth. That's right. Just like that." He dropped his head and took as much of her breast into his mouth as he could and suckled deeply.

"Hugh!"

"Shhh! We have to be quiet. Don't want anyone coming to investigate."

"Please," she moaned. "I need …"

"Hold on, baby. I'll give you what you need." He thrust his fingers back inside her sheath and spread her cream all about. With her moisture as lubrication, he rubbed in a circular motion around her clit with his thumb while he felt around inside until he located her g-spot. Then he rubbed firmly against it.

God, she was a moaner. Concerned she would attract unwanted attention, he placed his mouth over hers, swallowing the sexy sounds she was making. It didn't take much before she stiffened, her body clamping down hard on his fingers as the orgasm shook her. Damn, that was sexy. The next time she came, it would be around his cock.

He released her mouth and allowed her legs to drop to the floor. He was bringing his fingers to his mouth for a taste when Mary Elizabeth slid to the floor onto her knees. He reached out and tried to catch her, appalled that he'd allowed her to fall. Or at least, that's what he thought happened until he felt her hands on his belt, unbuckling it. She made short work of the belt and zipper. Then her hot, greedy hands reached in and pulled out his aching arousal.

He felt her hot breath on him a second before he felt the moist heat of her mouth. Oh hell, yeah. That felt good. He braced his palms against the door and watched her take him into her mouth. He was a large man. Her mouth was small and the fit tight. She worked his cock with an expertise that would have shocked him had his brain been functioning.

All he could do was feel as he began thrusting his hips, watching his cock slide in and out of her mouth. "That's it, baby. Suck me. Damn, that feels good." She had her hands fisted around his shaft, dropping one occasionally to lightly caress with his balls.

His scrotum began to draw up as he felt his orgasm approaching. Grabbing the back of her head with his hand, he held her head steady for his thrusts. His head hit the back of her throat, and she gagged. He tried to pull back but it was too late. He swore as he felt his seed erupt.

"Damn, baby. I'm sorry. I was rough right there at the end."

Mary Elizabeth leaned back against the door, coughing. "It's okay," she said once the coughing fit was over.

The mood broken, Hugh reached out and cut on the light. Mary Elizabeth blinked as her eyes adjusted. They were in the laundry room. Hugh crossed over to a small sink and washed his hands before adjusting his clothes.

"You need to straighten up unless you want everyone out there to know what we were doing." Not that it would matter. His scent was all over her. The bear in him roared in approval. *Mine!*

Now that the haze of lust was clearing from his mind, he questioned himself. If he really didn't want this human, why was he having such a hard time staying away from her? He had to do better than this. At least he hadn't fucked her, but he'd come close. His bear was still hungry. It knew what it wanted, and what it wanted was Mary Elizabeth.

He needed to take a step back and readjust his thinking. As hard as it was for him to believe, there was a strong possibility that Mary Elizabeth was his mate. Right now, he wasn't sure how he felt about it. If he'd tasted her like he intended to before being distracted, he would know for sure. Yes, he wanted a mate, but he wanted to do the choosing. Despite how his bear felt about the situation, it was the man who'd have to live with her. He had to be sure that she was the one.

* * * *

What the hell was she doing? The last thing she needed was a man in her life. First of all, she lived in his building, which was too much like living with him, and gave him a measure of control over her that she didn't like. Besides, she was a firm believer in not mixing business with pleasure. She'd seen firsthand the results of what happened when things went sour in those types of relationships, and they always did eventually. If this relationship went bad, she would have to move, and that might prove difficult since her apartment was the only available rental in town.

For once in her life, she was in control. There was no one telling her what to do, how to think, and what to wear. She was finally free. The only person she had to please was herself. Hugh would ruin all of that. The sad thing was, she was the one that instigated this whole mess. Therefore she was the one who had to fix it. It was time for some damage control.

"Mary Elizabeth, I think we need to take a step back and think about what we're doing before this goes any further. You're a nice woman, but you're my tenant. A relationship between us wouldn't be a good idea."

"Oh, I'm so glad to hear you say that. This is all wrong. I know I gave you the wrong impression just now. I'm really not the type for one night stands. The last thing I want is a relationship with you." She was so relieved. He understood perfectly how she was feeling and was on the same page. She tucked her breasts into her top and tugged on her skirt, making sure everything was covered.

Hugh's eyebrows came together as a ferocious frown crossed his face. "What's wrong with me?"

"What?" she asked distractedly, her mind already on something else. She had to drag her mind back to the conversation. "As far as I know, nothing." She inspected herself to see if she missed anything.

"You said, 'The last thing I want is a relationship with you.' Why me, specifically? Is it because of Charles?"

Mary Elizabeth snapped to attention. "Are you crazy? Didn't you just say a relationship between us wouldn't be a good idea?" Men! See, this was one more reason why she didn't need a man in her life. She turned and opened the door, peeped out to see if anyone was nearby.

Yes, but it was different when he said it. He never expected her to agree. Why was she so against a relationship with him specifically? He was a good catch. He owned his own business. He was decent enough looking and he was a nice guy. What more could she want?

Women always wanted him. He never had any problems attracting women. He was usually turning them away. He watched her reach under her skirt, pull off her thong and throw it in the trash before tugging her skirt back into place. Then she walked out the door. Knowing she was naked under her skirt caused the blood to drain from his head and flow straight to his cock.

He stalked out of the room behind her, determined to get an answer to his questions. What did she have against him and who the hell was Charles? She was his, not this Charles guy. It didn't matter that up until now he hadn't wanted her. That all changed the minute he discovered she didn't want him. What kind of game was she playing? The woman virtually threw herself at him and now she was saying it was a *mistake*? He caught up with her in the kitchen only to pull up short. Kiesha got to her first.

* * * *

"Kiesha, where have you been? I looked but didn't see you anywhere." Mary Elizabeth was so happy to see her. She could feel Hugh hot and heavy behind her.

"Carol had her baby." Kiesha was positively glowing with excitement. "And I got to watch. This is the first birth I've ever witnessed."

"What!" The shock of what she was saying caused Mary Elizabeth to forget all about Hugh, who was standing there glowering.

"I know. Unbelievable. Apparently she was having contractions and didn't tell Mark. She was determined to be here tonight. You saw that. Well, her water broke and Mark came to get Alex. Get this, instead of lying down and screaming for drugs as any sane woman would do, she set up the spare bedroom, turning it into a delivery room. She set up the equipment, laid out the supplies...Alex had to make her lie down."

"Get out of here. Are you serious?" The very idea of it was mind-boggling.

"Very serious." At that moment, Shannon walked up and asked Kiesha about Carol.

"How did you find out? I wasn't aware that anyone not in the bedroom with us knew what was going on. We tried not to draw any attention to ourselves."

"I was talking with Alex when Mark came to get him," Shannon explained.

"Carol's doing great. It's a boy. Mark is beside himself with excitement."

"What are they going to name him? Have they decided on a name yet?" Both Shannon and Mary Elizabeth spoke, their words overlapping.

"He's being named after his father, of course."

Mary Elizabeth looked at Shannon and they both rolled their eyes. They knew whose idea that was. Women rarely chose to name their sons after the father. There were just too many names to choose from, not to mention the confusion of having two people in the same house with the same name. No, that was a man thing.

Laughing, they pulled out chairs at the bar and settled in for a chat. They talked about other births that they had seen or heard about. Mary Elizabeth, who wasn't doing as good a job ignoring Hugh as she was pretending, heaved a silent sigh of relief when he finally stalked off.

As soon as he was gone, Shannon turned to Mary Elizabeth. "So, what was that all about?"

"I don't know what you're talking about." But her face turned red and she looked everywhere but at Shannon.

Kiesha glanced back and forth between the two them before turning to Shannon. "What's going on? What did I miss?"

"Nothing," Mary Elizabeth mumbled, hoping Shannon would let it drop.

"Oh, I don't know. Which nothing would that be? The nothing where you kicked Hugh after he kissed the breath out of you on the dance floor? Or the nothing where you two were going hot and heavy at it while dancing just before you disappeared together?" Shannon grinned, obviously enjoying herself.

"Really. Oh, my. Do tell. Mary Elizabeth, is there something you'd like to share? Miss, 'I don't have time for a relationship'. Come to think of it, where were you? I know you weren't in the kitchen when I first walked in. Then *poof*! I turn around, and there you are. But you didn't come from the living room."

Shannon leaned forward and sniffed Mary Elizabeth, causing her to jerk away. A devilish glint lit her eyes. "Hugh's scent is all over her. Wherever she was, Hugh was there, too."

Kiesha raised both eyebrows, silently demanding she tell all.

"There's nothing to tell."

"Of course not," Shannon stated with a grin.

"There isn't. So we got a little carried away. It doesn't mean anything."

"Not a thing," Kiesha echoed, obviously trying not to smile.

"Even if I were interested in him—not saying I am—

nothing could come of it. Think about it. The man's my landlord."

"Right. Landlord. Major problem," Shannon teased.

"It wouldn't work. He's too masculine…too dominant…too…too..."

"Alpha?" Kiesha suggested.

Mary Elizabeth snapped her finger. "Yes! That's it. He's too alpha. I've had enough of people telling me what to do. Tonight was interesting, but it just won't work. Hugh said the same thing."

Kiesha and Shannon looked at each other doubtfully.

"Really, it's true. We both agreed."

"Are you sure *both of you* are in agreement? That man looked mighty determined just a minute ago. I don't think you've heard the end of it from him."

Mary Elizabeth hoped Kiesha was wrong.

* * * *

Back in the living room, Hugh ran into Alex. "I heard the news. Everyone alright?"

Alex gave a great big smile. "Everyone's just fine. I wish all of my deliveries went as smooth as this one did."

Hugh grinned in return. "Did you really expect anything less from Carol?"

"No, can't say that I did." They shared a laugh. "I can't wait to see her running around after the little one. He's bound to have her stubbornness and attention to detail. Throw in Mark's sense of humor and it should be very interesting."

Alex looked around him. "Have you seen my mate? She disappeared while I was cleaning up."

"She's in the kitchen with Shannon and Mary Elizabeth." Who was trying her best to ignore him. Standing where he was, he should be able to see her the minute she exited.

"What do you think of her?"

"Who?" He hoped he wasn't talking about Mary Elizabeth. He hadn't made up his mind on the subject yet.

"Mary Elizabeth. What's your impression of her?"

Damn, he is. Hugh couldn't lie. Alex would be able to smell it. The best he could do was stall. He really didn't want to talk about his suspicions right now. "I haven't really been around her much. She's helped out in the diner a few times and what she did to that apartment was nothing short of amazing." He hoped Alex would let it go at that. He wasn't ready to tell anyone yet that she might be his mate. He was still having a hard time believing it.

"So she hasn't said anything about herself?"

"No. Why?" What did Alex know that he wasn't saying?

Alex looked as though he were debating on whether or not to continue. Hugh held his breath, mentally pushing Alex to tell him. Finally, Alex nodded as though coming to a decision. He motioned for Hugh to come a little closer to the wall, away from any ears that might overhear what he was going to say. "One of the reasons I wanted her to rent your place was so that you could keep an eye on her. You know that. What you don't know is that Mary Elizabeth just buried her twin. From what Kiesha's told me, the relationship between them wasn't a good one. But still, it was her sister. I was at the funeral with Kiesha when the mother threw herself over the casket and cried out that she wished it had been Mary Elizabeth that had died, not the other one."

Hugh whistled under his breath. "Man, that's messed up."

"There's more. Apparently she's the one the family relies on to do everything. The one that died was the beautiful, spoiled one. Mary Elizabeth is the caretaker who never gets acknowledged. Kiesha wanted her here to get her away from her messed up family."

Hugh digested that in silence before asking, "Do you know who Charles is?"

"If I'm not mistaken, that was the name of the sister's husband. Why?"

"Just something she said. So, she came here to get away and start over?" That might explain some things.

"Yes. I'm hoping that she'll be a match for one of my wolves. Kiesha would be happy to have her here permanently."

Hugh felt his beast stir, rejecting the idea of Mary Elizabeth with anyone but him. Then what Alex said sank in. "I thought she moved here for good. Are you saying this is temporary?"

"No, it's not supposed to be. Kiesha's concerned that once her family realizes just how dependent upon her they are, they'll put pressure on her to come back. They just lost one daughter. They can't be happy about losing Mary Elizabeth, too."

"You think she'll go back if they apply enough pressure?" Over his dead body. She wouldn't be going anywhere without him.

"It's possible. She has no family here and she's very family-oriented. The only person she knows here is Kiesha. There's the job but Kiesha wouldn't fire her if she wanted to return. If they play the guilt factor just right, she just may cave and head back. We'll have to see. They'll have to get to her before she has the chance to put down any roots. That's when she'll be the most vulnerable to their persuasion."

"If you hadn't told me she had just lost a sister, I wouldn't have known. She isn't acting grief stricken. Well, she seemed kind of sad when she first arrived, but nothing since."

"From what I observed at the funeral, Mary Elizabeth's not the type to let her feelings show. When her mother made that comment, there was this brief flicker of pain, then nothing. It's like she sucked it all deep inside. Kiesha doesn't believe it's hit her yet. She thinks Mary Elizabeth has been so busy taking care of everyone and everything else that she hasn't allowed herself time to grieve. We're both worried about what will happen when the grief does hit. She shouldn't be alone when it happens. That's where you come in. We need you to keep an eye on her without making her suspicious."

Hugh thought about it for a moment. "I think I know how to do it without her knowledge. She already spends a lot of time in the diner with Anne, though that may change when she starts work. She makes these amazing desserts. I can ask her if she'd be willing to make some for the diner. That would give me a reason other than being her landlord to keep in contact with her."

"You think it will work?"

"I don't know. Anne suggested it and she turned her down flat. All I can do is try. If it doesn't, I'll think of something else." It would give him the excuse he needed to get close to her without her suspecting a thing. He stopped talking when Kiesha walked up, looking around expectantly for Mary Elizabeth.

Alex reached out and pulled Kiesha close to his side. "How are you holding up?"

With a sigh, Kiesha looked at Hugh and rolled her eyes. "Alex, I'm still in my first trimester. I'm fine. Are you going to be like this the whole pregnancy?"

"Yes." Hugh and Alex answered simultaneously, both of them grinning at her.

"Are you hungry? Thirsty? Can I get you anything? Do you need to sit down and rest?"

"No, I grabbed a plate while I was in the kitchen talking to Shannon and Mary Elizabeth. Mary Elizabeth told me about this drink she tried and how good it was. She said it was real fruity and you could barely taste the alcohol. I wish I could drink. I want to try one."

Hugh and Alex looked at each other in concern.

Alex asked, "Did she happen to mention the name of this drink?"

"Shifter something. I thought it was kind of cool that ya'll had a drink named after you."

"Us, baby. You're one of us now," he reminded her. "Was it Shifter Surprise?"

Kiesha snapped her finger. "Yes, that's it."

"Where is she now?" This time the question came from Hugh. He was looking around, trying to spot her.

"She went home." Kiesha was grinning like she knew something he didn't.

"What!" Again Hugh and Alex spoke in concert, this time in stereo.

The grin slid from Kiesha's face to be replaced by a frown. "I said she left. She was getting tired. Is that a problem?"

Hugh turned to Alex. "I'll go after her and make sure she's okay. You explain to your mate." *And when I find mine, I'm going to turn her over my knee.* Hugh turned and left.

"What's going on? Why is he going after Mary Elizabeth? If she's in trouble, you'd better start talking...Now. This is my friend you're talking about."

"Shifter Surprise is a drink made especially for shifters. Because of our high metabolism and lean body mass, it's difficult for us to become intoxicated, no matter how much we drink. The alcohol doesn't stay in our system long enough to even get a buzz. To get around this, some of the guys created a special drink—the Shifter Surprise. It's made with several different liquors and fruit juice, plus one extra ingredient that forces the alcohol to hit the bloodstream fast and hard, before our metabolism can burn it off. It's like having five shots hit your system at one time."

"So this drink is really strong, I get that. Why did Hugh run after her? She seemed fine to me."

"Is Mary Elizabeth a hardcore drinker?" He was allowing her brain time to come to the correct conclusion.

"No, she's not. She gets drunk off wine coolers."

"What's going to happen when all of that liquor hits her system, especially if she happens to be driving down a dark mountain road at the time?"

Kiesha's mouth formed a silent "O" as she finally understood what he was getting at. Before she could comment, Shannon joined them. "What's wrong, Kiesha? I can smell your fear."

Alex answered Shannon, knowing she would understand his concern. "Mary Elizabeth drank a Shifter Surprise."

"I know. I watched her drink it."

"You saw her with it and you didn't stop her?" Alex couldn't believe it.

"No. She only had one and she was eating the whole time she was sipping on it. If it were going to have a major impact on her system, it would have done so by now. Is that why Hugh left?"

"Yes. He went to ensure she makes it home in one piece."

"Well, she should be okay. Mary Elizabeth's a smart cookie. I don't know why ya'll are so worried.

"Maybe not," Kiesha said slowly, a pensive look on her face.

Her tone got both Shannon and Alex's attention. "Why do you say that, honey?" Alex didn't want any more bad news. He was just starting to relax.

"She liked that drink so much that she got another one on her way out the door."

* * * *

Mary Elizabeth arrived home, drink in one hand and purse in the other. What a night! She tossed her purse onto the coffee table and sat down to unlace her boots. With a sigh of relief, she wiggled her toes. That was much better. She took off her jacket, propped her feet on the coffee table, and sat sipping her drink. She had an excellent time at the party, but now she was tired.

Enough reminiscing. She'd better move, otherwise she'd wake up on the couch. She finished her drink and tossed the cup on the table. She'd get it in the morning. After turning off the lights, she headed for her room, stripping as she went. At the last minute, she detoured to the bathroom. She was sweaty from all of the dancing and needed a shower. The abrupt change of direction caused her to stumbled, and she fell against the wall, feeling a bit woozy. The sooner she laid down the better. She was so tired, she was dizzy.

She intended to rush through her shower, but the hot water felt so good beating on her weary muscles that she lingered. Another wave of dizziness hit and she decided she'd better finish. She rushed through the rest of her shower and almost fell over trying to wash her legs. Man, she better get to bed quick. She turned off the water, and left the towel on the rack. No sense drying off. She'd just fall on her face. No one could see that she was naked. She opened the door, her mind focused on getting into bed and stopped liked she'd run into an invisible wall.

Chapter Six

Hugh left the party in a controlled panic, trying not to think of all the things that could happen to his mate before he got to her. Alcohol poisoning was just one of the few things to cross his mind. He drove slowly, scanning both sides of the road just in case she'd lost control of her vehicle and run off the road. With all these trees, it would be too easy to drive right by the site of an accident and not see it until it was too late.

His nerves hadn't been stretched this tight since his last mission. He'd given Uncle Sam twenty years of his life, going on missions and putting his life on the line for his county. In a way, he could understand Mary Elizabeth. He knew what it was like to have other people controlling your actions, always having to answer to someone other than yourself. While he understood how she felt, it didn't change a thing. She was his mate. She'd just have to adjust.

If he'd had doubts before, he didn't now. His beast was straining at the leash, urging him to hurry. Its mate was in danger and it wanted out. He controlled it, knowing patience was the key. He couldn't afford to screw this up by rushing. It might cause him to miss something he needed to see.

To calm himself, he thought back to his conversation with Alex. The thought of her leaving caused a growl to rumble out of his chest as his beast rattled against its cage. He and his beast were in perfect agreement. His mate was going nowhere, not if he had anything to do with it.

His thoughts returned to the mysterious Charles. Why had she mentioned him? Did she have something going with her brother-in-law? She didn't seem like the type to do something like that. Maybe she was referring to someone else. It didn't matter. She belonged to him, no matter what anyone else thought. He wasn't sure why, but something about this woman brought out the caveman in him. He wanted to grab Mary Elizabeth by her hair and drag her into his cave, using his club on anyone who got in his way.

Once he was sure she was okay, he was going to set her straight on a few things. It didn't matter what she wanted. She was his. She could just get over any issues she had with him. At the first opportunity, he was claiming her. Given the way she felt, he'd probably have to trick her. Giving it some thought, he set up his battle plan. Once, he'd excelled at strategic planning. Claiming Mary Elizabeth was the most important mission of his life. He'd need all of his skills to accomplish it.

First, he needed to build upon the attraction she felt for him. She could deny it all she liked, but there was something powerful between them. Something explosive. All he had to do was to convince her to explore their attraction and let nature take its course. Let her think it was her choice. Get her to let her guard down and the mating heat would do the rest.

It seemed to take forever but he made it all the way into town without spotting her vehicle. He saw the diner, and drove around back. Her truck was parked haphazardly in the lot. He viewed it with trepidation, relieved that she'd made it home but concerned because she usually parked with more care than what he was seeing.

He took the stairs two at a time until he reached the top. Hugh banged on the door, and then waited in vain for a response. The walls of the apartment were too thick for him to hear anything inside, even with his sensitive hearing. When he'd waited what he thought was a reasonable amount of time for her to answer the door, he pulled out his keys and let himself in.

Once inside, he could hear the shower running. He wasn't leaving until he saw for himself that she was fine. He closed the door, and as an afterthought, locked it as well. There was a cup sitting on the coffee table, one he recognized from Alex's house. He could smell the alcohol from where he stood. Damn, she must have grabbed another drink on her way out of the door. The shower cut off. As he turned toward the bathroom, he spotted her skirt lying on the floor. A few paces beyond that lay the top she'd worn.

He took off his jacket and tossed it onto the couch as his temperature suddenly spiked. He paced back and forth, waiting for her to come out of the bathroom. Screw that! It was taking her too long. He was going in there to check on her. As his hand reached for the knob, the door opened and out stepped Mary Elizabeth—wet, naked, and glistening.

The blood instantly drained from his head to his groin. Everything but the need to mate forgotten, he reached for her. Mary Elizabeth spotted him and turned sheet white, and then an interesting shade of green. She slapped a hand over her mouth, her eyes mirroring her distress right before she spun around and hurled herself at the toilet. Sounds of retching could be heard as her body released the contents of her stomach.

Oh hell, he'd been afraid of this. Pushing up his sleeves, he followed her into the bathroom. She knelt on the floor hugging the toilet as her body heaved and spasmed. He gathered her hair, pulling it up and back, and made soothing noises. He stayed like that until her stomach was empty and she was dry heaving.

Hugh wet a washcloth with cold water and placed it on her hot, sweaty forehead. Using her hair like a handle, he tugged her head back until it rested on his thigh. When she stopped heaving, he helped her stand and supported her while she rinsed and gargled. Then he carefully lifted her into his arms, carried her into the bedroom, and laid her on top of the bed.

He searched until he found her pain reliever. A glass of water in one hand, and pills in the other, he returned to the room and sat on the bed beside her. He slid his hand under her neck and lifted her into a half-sitting position.

"Drink this. You don't want to dehydrate. Take small sips and it won't upset your stomach. If you keep the water down, swallow some pain reliever."

He brought the cup to her mouth and held it there, helping her hold onto it just in case in her weakness she dropped it. She cautiously took a few small sips, and when those stayed down, she took a few more. When she'd had enough, she pushed the cup away and turned her head. Hugh brought the cup back to her mouth and pressed it against her lips.

"If you can, try to drink all of it. Your body's had a shock and the more water you drink now, the better you'll feel later."

She swallowed a bit more of the water, and then turned her head away, her lips pressed tightly together. "No more. It's trying to come back up."

Hugh took the cup and set it on the nightstand, and then lowered her body back to the bed.

"What's wrong with me? Was it something I ate? And what are you doing here?"

"No, nothing was wrong with the food. It's not what you ate that's the problem. It's what you drank. Shifter Surprise. Didn't the bartender warn you not to drink it? Your body's reacting to the alcohol." If she didn't look so miserable, she'd be over his knee right now, getting the spanking of her life.

"The bartender mentioned something about the drink

being strong, but I wasn't in a mood to listen. How did you find out?"

"Kiesha told us, thank God. You have no idea how worried we were, especially when we discovered you had already left. Anything could have happened." And that was before he knew she'd gotten a second one. He'd have been a basket case had he known. "The next time a bartender tells you a drink is too strong, listen to him."

She didn't get a chance to answer. She lurched off of the bed and sprinted back into the bathroom for round number two. Hugh followed closely behind and assisted as he had before, until she was back in bed again. They went through this twice more until her system was totally purged. After laying her on the bed the last time, he called Alex and let him know that she was okay. Alex wanted to send someone over, but Hugh convinced him not to. He'd played nursemaid to plenty of drunken soldiers in his time, so he knew exactly what to do.

Back into the room, he expected to find her sleeping. Instead, she was in the fetal position, shivering. Cursing, he rushed to her side and placed his hand on her forehead. She leaned into his touch.

"Cold. So cold," she managed to get out through clenched teeth.

Without delay, Hugh scooped her up, flipped back the covers, laid her down and tucked her in. He waited to see if that would help. It didn't. She was curled up so tight she was nothing but a small lump under the covers.

Damn, her body was reacting to the alcohol. He had to get her warm. If he couldn't, he was going to have to take her to the emergency room for alcohol poisoning. He flung off his clothes and climbed under the covers with her. He reached over and uncurled her body, pulling her to him, and wrapped his arms around her. She fought him like a weak kitten until the heat from his body began to soak in. Then she wrapped her body around his like a clinging vine. He groaned and felt his body respond as her bare breast disturbed the small smattering of hair on his chest, her puckered nipples poking into him. His erection rose, nudging against her opening.

He gritted his teeth and forced his body to stand down, resisting the urge to thrust up and sheath his body in her heat. Now was not the time, but soon. Very, very soon. He made himself think of mundane things until he had control over his baser instincts. When he gained it, he forced his body to relax and rest while it could. It was shaping up to be a long night.

Chapter Seven

"Mary Beth. Mary Beth."   She heard a voice calling her name. "Mary Beth." That was Babs! Only one person called her by that name.

"Babs, where are you?"   Her eyes snapped opened, but still she couldn't see. Her bed and room had both disappeared. There was a heavy fog blanketing the place where she stood.

"Mary Beth, where are you? Mary Beth!" the voice cried out.

"Babs, I'm here. Where are you? I can't see. The fog's too thick." She twirled around in a circle, trying to pinpoint the direction from which Babs' voice was coming. Fog was everywhere. She could barely see two feet in front of her.

"Mary Beth, I needed you and you let me down. It's all your fault. I'm dead now because of you. Why didn't you stop me?" The voice came again, this time to her left, its cry more urgent.

"I tried. You wouldn't listen. It's not my fault." As she stepped to the left, hands held out in front of her, something shadowy went by on her right, disturbing the fog. She spun around in that direction, only to find nothing there. "Babs! Where are you, Babs? I'm coming."

"You were supposed to protect me, Mary Beth. You let me down. Failed me when I needed you the most."

Something shadowy went by on her left, and she spun in that direction, trying to see what it was. "You made your own decision. You didn't listen. You never listened."

"You're supposed to watch over me. Mother told you to protect me." Babs' face appeared out of the fog. It was gray and freakish-looking, like something out of a horror movie. Mary Elizabeth flinched and jerked away, falling on her behind. In the background, like an evil voiceover, she could hear her mother. "You're such a failure, Mary Elizabeth. Can't even do the simplest things. Now your failure's cost your sister her life."

"It's not my fault. I'm not responsible for Babs." She backpedaled, trying to get away from the ghostly apparition masquerading as her sister Babs.

Babs and her mother's disembodied heads spun around her in a circle, cutting off all avenues of exit, their voices chanting, "Your fault. Your fault."

Mary Elizabeth jerked awake, gasping for air. Tears ran down her face and her heart pounded like it would jump out of her chest. Their words echoed in her mind.

A light clicked on, causing her to blink rapidly as her eyes struggled to adjust.

"What's wrong? Are you sick again?" Hugh's voice was groggy with sleep. He sat up and rubbed his hand across his face, like he was trying to wake up.

Mary Elizabeth shook her head. She lay down and turned her back toward him, hoping he would go back to sleep. Her throat was too tight for her to give him a verbal answer. There was a heavy silence. She could feel him watching her. She hunched her shoulders defensively, resisting the urge to wipe the tears from her face. She really didn't want him to know she was crying. Let him think she was drifting back to sleep.

She could feel his eyes, boring a hole in her back like he had x-ray vision. It was causing her nerves to draw up tight. She could feel the tension in her neck and shoulders.

"If you're not sick, what's wrong?"

Silence.

"I know something is wrong. You're body's too tense for you to be sleeping."

When she refused to respond, he gave a long, drawn out sigh, like she was vexing him. She slid her legs off the bed, needing to get to the bathroom where she could have some privacy. Before her feet touched the floor, Hugh's arm reached out and snagged her by the waist, dragging her across the bed and into his lap. "If you're not sick, it must be something else."

She kept her face turned away from him, still not answering. She was doing all she could not to break down and cry. If she opened her mouth, it would all come out.

"Alex told me about what happened to your sister. Must have been rough. Want to talk about it?"

At his words, she jerked and shook her head rapidly, and a sob escaped before she could choke it back. She was not going to cry. She hated to cry.

Hugh wrapped his arms around her, resting his chin on her shoulder. "It's okay to cry, you know. You need to grieve. Let it out. Don't hold it in. You'll only make yourself sick if you do."

She pushed against him, trying to get away. He held her tight. "Let go."

"Not until you release those tears you're holding back and get it out of your system."

"I'm not crying. I detest crying. There's nothing to cry about. She's dead and gone and crying won't bring her back. I tried to stop her, but she wouldn't listen. She wouldn't listen and now she's dead. Oh God, Hugh, she's dead. Why didn't she listen to me?" With that, the dam burst and she began crying in earnest. Fighting Hugh, she tried to free herself and get away from him, not wanting anyone to see her like this.

Hugh locked her in an iron grip, refusing to release her. Instead, he gathered her even closer to his body, rocking her and making soothing noises. Still, she fought him even as she fought against the grief, until she'd exhausted her strength. Giving in, she slumped against him and let it out—all the sorrow and the conflicting feelings she felt for her sister that she loved yet now could admit that she hated with equal passion. She cried for years of mistreatment by her mother, but most of all she cried for what should have been and never was.

The tears went on and on, until all that was left were the hiccups. Hugh lifted her off of his lap and went into the bathroom. She curled up on her side, facing away from him. He climbed back under the covers and pulled her close before handing her the tissues. She wiped her still streaming eyes and blew her stuffy, clogged up nose. Her face felt hot and swollen, and her body sore.

Hugh curved around her back like a spoon, with her head tucked under his chin and his arm around her waist, holding her tight. She closed her eyes and tried to stop the flow of the tears tracking silently down her face. They wouldn't stop. Memory after memory, of good times and bad, flowed through her mind like a river. With each memory came a fresh flood of weeping. She needed to stop crying. She had to do something get her mind off of the past. Enough was enough.

She turned in his arms, shifting to face him, and pushed steadily against his chest until he was half lying on his back. Then she threw an arm around his waist and began to spread kisses all over his chest.

"Uh, Mary Elizabeth. What are you doing?"

It should be obvious. If he had to ask, she wasn't doing it right. She pushed him again until he lay completely on his back. Her hand slid down to stroke his rapidly hardening cock.

"Honey, that feels good, but I don't think this is a good idea. Let's wait until you're feeling better."

Mary Elizabeth ignored him. She threw her leg over

his and straddled his thighs. Sliding backwards, she worked her way down his torso with her mouth.

"Mary Elizabeth, stop. Let's discuss this. *Baby, please*. I don't think you know what you're doing."

Why won't he shut up? She didn't want to talk. Couldn't he tell?

Hugh had a decision to make. He didn't want to take advantage of her fragile emotional state. It might jeopardize his long-term objective, but he couldn't allow her to continue with her current course of action.

His body jerked in reaction to the feel of her hot, moist breath on his penis. She grabbed his cock with both hands and was frantically sucking the head. This was nothing like before. Her head was bobbing up and down like she was in a race to finish him off as fast as possible. He reached down and tried to pry her off of him. She fought against him, tightening her teeth on his cock in warning when he persisted. Hands in the air, he surrendered and let her have her way.

This wasn't right. He wasn't sure how he'd envisioned their first night together, but this wasn't it. How to stop her without hurting her or worse, inflicting pain upon his most valuable asset? While he was strategizing the options available to him with the least amount of collateral damage, she abruptly stopped.

Rising above him, she positioned her body and tried to impale herself on his cock. It didn't work. One, the woman obviously didn't know what she was doing. Two, she was tight and dry. She was not forcing him inside, no matter how hard she tried. Finally, she gave a shriek of frustration and slapped him on his stomach. "Help me!"

He casually reached out and caught both of her wrists in his hand and pulled until she lay flat on top of his body. Then he rolled them until he was on top. "If you want me to help you, you have to tell me what it is you are trying to do." His tone was utterly reasonable, but there was a hint of steel underneath.

She held his gaze for only a moment before her eyes to slide away in shame. Tears once more filled her eyes. She was such a failure, just like her mother stated. Here she was, naked and willing, and she couldn't even seduce the man into having sex with her.

"Unh, unh, unh. Look at me."

She gathered her courage and then raised her eyes to meet his, which immediately drilled into hers. "I'm sorry, Hugh. I just wanted a distraction, something to take my mind off of Babs and all of the memories. I just can't deal with them right now."

He studied her for a moment, gauging her sincerity. He was quiet for so long that she began to squirm. "I can help you, if that's what you want. But know this. This won't be a one-time deal. You will not use me tonight and then toss me away tomorrow. Understood? Know what you're asking because if we do this, it's just the beginning. There won't be any turning back. I won't let you go. Do you accept my terms?"

She blinked at him while nervously chewing on her bottom lip. He could almost see her mind churning as she cautiously examined his words, looking for the trap contained within. He watched her like a predator with his prey, willing her to agree to his terms. One simple yes, and she was his.

"I understand. I accept your terms," she said solemnly.

His beast roared in triumph, but the man was more subdued. He wouldn't pass up this opportunity, but it wouldn't be the fierce claiming his nature demanded of him. That would have to come later, and there would be a later. She was exhausted, both physically and emotionally. She didn't really want sex. What she wanted and desperately needed was sleep. She sought a way to shut her mind off so she could rest, and he needed to mark her, claim as his. He would give them what they both desired.

He repositioned his body so that his legs lay on the outside of hers, his erection heavy against her mound. He braced his forearms on either side of her head and resting his weight on them. Then he lowered his face until they were eye-to-eye. Her eyes immediately shied away. "No, look at me. Look me in the eye."

His eyes were two inches away. She didn't she'd ever been this close to anyone in her life. Eyes were such strange things. From a distance, his appeared to be black. Now that she was close, she could see there were specks of gold in his eyes. She felt her eyes losing focus.

"Hey, keep your eyes and your mind focused on me."

She snapped back to attention, unaware that her mind had drifted. This was so uncomfortable. If the eyes really were the windows to the soul, she wondered what hers revealed. Could he see what a failure she was? Did all her disappointments show? Maybe her mother was right. Maybe she was too old and too fat to be trying to attract a man's attention now. What did she have worth offering?

"Mary Elizabeth." He cupped her face, and put the tip of his nose right against hers. "Look at me. Not through me. I need you to focus, honey. Don't let your mind wander. Breathe with me. Inhale when I exhale. Focus your attention on me. Can you do that for me?"

"I'll try."

"Good girl."

Mary Elizabeth concentrated on matching her breathing to his. She focused on the feel of his chest, rising and falling; the soft caress of his breath against her lips, all the while staring deep into his eyes. When he inhaled, she exhaled and when he exhaled, she inhaled. On and on it went—inhale, exhale, inhale, exhale—until his very essence permeated her body.

It was the most intimate thing she'd ever done. She never realized just how rarely she gave complete eye contact with anyone. Mary Elizabeth saw him, really saw him, like she was looking into his soul.

Their breathing synchronized on its own and she no longer had to keep track. She felt his body surrounding hers. Felt the heat of his sex, nestled against hers. Felt his breath upon her face as they breathed the same air. She inhaled deeply, trying to breath in more of his scent. She could feel her body softening under his, the tension leaving it. Her nipples began to tighten into little buds that brushed against his chest with each inhalation. Moisture began to pool deep within before leaking out to dampen her mound and run down her thighs.

Slowly, their breathing increased, his keeping pace with hers as arousal coursed through her body. Yet he did nothing more than looking at her. Look into her, like he could see her soul and was entranced by what he saw. She moved restlessly, seeking closer contact.

"Be still," he whispered. "Be still and feel."

"I'm trying." She could feel something building inside of her. Something strong. She wanted, no, needed something that she knew he could give to her.

Slowly, oh, so very slowly, he closed the distance between them and laid his lips on top of hers. He didn't move. He didn't try to kiss her. He just lay there with his lips pressed against hers, forcing her to breathe through her nostrils, his eyes maintaining contact the whole while. She forced herself to lie there as he instructed and follow his lead. Finally, as though rewarding her for good behavior, he gave her more.

He gently licked at her closed mouth, first one lip, then the other. He outlined her lips with his tongue, starting with the seam between her lips. Pulling her bottom lip into his mouth, he suckled and nibbled on it, before switching his focus to the top lip. He brushed his lips back and forth across hers softly, never once losing eye contact. Extreme pleasure caused her eyes to fall to half-mast.

"Keep your eyes open. Let me see you," he instructed and went back to suckling her top lip, biting it gently and teasing it with his mouth.

Unable to take it anymore, she raised up, trying to capture his tongue. She wanted to taste him. At her urging, he slowly deepened the kiss. He licked the inside of her lips before plunging inside for a deeper taste. He kissed her thoroughly, leaving no part untouched. The whole while he kept his eyes opened, his gaze piercing hers.

Taking things to another level, he began to rub his erection against her mound, working his way between her cream-dampened, thighs. She tried to open her legs, but his legs blocked her. She spoke into his mouth. "Hugh, let me open my legs."

"No. Keep them closed." He took her mouth again in another bone melting kiss. He kept up a steady rhythm with his hips, slowly working his way between her thighs. It was a slow, sensuous motion, applying steady pressure against her clit.

"Hugh, come inside of me." She tried arching against him, to move him closer to her opening, but he was too heavy.

"No, not yet. There's no need to rush."

"But, Hugh..." She couldn't find the words to tell him what she needed. Her mind was blank. Her body had taken over.

"No, buts. You're tired. Trust me. I'll give you what you need. Just let go and let me take care of you. All you need to do is lay here and let your mind relax. Feel me. Feel what I do to you." He was determined to make this last as long as possible. He was taking his time, overwhelming her with sensation. He kissed her to keep her from speaking.

As the pleasure built, she dragged her mouth away

from his, panting, trying to get more air. She couldn't move. Her head was gripped solid between his palms, preventing it from twisting from side-to-side. She needed to find an outlet for the pressure building inside of her but there was nowhere for it to go. He held her tight enough to prevent her from moving but not so tight that it would hurt.

"Hugh, let me go. I need to move."

"No, moving. Just feel."

He kept up the sensuous pressure, stroking his cock steadily against her clit. It was making her crazy. Every nerve in her body went haywire. Her toes curled, her calves and thighs hardened and the muscles in her butt clenched. Her stomach contracted. Her arms, trapped against the sides of his body, tightened until she could feel each individual muscle.

"Harder. I need more pressure."

"No. Slow and steady, just like this."

"Hugh," she complained. She opened her hands, the only part of her body she could move, grabbed a hold of his waist and dug her nails into his flesh. She was right on the edge. She could feel the climax hovering just out of reach.

He grunted at the small pain and kissed her again. Watching her closely, he saw her eyes dilate, signaling her approaching orgasm. When her eyes began to close, to better capture the sensation, he spoke. "Open your eyes. Let me watch you come." He lowered his head until his forehead touched hers, forcing her to keep her eyes on his.

She should have felt self-conscious, knowing he was watching, but she was too far-gone to care. Her orgasm built and built, until like a tidal wave it crashed over her. It went on and on as Hugh kept up the steady pressure, pushing her past one orgasm and into another. As the last one faded, Hugh pressed a meaty thigh between hers and maneuvered her legs open.

Changing angles, he drove deep into her pussy, until he was embedded to the hilt. Instead of immediately thrusting as she expected, he rotated his hips in a circular motion that put continuous pressure on her clit, both inside and out, hitting all of her g-spots.

"Ohmygod, ohmygod, ohmygod! What are you doing to me? Stop! Wait, don't stop. Stop! I can't take anymore. It's too much. Wait! Hugh! Ohmygod. It's coming! If you stop now, I'll kill you! Harder, Hugh, harder! "

Her next orgasm, when it hit, was fierce. It shook her from head-to-toe. Her mouth opened in a silent scream and her eyes rolled back into her head. Tears coursed down her face. She saw spots and everything faded to black as her body struggled to handle the intensity of it.

As her sheath rippled around his cock, Hugh widened the opening between her legs. He hooked her under the knees and lifted her legs until she was almost bent in half. With her body wide open, he thrust heavily, trying to reach the opening to her womb. Instinct demanded he plant his seed and bring forth new life, claiming his mate in the most basic of ways. He felt his eyes change and his teeth lengthening into fangs as his beast came to the forefront. He hid his face against her neck so she couldn't see his partial shift. His teeth locked on the curve of her neck and shoulder as he strove for his own release. When it struck, he bit down hard until he drew blood, marking her as his mate for eternity.

Mine! At last he had a mate. He held her tight, crushing her in his arms as his body shook with his release. When it lessened, he rolled onto his back to keep from crushing her with his weight, dragging her with him. Her body lay limp like a cooked noodle on his. He'd totally drained her. His cock, still embedded inside, was hard as steel. He ignored it. This little taste of her would have to be enough.

"Go to sleep." He rubbed his hands up and down her

back.

"'Kay," she mumbled, already halfway asleep.

He held her while she slept. Mentally, he reviewed his battle plan. Phase One of his plan was complete. Tomorrow would be soon enough for Phase Two. Objective met, he allowed himself to sleep.

Chapter Eight

Always a light sleeper, Hugh heard ringing and woke. A glance to his left assured him that Mary Elizabeth would not be getting up to answer the phone. He doubted she even heard it. She lay sprawled on her stomach with her arm pillowing her head. The other arm dangled off of the edge of the bed and still, the phone continued to ring. She must not have voicemail or it would have picked up by now.

He considered letting it ring until whoever was on the phone gave up. He didn't for two reasons. Mary Elizabeth needed her sleep. She'd had a rough night with everything that happened, and he didn't want her being disturbed. Also, she only knew a few people here in town. Judging by the way the phone continued to ring, whoever was on the other line must be family. Reluctantly, he lumbered into the front room to answer it.

"Hello?" He answered around a yawn, his voice heavy with sleep.

"Sorry, wrong number." The male caller disconnected before Hugh could speak. With a shrug, he hung up and turned to go back to bed. He hadn't had nearly enough sleep. He didn't make it two steps before the phone rang again.

He sighed and answered. "Hello."

There was a pause, and then a confused, male voice said, "There must be some mistake. I'm trying to reach Mary Elizabeth Brown."

"This is her residence. She's asleep right now. If you

104

tell me who's calling, I'll give her the message."

"Who the hell is this? If she's asleep, then what are you doing there? Why are you answering her phone?" The confusion left the caller's voice and his tone became arrogant and demanding.

"I'm the man who answered the phone. What's it to you?" Hugh operated on a "need to know" basis. As far as he was concerned, this person did not need to know who he was or what his objective was for being there.

"This is Charles Remington, III, and Mary Elizabeth is my fiancée. I have a right to know what you're doing in her apartment, answering her phone at eight-thirty in the morning while she's still asleep."

Hugh's stance became battle ready and his hand clenched the phone. "Well, Mr. Charles Remington *the Third*, she may have been your fiancée but she belongs to me now. I'll tell her you called."

"Now listen here. *WHO ARE YOU?* I demand an answer!"

"I'm the man who spent the night fucking your fiancée," Hugh said calmly, and disconnected the call. As an afterthought, he pulled the plug from the wall. Wouldn't want Mr. Charles Remington the Third calling back, at least not before he got some answers.

So that was Charles. Seemed he and his mate needed to have a little talk. Clarify a few matters. He walked back into the room and stood there contemplating her. She lay there completely oblivious to the turmoil swirling about her. If there truly was a fiancé in the picture, this was going to require a minute adjustment to his strategy. His objective was still the same, but he needed to change in his methodology. His timetable just got upped. He'd planned to be subtle in his maneuverings, but now that approach was out the window. He was going to have to be more direct, more in charge. The image of a human steamroller came to mind. His mate wouldn't know what hit her.

* * * *

Shannon met with Alex at his office at nine the next morning as scheduled. She was nervous but excited. Maybe now she would get some answers. Knowing was always better than not knowing, in her opinion. If she knew what was happening, she could take action. This not knowing what was wrong with her was slowly but surely killing her.

"Tell me what's going on with you. I want to know everything. Don't leave anything out. I want to know if you're eating, how much you're eating, if you're sleeping at night and how frequently you wake up. Tell me about any pain or discomfort you're having and where it's located. Be totally open and honest. No symptom is too small or too strange. Anything and everything you tell me will help narrow down possibilities of what's going on in your body."

She told him everything. Her restlessness, and feelings of being watched. She mentioned the tingling in her legs and periods of extreme heat. She spoke of being thirsty all the time and strange dreams that she could never fully remember. Dreams that left her wet and wanting but never completely fulfilled.

"What about the attack? Have you remembered anything else from that night?"

"You think this is somehow related to the Hunt?" The thought crossed her mind, but she didn't see how it could be related.

"Anything is possible. I'm trying to cover all my bases. So? Did you remember anything else? Without access to your previous medical history, I have no way of knowing whether something that night is responsible for what you're experiencing."

"I remember the fights, and then the rest is a blank

until I woke up in Carol's house." No one would tell her who found her and brought her to them. They said it would better if she remembered on her own.

"Alright. Now I want you to go into the exam room and undress. There's a paper gown on the examination table for you to change into. Once you're ready, I'll come in and do a full exam and withdraw blood for testing."

When he finished examining her, he threw his gloves into the trashcan and helped Shannon to sit up. "Get dressed and go into my office. I want to run some tests and then I'll be in to speak with you."

Shannon dressed and then went into his office to wait. Flipping mindlessly through all of the health and fitness magazines displayed, her mind went through scenario after scenario of what the diagnosis would be.

Alex breezed into the office. Settling into his chair, he placed her chart on the desk before him. "Have you ever heard of a condition called Polycythemia?"

"No. What is it? Is this 'whatever you called it' what's wrong with me?" Shannon was irritated to discover that she was vaguely alarmed and she didn't even know what it was yet. Getting a grip, she waited impatiently for him to answer.

"PV is a blood disorder in which the body produces too many red blood cells, thickening the blood. It's extremely rare and it explains some of the symptoms you're experiencing."

"Are you sure? I mean, if it's so rare, how would I have it?" This is not what she was expecting. Of course, she didn't really know what to expect. Shape-shifters were rarely sick. It had to do with their rapid healing abilities.

"No, I'm not one hundred percent sure. I would need to run more test. Your red blood count is higher than normal, which caused your blood to thicken. I noticed it when I drew blood. In conjunction with your other symptoms and after a little research into the matter, this is the diagnosis I settled on.

"So this is PV is what's causing my problems?"

"Not entirely. This is only a part of it. It would explain the tingling in your legs, itchy skin, and possibly your lack of sleep. It wouldn't normally be a major issue, not in its milder stages like what you have, but there are complications. Something has thrown your body into a second heat. You're not mistaken. You're going into heat and that's going to create a problem."

"You think?" she asked sarcastically. Once a year was bad enough. Twice in one year was mind-boggling. Males had no idea what a female went through when her body went into heat.

"There's more. Do you take birth control of any kind?" He sounded downright grim. She didn't know where this was headed, but she didn't have a good feeling about it.

Many she-wolves took birth control to control the heat. It helped the female not to mount any penis that presented itself at the peak of their heat. That's when a female was most vulnerable. The instinct to mate and reproduce could literally have her acting like a bitch in heat, accepting any and all comers.

"Yes, I'm on the Pill." She named the brand.

"You have to come off of them."

Her mouth dropped open and she bit back the urge to rail at him. Did he understand what he was asking her to do?

"Alex, you know I can't do that, especially not now." If she did, she might as well lay down in the street naked and hang a sign around her neck that said, "Fuck me." It would be the same thing.

"Shannon, I'm sorry, but you really don't have any alternatives. I hate to sound melodramatic but it really is a choice between your virtue and your life. With the extra blood your body is producing, the Pill dramatically increases your chances of forming a blood clot, which I don't have to tell you are deadly. That's not a risk I'm willing to take. You need to come off of the Pill and any other natural substances you're taking to control the heat. All of them have the same threat potential."

Shannon had never gone through the heat without some type of buffer. She didn't know how. Only mated females did it without taking anything. Wouldn't Rory get a kick out of this? "Alex, if I can't control this thing, I could end up mated to any wolf that was cunning enough to get to me, whether I want to be or not."

"I know the risk, Shannon, but would you prefer losing your life? This is serious business. I don't want your choices taken away from you any more than you do. Look, here's the problem. The increased blood production thickens the blood in your veins, increasing the potential of blood clots forming in your body. Because of the hormones in your birth control pills, they also dramatically increase the blood's likelihood of clotting. The hormones produced by your body which is throwing you into another heat, also increase your risk factor. I can't control the blood production because there is no treatment or cure. All we can do is monitor it and take measures as needed. I can't stop the heat because I don't know what's causing it. The only factor in this equation that is in our control is the birth control. Anything that we can do to decrease the potential for blood clotting needs to be done."

Shannon didn't want to give up her pills, but she could see that she had no choice. Still trying to gain some control over her circumstances, she tried to find another way out. "Is there anything you can do about the pack? Make the unmated males leave me alone or something? "

He looked at her sorrowfully and shook his head. "Under normal circumstances I could try, but your season is scheduled to hit its peak right during the week of the full moon—a blue moon."

She stared at him in horror as the implications of what he was saying set in. A blue moon was a second full moon falling within the same month. It only happened about once every two years. Weaker shifters had little to no control over their beast during a regular full moon. Blue moons were worse because they triggered a sexual frenzy. Unmated males secretly referred to the week of the blue moon as the "FuckFest." The urge to mate became all-consuming and everyone was effected, even the alphas. There were always more pregnancies after a blue moon phase. Oh, shit! Her heat was hitting its peak during a blue moon. There wasn't a worse time for this to happen.

"It will be alright, Shannon. We'll figure something out, okay? I promise. In the meantime, let me give you something to help you sleep at night." He reached into his coat pocket and handed her some pills.

"Thanks, Alex. I appreciate your help. At least now I know what's going on. Do me a favor. Don't say anything to anyone about this, please?"

"I couldn't. It would violate doctor-patient confidentiality. Try not to worry. The last thing you need right now is stress. Relax, at least now you know you're not going crazy." He tried smiling at her, but it wasn't much of a smile.

"I think I would have preferred going crazy. I'd probably handle it better. I'll see you later, Alex. Thanks for the sleeping pills."

She got up and left, leaving a very worried alpha behind.

Shannon sat in the truck, trying to get herself together. *Think, Shannon, think.* This was no time to panic. She was an intelligent woman. There had to be something she could do.

Okay, let's look at this logically. What was that serendipity prayer? Something about not worrying about the things she can't change. To focus on changing what she could. All right, what about this messed up situation did she have the power to change?

She couldn't do anything about what was going on with her blood. Ditto, the heat. The PV whatever took away whatever control she might have had over that. Okay, get over it already and move on. If she didn't want to fall on the first exposed penis she saw, then she was going to have to make it difficult for the penises to get to her.

Leaving was out of the question. Shape-shifters were everywhere and the last thing she wanted to do was be surprised by some out of area wolf-shifter. Right now the advantage was on the side of the male. Once her heat was at its peak, all a male had to do was show up and she would do the rest. What she needed was a way to keep the males from getting to her. She might not be able to control them but she just might be able to limit or prevent them access to her body.

Realizing she was on to something, she let that thought play out in her mind. If she could make it difficult enough to get to her, she might just make it out of this heat unmated and in one piece. What she need was somewhere secure where she could lock herself in and everyone else out. She needed a panic room, 'cause Lord knew she was going to be in a panic when the blue moon rose.

That's it. That's what she'd do. She'd create a safe room in her house. She was sure Alex wouldn't mind. He'd probably help if she told him what she was about to do. She backed out of the parking lot and drove to the home. She needed to find a room suitable for her purpose. She was so grateful that she'd spent time helping Rory with his construction business. Every bit of knowledge she'd gained was going to come in handy now.

Chapter Nine

Mary Elizabeth's nose twitched, and she inhaled deeply. *What was that smell?* Its divine aroma lured her out of sleep. She forced her eyes open, and waited for them to focus. They were dry and gritty, her vision cloudy and blurry. She lay on the very edge of the bed, with one arm and leg dangling off. She followed her nose to the nightstand, on which her sense of smell told her the coffee lay.

Carefully so that she didn't fall off the bed, she propped up on one elbow, and groaned inwardly when an evil drummer started a vicious beat inside of her head. She closed her eyes and prayed that her head would fall off. She could live without a head, couldn't she? And if not, well, right now, death didn't sound like a bad thing.

She desperately needed that coffee. She couldn't see it, so she felt for it, being careful not to knock the cup over. She burnt her hand when one of her fingers slid inside of the cup, but it was nothing compared to the pain in her head. She brought it to her mouth. Ahh! She closed her eyes and savored the flavor. It wasn't how she liked it, but it was strong and hot, just what she needed.

Half of the cup was gone before her vision improved enough for her to see. As the caffeine worked its magic, she slowly alerted to the fact that she was naked. *Hmmm, when did that happen?* She didn't normally sleep in the buff. It wasn't until she was placing the cup back on the nightstand that she noticed the glass of water and the bottle of pain reliever sitting there.

Just what she needed. She opened bottle and took two. She was about to close it when that villainous drummer played a particularly painful combination. She tossed another two pills into her mouth and chased them with water. Too weak to get up, she lay down wondering if she'd ever feel human again.

She must have dozed off for it was the intense pressure on her bladder that woke her the next time. Her eyes still felt like sand paper, but she was more alert. The evil drummer had given up his wicked ways and was silent for now, for which she was extremely grateful.

She crawled out of bed and stumbled to her feet. She hoped someone got the tag number of the truck that hit her. If she hadn't been in an accident, then she was mugged. There was no other explanation for the way that she felt.

She relieved her bladder and climbed into the shower, standing under the hot stream, letting it run over her head and down her body while still half asleep. After awhile, she roused herself enough to wash her hair. Becoming more alert, moment by moment, she finished washing and stepped out of the shower.

Now that she was awake, her mouth tasted like something crawled in it and died. She brushed her teeth and tongue and spent a long time with the mouthwash. When she rose from rinsing, she glanced in the mirror and shrieked. Her eyes were puffy and swollen with dark circles, her skin pale and wan. She looked horrible.

She was in the bedroom getting dressed when the bed caught her attention. Actually, it was the pillows she noticed. The pillows on both sides were dented as though two heads, and not one, slept in her bed last night. The decorative pillows that she kept on the bed were on the floor, as though they had been tossed there during the night. Her entire bed was a mess, which was surprising because she rarely moved in her sleep. She kept to one side of the bed and that was it.

As she stood there, memory kicked into place. In a rush, it all came back to her. The party. The drinks. Crying over Babs' death and Hugh. Oh lord, she'd slept with Hugh! She looked around anxiously. Where was he?

Fool! It's not like I could miss him. He's too big. He must have left. Where did he go? What time is it? Almost one. No wonder he'd left. He was needed at the diner. Saturdays were busy.

She dressed and straightening the room. Her linens smelt like sex and Hugh. She stripped them off the bed and replaced them with fresh ones. Once the bed was made, she went into the kitchen to find something to eat. On the refrigerator was a note from Hugh.

Sorry I had to leave. Waited as long as I could. When you're ready to eat, come down to the diner and I'll feed you, Hugh.

How considerate of him, but she wasn't ready to face him just yet. It wasn't every day a woman gained a new lover. At least she'd been spared the embarrassing morning after scene she heard so much about. Although if he were here, they'd be past it now.

A cursory glance at the contents in the refrigerator showed there was nothing appealing inside. She was hungry, but didn't feel like cooking. Looks like she'd be taking Hugh up on his offer after all.

* * * *

Hugh placed another order in the window and rang the bell. "Pick up!" His mind was on Mary Elizabeth. Was she up? He wished he could have stayed and eased her awake. It was probably better for her that he'd left. She had a rough night. With getting sick, grieving for her sister and then him, she needed all the rest she could get. She'd better get it while she could because she wouldn't be sleeping much tonight either.

It was after one o'clock when she finally walked through the door. He examined her carefully. She was a little rough around the edges, but otherwise okay. She went directly to her seat at the counter and picked up the menu. She caught sight of him and blushed to the roots of her hairline. Hmm, interesting reaction. He'd find out later what that was about.

He pulled another ticket from the turnstile in the window and got back to work. If he wanted time with his mate, he needed to hire more help. While he worked, he made a list of reliable people he would call.

The next order was Mary Elizabeth's. He recognized the handwriting. Hugh delivered her food when it was ready. He eyed her possessively. "Good morning, feeling better?"

"I'm okay." She blushed again and played with her food.

His mate was looking distinctly uncomfortable. From the way she was subtly glancing around, she was concerned about public opinion. Smiling wickedly inside, he put Phase II of his operation in action: The Claiming. His mark was already on her, serving notice on all shape-shifters that she was taken. Now it was time to let the rest of the population know. "I want you to take it easy today. Get plenty of rest. I didn't let you get much sleep last night." He spoke low, but knew his voice carried.

Her mouth opened in shock. Silence fell in the diner and all eyes turned their way. Seemingly oblivious to the firestorm of gossip he'd just started, Hugh leaned forward and kissed her lingeringly on the mouth, just in case there was any doubts about how he kept her woke. "I'm needed in the kitchen. I'll see you when I get off." He sauntered back into the kitchen.

Belatedly, it occurred to Mary Elizabeth that when she agreed to Hugh's terms, maybe she should have heard what those terms were. Now because of her blanket agreement, he had the upper hand. Just what had she let herself in for? Well, other than sex. Great sex. Fabulous sex. Okay, so she thought the affair would be their little secret. How unrealistic of her. She could deal with it. She could deal with almost anything as long as he kept delivering like he had last night.

Or so she thought. She questioned her ability to handle things when she got to the register to pay for her meal. Hugh's voice boomed from the kitchen. "Cyndi, Mary Elizabeth's meal is on me. Just tear up the ticket."

Cyndi gave her a knowing look and once again she could feel everyone's eyes on her. Giving Hugh an evil look, she walked out of the diner and back to her apartment where it was safe.

* * * *

Shannon drove home, mentally reviewing the rooms in her house. She needed an area with only one point of entry, and it couldn't be too small for she wasn't sure how long she would be in there. She could use her bedroom. It had a bathroom, but the problem was the windows. There was a small one in the bathroom and a large one in the bedroom.

She parked and studied the house. It was a cute little wood-framed, complete with an old-fashioned front porch. The house wasn't as small as it appeared to be. There were three levels to it—the attic, the main level, and a basement. The attic, used primarily for storage, might be an option, but there was no bathroom, and possibly no electricity other than the single light socket in the ceiling.

She started there. No, this won't do. There were too many windows, and no way to block them all. She left and headed for the basement. Now this was more like it. It was partially remodeled. The floor and walls were made of concrete, which were insulated and covered with dry wall. There was a half-bath and plumbing for the washer and dryer connections.

It was easily defendable. There was only one point of entry. There were two windows at ground level but they were extremely small. Still, she could easily reinforce them with steel grills or bars, just in case. She would remove the door at the top of the stairs and install a heavy-duty, steel-reinforced one in its place, complete with deadbolts. If she walled up the stairway, she could install another steel door at the bottom as an extra security measure.

The basement was large, running the whole length of the house, with just one section walled off for the bathroom. It was empty except for an old bedroom set, which was still in good condition. She'd use it and save herself the hassle of dragging hers downstairs. She was going to be locked in for quite a while, at least a week. As long as she had food, water, a bathroom and a place to sleep, she could get through most of it.

The inside taken care of, she moved to the outside. She needed to set booby traps around the perimeter of the house. Not to kill, but to slow them down. She had to give it more thought.

Scent. It would be a big problem. Her scent would broadcast her heat to every shifter in the area and bring them running. Their scent would trigger a sexual response in her. If she smelled them, all of her efforts would be for nothing. She needed something strong enough to block their scent, but not so strong that it damaged her nose. If she could temporarily disable their sense of smell, especially while they were in wolf form, it would cut down on the number of pursuers.

All of the weak males, the omegas, would be in wolf

form. Eliminating them would be easy, leaving only the strongest, the betas and alphas. They could control their change and could easily switch to their human form to hunt her. The only way to protect herself from them would be to put up plenty of barriers and hope they couldn't get through.

The only hope she had was that the harder it was to get to her, the less shifters there would be making the attempt. Each delay would cause them to fight among themselves until only the strongest remained. That's when all of her security precautions were going to be put to the test.

Maybe she should call Rory for help. No matter what differences they may have, she knew he would come to her rescue if she asked. The question is, in the final analysis, would she be able to trust him? If he set up her safe room, how did she know that at her weakest moment, he wouldn't slip someone inside? Every room had weaknesses and no plan was foolproof. How did she know that he wouldn't use it his advantage? She didn't, and that was a risk she couldn't take.

She couldn't ask any shifter to help her. Well, not any wolf-shifter and she didn't know too many of the other types, but maybe she could hire a human. Someone who wasn't local. She'd pay enough to make it worth their while as long as the room was ready when she needed it.

She measured the doorjambs and the windows, calculating how much material she needed. This room was perfect. All the control panels and valves were located here, along with the furnace. They couldn't force her out. She needed another source of heat and light, just in case they knew something she didn't. The nights were cold and she didn't want to freeze and it was too risky to switch to wolf form just to keep warm.

There was no phone, but that was fine. Who would she call? Everyone would be out of his or her head with lust because of the blue moon. She was on her own. She just had to plan really well. She headed to Colbyville to get the things she needed.

Chapter Ten

Hugh pulled strings, offered overtime, and got out of the diner early. It was six o'clock when he let himself into Mary Elizabeth's apartment. A soon as he opened the door, the scent of chocolate chip cookies with an underlying scent of fear hit his nose. Closing the door quietly behind him, he went looking for his mate. The fear was emanating from her.

She was in the kitchen. He would have smiled at the picture she presented if he wasn't so concerned. There was flour on her sweatshirt and pants and a streak of chocolate on her face. Hair escaped from her ponytail, leaving strands in disarray around her face. She was pulling a pan of cookies out of the oven.

"What's wrong?"

She jerked and the pan of cookies dropped onto the counter. *Hmmm, must not have heard him enter.*

"Damn it, Hugh! You scared me. What are you doing here? Why aren't you at work?" She was screeching. There was definitely something wrong.

"I left early. You didn't answer my question. What's wrong? You're tense."

Mary Elizabeth closed her eyes and visibly gathered her resolve before blurting out, "Hugh, I'm sorry, but this won't work. I know I agreed to your terms, but I simply don't have what it takes to handle an affair. I mean, look at me. I'm a nervous wreck. I have no idea what I'm doing, or how to proceed."

She had the most beseeching expression on her face.

He widened his legs and crossed his arms over his chest, leveling a look on her. "Well, you did agree and I'm not letting you loose. I told you last night, this isn't a one-night stand." He said nothing about her misconception that they were involved in an affair. If she was already panicking, she'd run scared if she knew what he really wanted—forever.

She transferred the cookies to a plate, avoiding his gaze. "We never discussed birth control, disease, and the like. You didn't use any last night and I didn't think to ask. How do you know I'm safe? How do I know you're safe? What if I'm pregnant?"

Her bashfulness amused him. He needed to put her at ease. That wasn't going to happen as long as she was in this kitchen. "You're right. We do need to talk, but we aren't doing it in here." He took her hand and dragged her into the living room. He sat on the couch and pulled her onto his lap, locking his arms around her when she tried to squirm off.

"Be still. I'm not letting you up."

He waited until she settled before starting. She looked everywhere but at him. His mate had a definite problem with intimate conversation. "Now, first things, first. You are not pregnant."

This got her attention and made her look at him. "How do you know?"

"I know." He didn't tell her he would be able to tell by the change in her scent. "Now on to your second issue. I'm clean. We're tested regularly in the military and I haven't been with anyone since I've been out. The few sexual encounters I have had, I used protection. What about you?" He didn't tell her that as a shape-shifter, he couldn't catch any disease. His body was resistant to them all.

She blushed and ducked her head. "There was only one," she mumbled.

He placed a finger under her chin and lifted her head so he could see her face. "One what? Lover?"

"Yes, well, no. It was only that one time. I don't think that qualifies him as my lover."

"You've only had sex one time? I thought you were engaged?"

"You know about that? I'm surprised Kiesha told you. I never slept with Charles. I wasn't attracted to him in that way. In hindsight, I guess I shouldn't be surprised Babs stole him from me. We were more friends than anything else."

"You're engaged to your brother-in-law Charles?" He was missing something here. He planned to keep digging until he got to the bottom of the story.

"No."

She must have saw his confusion and elaborated. "I met Charles in college. For reasons I won't go into, I hadn't dated much growing up. We met in a study group and started hanging out. He was nice and everyone was pairing up. When he asked me to marry him, I said yes. Then he met Babs, and that was that."

He could see something in her eyes. Some information she was withholding. "So that was it? No harm? No foul?" There had to be more to the story than this.

He could see her debating whether to tell him the rest and held his breath, willing her to trust him. "No, that wasn't all. Babs followed me to the university. I introduced her to Charles after we were engaged. You know, the whole, 'this is my family' thing? It was time for end of semester finals and I had a heavy class load. There wasn't a lot of free time, so I didn't see much of Charles. He said he understood. He was studying, too. When the semester was over, he was coming home with me to meet my parents. I was going to surprise them with my engagement. When we got home, I was the one who was surprised." She shrugged ruefully. "Babs and Charles announced their engagement to our parents. I had no idea they were seeing each other. I still had the ring Charles gave me in my purse so my parents wouldn't see it until after we made our announcement."

Hugh's hands were digging into her waist by the time she finished. "Son of a bitch! No wonder you didn't want to go into detail. Someone should have beaten the shit out of both of them. What happened then? Do you still have feelings for this chump?" What kind of man did something like that? And that sister. What kind of bitch must she have been?

"No, I don't have feelings for him anymore. I wouldn't have sex with him when we were together. I had this quaint notion of saving myself for marriage. I realize now if I really loved him, I wouldn't have waited. After they betrayed me, I took the ring he gave me and sold it. I used part of the money to finance a vacation for myself and banked the rest of it. I had to get away from all of them. That's when my little one-night stand happened. I was angry with Babs and Charles, but angrier with myself. I figured since there wasn't going to be a wedding, there was no need to hold onto my virginity. The experience was so awful that I didn't bother repeating it."

His mate wasn't a virgin, but she was close. He liked knowing he was her first, and if he had anything to do with it, only lover. The clown that took her virginity didn't count. He shifted slightly, repositioning her on his legs to increase the circulation. He thought over all he'd learned. "You said you hadn't dated much. Why was that?" He wanted to know everything about her that he could.

"I might as well tell you the rest. Babs was the beauty in the family, and extremely popular in school. Whenever anyone befriended me, I never knew if it was me they were interested in or if they were just using me to get to Babs. And it wasn't just the guys. Girls did it, too. When most girls were going out on dates and learning how to handle themselves with boys, I was home studying or baking. It's the reason I had my choice of four-year scholarships to several colleges after high school. I didn't have much of a social life."

He pulled her close and laid a long, lingering kiss on her lips. "Here's what we're going to do. We are going to go back and pick up a few of the things you missed out on. Go, take a shower, and get dressed. Put on some jeans. When I come back, we are going out on a date. We are going to neck and fool around, and if you play your cards right, I just might let you get to second base."

She looked at him and smiled. It was like the sun coming at the end of a dark, gloomy day and warmed his heart just as much. "Really? That sounds like fun."

She hugged him tight before jumping up off of his lap, and rushed to go get ready. Before she reached the bedroom, she turned back. "How long do I have?"

He looked at his watch. The movie started at seven-thirty. "Can you be ready in an half an hour?"

"Yes. I'll be ready and waiting." Then she turned and rushed into the bedroom.

He watched her enter her room before leaving. He had a half an hour to get ready and put his plan into motion.

* * * *

Mary Elizabeth couldn't believe how excited she was. She felt like a teenager who'd been asked to the prom by the one boy she'd secretly has a crush on for years. What to wear? Hugh said jeans. Should she go with the jeans or should she try to "wow" him? She'd better stick with the jeans. She didn't know where they were going. Hadn't even thought to ask. She'd been too excited.

She pulled out a pair of low-riding, hip-hugging,

black jeans with boot-cut legs that flattered her. She paired it with a boxy, v-necked black cardigan that buttoned in the front. Underneath it she wore a vibrant red, scoop-necked camisole. She stumped into a pair of black, cowboy boots with a low heel, threw her hair into a braid, added a touch of makeup and she was ready to go.

Not a moment too soon. A very commanding knock sounded at the door. Had to be Hugh. She wiped her suddenly sweaty hands on her thighs and then went to answer the door. Her mouth drooled at the sight of him. He looked that good. He was dressed in basic black. He had on a long-sleeved, black t-shirt that lovingly clung to his every muscle, and he had a lot. His jeans were form-fitted, drawing her eyes to the enticing bulge between his legs.

While she was checking him out, he'd been doing the same. He whistled and handed her a rose. "A flower for my lady. Are you ready?"

She smelled the flower then ran the petals across her lips, feeling its softness. Hugh moved the flower from her lips and replaced it with his own. The kiss was soft and sweet, very romantic.

She sank into the kiss, wanting more. He deepened the kiss and then pulled away before things could get out of hand. Resting his forehead against hers, he asked again. "Are you ready? 'Cause any more of this and we'll be staying in." He rubbed his erection against her stomach for emphasis.

Though she was tempted, she really wanted this date. "I'm ready. Just let me grab my purse." She turned to retrieve it from the bedroom.

He caught her by the hips and turned her back around. "You don't need it. Just bring yourself. I'll take care of the rest."

He was serious. She always took her own money, but this wasn't about money. It was about trust. Would she trust him to take care of her? That's what he was asking. She took her house key and slipped it into the pocket of her jeans. "I'm ready."

He smiled approvingly before escorting her out the door. He led her to a green Hummer, helped her inside before walking around to the driver's side and getting in.

She waited until they pulled off before asking, "Where are we going?"

"To the drive-in movie theatre." He smiled wickedly. "Think of all the fun we can have. There are some rules, though. No removing of clothes and no sex. It's a family owned operation. They have guards that walk around with big, powerful flashlights to keep the couples from getting out of hand."

He reached out and took her hand, holding it while he drove. She never realized how special something simple like a man holding your hand while he drove could make her feel.

Tonight's movie was a Disney Pixar film that was geared toward families. The drive-in was packed. The back parking spaces were filled with teenagers who were probably more interested in making out than in watching the film. There were quite a few families and a few seniors spending the night out on the town, as well. Hugh found a place near the front and off to the side, but not too close. He parked and tuned in to the radio station on which the soundtrack was broadcast.

He pulled his seat up as far as it would go, told her to do the same, and then motioned for her to climb into the back seat. Raising an eyebrow at him, she did as he instructed. Once they were back there, he pushed the back of the bucket seats forward as far as they would go. Hugh reached behind the backseat and into the cooler. "Dinner is served. There's fried chicken, potato salad, veggies and dip, and sodas to drink. I also picked up some chocolate chip cookies for dessert, although I'm sure they are not as good as yours."

"Wow, you thought of everything." She watched as he pulled out plates and utensils and distributed them.

"I told you I would take care of you." He pulled the food out, one container at a time until both plates were filled. Stacking everything back into the cooler, he pulled out the drinks and placed them in the cup holders. By this time the movie was starting. He leaned forward and adjusted the radio volume to a comfortable level and then settled back to eat.

They sat in companionable silence as they ate and watched the film. When she was finished eating, Hugh took her plate and placed it into the trash bag he'd brought. Reaching back into the cooler, he pulled out a moist wipe for her to clean her hands and did the same when he was finished.

Once more he reached back, this time coming out with a blanket. "What else do you have back there?" She couldn't see a thing, but obviously he could because he didn't hesitate or scrounge around for anything. He stuck a hand back and came up with whatever he was aiming for.

"Just the things we needed for tonight. I believe in being prepared. Come over here."

She slid across the seat until she was snuggled up next to him and he laid the blanket over them. He slouched down in the seat, finding a position that was comfortable. Placing an arm around her shoulder, he pulled on her until she laid head against his shoulder.

Chapter Eleven

Mary Elizabeth was totally engrossed in the movie when Hugh made his move. He began by placing small kisses against her temple, working his way down to her ear. He nibbled and played with her earlobe, running his tongue around the outer edge. Keeping her eyes focus on the movie, Mary Elizabeth tilted her head to the side, giving him easier access.

Her focus shifted from the movie to Hugh when his kisses began traveling toward her neck. Just for fun, she tried pretended that it was the movie that held her attention. She ignored the goose bumps breaking out on her skin and tried to control her breathing. She didn't know that Hugh could scent her rising arousal.

Getting into the game, Hugh decided to see how long she could keep up the act. While he suckled and nibbled on her neck, he unbuttoned her sweater. When it lay open, he laid his hand on her stomach directly below her breast. He let his hand lay there, building her anticipation of what he would do next.

He ran the tip of his tongue up her neck to the underside of her jaw. From there, he placed small kisses along her jaw line, working his way toward her mouth. Still, she ignored him. There was a small smile on her mouth that told him she was enjoying this. Time to up the ante.

He eased his hand up until it lay against the underside of her breast. With his thumb, he lightly stroked her breast, causing her nipple to pucker. At the same time, he teased the corner of her mouth with the tip of his tongue. He smiled when she turned her face toward him, trying to capture his mouth with her own.

Playing with her, he moved his lips away from her mouth and kissed along the underside of her jaw. When she turned back to the movie, he kissed his way back to the corner of her mouth. She waited a little longer this time before turning toward him for a kiss. Once again, he veered away from her mouth. This time, traveling back to her ear. She gave a little huff of frustration as she once again returned her attention to the movie.

He slid his hand until it covered the whole breast. Then he cupped it, playing with its weight. A small shiver shook her body. He used the fingers of the hand that lay across her shoulders to lightly stroke her neck while he kissed his way back to her mouth. Once again, he teased the corner of her mouth, this time with small kisses.

No response. She locked her jaw and kept her eyes on the movie, stubbornly refusing to rise to the bait. He backed up a few inches and stared. Nothing. She didn't so much as glance in his direction. Hmm, a challenge. This was going to be fun.

How much could she take before she broke? It would be his pleasure to find out. Watching her reaction closely, he allowed his hand to drift from her breast to her waist. He slipped his hand under the blanket and toyed with the button on her jeans. No reaction. She didn't even blink. He pulled it loose, then ran his finger along the zipper, keeping the pressure light.

Her pupils dilated, but other than that involuntary reaction, nothing. He let his finger glide lower, past the zipper and onto the seam running between her legs. He went back to playing with her neck. She had a hot spot where she was particularly sensitive right below and slightly behind her earlobe. He worked that spot as he increased the pressure of his hand, which was rubbing back and forth, right over her clit.

Her legs relaxed, falling open to give him better access as her head fell back to lie against his supporting arm. Her chest moved up and down as her lungs struggled to get more air. She bit her lower lip to hold back the moan he could hear at the back of her throat. But still, her eyes never left the movie screen.

The scent of her arousal caused his control to slip. It was making him crazy, causing his beast to rise. He wanted to lay her down and taste the sweet honey he could feel dampening her jeans. He wanted to remove her shirt and suckle the nipples he could see poking proudly through her shirt. He scraped her neck with his teeth, resisting the urge to bite down. The game he was playing backfired on him as he was caught in a trap of his own making.

He lowered her zipper and slid his fingers within, needed to feel her skin-to-skin. His finger glided between the folds of her sex, causing her back to arch as pleasure ripped through her body. He dipped his finger lower, lubricating it and then rubbed her clit. With a whimper, she caved. She reached up and grabbed him by his hair, pulling his face down to hers for a kiss. He never even thought to resist. Playtime was over.

His mouth devoured hers. She draped her leg over his thigh, opening herself for more of his torture. Her hips were pumping, trying to force his hands deeper to the emptiness inside. The hand that was stroking her neck slid down her shoulder, taking the thin straps of her camisole and bra with it. Her top and bra slid down until it barely covered the tip of her nipple. His hand pushed it the rest of the way as he cupped her bare breast, gently stroking and pulling her nipple.

With his upper body he leaned forward, slowly forcing her body back until she almost reclined on the seat below. He tore his mouth from hers and dropped it down to cover her breast. Freeing his hands, he grabbed the waist of her jeans in preparation of stripping them from her body. The sound of her ragged breathing drowned out the movie soundtrack playing through the speakers of the radio. Right when his hands had a good grip and he was ready to pull, the high power beam of a flashlight cut through the darkness of the interior of the vehicle.

With a succinct curse, he yanked Mary Elizabeth upright, pulling up the strap of her top at the same time. Cupping her head with his hand, he pulled her tight against his body, in an attempt to shield her from prying eyes. The guard tapped on the foggy window, indicating for Hugh to lower it.

After making sure that the blanket covered their lower bodies, Hugh slightly lowered the window. "How you doing, Bobby?"

"Just fine, Hugh, just fine. Mighty good movie, don't you think? Of course, you might be having a hard time seeing it with the windows of this here Hummer all fogged up like they are. Maybe you should cut on the defroster. Help yourself out a bit." He smiled wickedly and halted his motion to get a gander at the woman Hugh was with when he heard him growl.

Hugh gave Bobby a look that promised retribution. Bobby was a shape-shifter. As soon as the window opened, he would have smelled the scent of their arousal and know that watching the movie was *not* what they were doing. "I'll do that. Like you said, wouldn't want to miss such a good movie."

"Well, I'll be going now. Got to make my rounds. You know how it is. Got to make sure nobody's doing anything illicit or indecent-like. This here's a family operation. Got to think of all the little kiddies here with their families. Wouldn't want to shock anyone, now would we?"

"You go on and make your rounds. I'll be talking to

131

you later." The warning was given without heat. He was caught flatfooted and he knew it. The last time he'd been caught going at it hot and heavy, he'd been a teenager testing out his sexual prowess right here at this very drive-in. It was just as embarrassing now as it had been then.

He powered up the window and turned to Mary Elizabeth. They looked at each other and then burst into gales of laughter. Mary Elizabeth laughed until her side hurt. When the laughter faded, she lay against Hugh, totally exhausted. "I can't believe we got caught like that."

Hugh smiled down into her face. "Just be glad he came when he did. A few minutes more and I'd have had you naked and screaming my name." At the thought of it, his face hardened in renewed arousal as heat filled his eyes. He reached for her, intent on finishing what he'd started before they'd been so rudely interrupted.

"Oh, no, you don't." She scrambled backwards, trying to evade the hands reaching for her. "You're not starting that again. We almost got caught the last time." She slapped his hands away from her.

"We'll be quick. We could be done before he makes his next rounds." He smiled winningly at her, still attempting to grab her and pull her to him.

"No, no, and no. Once was enough." She laughed as he tried to mess up the clothes she was straightening. While she zipped up her jeans, he was baring her breasts. When she pulled up her top and straighten her bra, he undid the zipper on her jeans. The struggle turned into a wrestling match, with lots of laughter on both sides.

She wriggled and twisted away until Hugh finally managed to pin her down on the seat. He captured her hands and pinned them above her head. He laid half on the seat and half off, his body cradled between her thighs. Things turned serious when she felt his erection pressing against the heat centered between her legs. She wanted him in her and she wanted him now. Her body still pulsed with arousal. He'd lit a flame in her that he had yet to put out. Groaning, she arched up against him, rubbing her pussy against his arousal.

"Do that again and I won't care where we are or who drops by." His teeth were gritted as he fought a battle with himself to resist what she offered. Now was not the time, but they would definitely be finishing what they started.

She rubbed against him again, tempting him. "If you don't want me tempting you then you need to get off of me. I can't think with you like this." She arched against him again, wanting him to say to hell with everyone. She never knew lust could be so consuming. She was almost to the point where she didn't care where they were or who was watching. She just wanted him to finish what he'd started.

His chest rumbled at the picture she made laid out under him. Her lips were swollen and wet from his kisses. Her hair had come loose from the braid and was tousled around her head. Her eyes were shiny with need. In the struggle, her straps had lost the battle to stay on her shoulders and lay down around her elbow. The only thing preventing her breast from showing was his weight upon her body.

He hated to quit but he knew Bobby. Bobby would come by just to make sure Hugh was doing the right thing. And he was right. This wasn't the place for it.

"We'll finish this later." He sat up and pulled Mary Elizabeth with him. He kissed her lightly on the mouth, pushing her away when she tried to deepen it, before helping her to straighten her clothes. Cracking the windows to let in some air, he pulled her back into his arms and settled back to watch the rest of the movie. He had no clue what was going on, having lost the thread of the storyline a long time ago. He did it to gain a measure of self-control. He was looking forward to getting her home and concluding what they'd started.

Chapter Twelve

The ride back to the apartment was silent, each one preoccupied with their own thoughts. A subtle hum of anticipation hovered in the air. Hugh brought the Hummer to a stop directly behind her truck, blocking the exit. As long as he was there, she would be going nowhere. He wondered if she caught the subtle meaning of his actions.

He took the keys out of the ignition, walked around to the passenger side and opened the door. She grabbed her rose and slide out onto the pavement. Taking her elbow, he closed the door and escorted her up the stairs to the apartment.

At the door, she placed her key in the lock and then leaned her back against its solid strength, denying him entrance. "I had a really good time tonight. Thank you."

Wondering what game she was playing, he arched an eyebrow at her. "It's still early. Aren't you going to invite me in for coffee and dessert? We never did get around to eating the chocolate chip cookies."

"I don't know. My parents aren't home. I'm not allowed to have company when they're out." The tone was young and innocent, but the expression on her face was wicked.

He braced his arms on the door above her head and leaned forward, bringing his face even with hers. "Let me in, baby. I'll be good. Trust me. They'll never know I was here." He wiggled his eyebrows at her, his tone cajoling, more than willing to play her game.

She bit her bottom lip, and glanced around

uncertainly. "I'm not sure. You saw what happened at the movies. We almost got caught. If I let you in, you have to promise to be very, very good. And you have to leave when I tell you."

He placed his hand over his heart and solemnly promised, "Oh, baby, I promise you, I'll be sinfully good." He twisted the key in the lock and opened the door in the same motion, and then backed her into the apartment.

As he closed and locked the door, Mary Elizabeth headed toward the kitchen. Hugh reached out an arm and snagged her by the waist, pulling her back into his hard body. "Where do you think you're going?" He plucked the rose out of her hand and tossed it onto the couch.

"To make coffee, of course. Didn't you say you wanted some?" Her voice came out breathless. Hugh had found the spot on her neck that made her weak in the knees and was plying it.

"Forget the coffee." He unbuttoned her sweater and slid it off of her shoulders.

"How about dessert? I have some freshly baked chocolate chip cookies." The camisole Hugh was pulling over her head muffled her voice.

"I don't want any cookies." He unsnapped her bra, pulled it down her arms and let it drop to the floor with the rest of her clothes. He kissed the underside of her jaw, working his way down her neck as his hands caressed and massaged her breast.

Her earlier arousal came roaring back. She reached back and circled her arms around his neck. Arching her back, she pressed her breast firmly into his hands. "How about some ice cream? Don't you want something sweet to eat?" She moaned as her breasts swelled and her nipples tighten.

He unbuttoned her jeans and lowered the zipper. Sliding his hand inside, he cupped her sex, drawing a ragged breath from her lips. "I want some of this honey that's been driving me crazy all night." His fingers were flexing and rubbing, trying to go deeper, but his movements were hampered by the tight fit of her jeans.

With his other hand, he tugged on her jeans, trying to pull them down without dislodging the hand between her legs. She helped push them until they were below her knees. She raised her leg, trying to get the jeans off and almost fell over sideways. Only the hand he had cupped between her legs kept her from falling.

"Whoa, take it easy there." He steadied her as she clutched at his arm, trying to regain her balance.

"Oops. Forgot about the boots. They have to come off before the jeans can." She couldn't believe she'd done something so stupid. Before she could feel self-conscious about her non-sexy move, Hugh spun her around. He bent over, pressed his shoulder against her stomach, and then lifted her into a fireman's hold.

She gave a shriek of surprise and grabbed a hold of his belt to balance herself. He held her legs as he turned toward her bedroom. Wanting to impress her, he bounced her up and down a little on his shoulder.

"Hey! Stop that!" She smacked his butt, hard. Then, impressed with the shape and feel of it, cupped it with her hands, giving it a small squeeze. *Nice.* It was high and firm, not flat or non-existent like some men. She couldn't believe how bold she was being.

Her world went topsy-turvy as Hugh flipped her off of his shoulder and onto the bed. "Oomph!" She landed with a bounce, arms spread wide in an attempt to catch herself. She giggled, amazed that he was being so playful.

Her laughter brought a smile to his face. He grabbed the heel of her boot, turned and straddled her leg. Getting a good grip on it, he pulled—hard—attempting to pull it off. The boot stayed in place but her body slid to the edge of the bed. He rolled his eyes as Mary Elizabeth laughed like a lunatic.

"Brace yourself so that I can pull off your boot." She propped up on her elbows and braced her other foot against his rear as he tugged. With a small suctioning sound, the boot came off and he tossed it to the side. "Give me the other one."

She slowly dragged top of her stocking foot along the ridge of his arousal, between his legs and across his balls until she had it braced against his left cheek.

"Careful. You're playing with fire," he cautioned as her action caused fire to streak through his veins.

"Oooh, burn me," she playfully responded. She slid her other foot through the opening in his legs and held it aloft until he grabbed a hold of it.

Hugh tugged the last boot off and without letting go of her leg, turned to face her. She watched to see what he would do next. He got a good grip on the legs of her jeans and tugged, pulling them completely off of her body. When he was finished, she lay there dressed only in a pair of lace-top, thigh high stockings and a matching pair of lacy black, boy-cut panties.

A man on a mission, he reached for her panties to take them off. She slapped at his hands, causing him to draw back in surprise. "Not so fast, buster. You are seriously overdressed. How about evening things up a bit?"

His eyebrow arched as he considered her words. He looked down at his attire, then back at her. "What would you like for me to remove?"

Oh, she liked this. Smiling broadly, she looked him up and down slowly from head-to-toe as though searching for something. "Get rid of the shirt."

He pulled his shirt free from his jeans, grabbed the hem and pulled it over his head before letting it drop to the floor next to her jeans. He stood awaiting her next command.

Mmm, look at all those muscles. Her eyes traced his

bulging shoulders and biceps, straight down to a flat stomach that rippled with muscles. Although he'd been bare-chested with her before, she hadn't been in any condition to appreciate it. She planned to enjoy every minute of it this time.

To Hugh, she appeared to be in a trance. He placed his hands on his waist and waited for her to snap out of it. Finally, tired of waiting, he asked, "Would my lady like me to remove anything else? Or can I get back to what I was doing?"

His words caused her to snap out of her daydream in which she was running her hands and mouth all over his body. She squirmed uncomfortably as her heat index rose and surreptitiously checked her mouth to see if she was drooling. "Your pants." Her voice broke and she had to say it again. "Take off your pants."

She watched avidly as his hands went to his belt and undid the buckle. He undid the button and pulled down the zipper. Sliding his thumbs into the waistband of his pants, he pulled them down. Once around his feet, he hesitated, clearly remembering what happened to her. "I need to take my boots off first."

"Let me." She jumped up from the bed and pushed him down to sit on the edge. She bent over with her breasts hanging and grabbed the heel of his boot. Getting a good grip, she gave it a fierce tug. Nothing happened. She looked down, surprised.

"Perhaps if I unzip them first?" he suggested dryly. She looked at him, then at the boot in her hand. His foot hit the floor with a thud as she propped her hands on her hips. Arching her brow, she asked sarcastically, "You couldn't have said anything sooner?"

"I was enjoying the view." He unzipped both boots and kicked them off before standing and stripping off his jeans. Then he stood before her totally nude. The retort she was going to make died on her lips as she got a good look at him. The man was huge. Talk about being well hung. She didn't see how he had managed to get that monster inside of her.

He watched her eyes grow to the size of saucers. "Don't worry. It will fit."

She looked at it doubtfully. "I can't believe you got that inside of me last night." Fully erect, his penis reached to his navel. She wasn't an expert on these things, but he had to be at least nine inches.

He hooked an arm around her waist and fell back onto the bed with her on top. He quickly flipped them so that she lay on her back with him on top. He made a place for himself between her legs, bracing on his forearms above her. "We fit. We were made to fit together." Not giving her any further opportunity to think about it, he lowered his head and kissed her. He already knew that she loved his kissed. His kissed her deeply, pouring all of his passion for her into it.

She forgot about everything but his mouth on hers, and the feel of his hard body pressing into hers. She wrapped her legs around him, rubbing her cloth-covered mound against his erection. Her hands came up and cupped the sides of his face, holding his mouth against hers as she fell head long into the passionate kiss.

Their mouths stayed fused together until their oxygen supply ran short. She snatched her mouth away from his, needing to breathe as his mouth traveled down her body to her breast. When his mouth latched onto it, she gave a keening cry as her back left the bed. Oh God, she hadn't known her breasts were so sensitive.

She pushed against his head, trying to push him off. It was too much. The sensation was too intense. Hugh grabbed her hands and pinned them to the bed above her head. Holding her in place with one hand, he went back to plundering her breast. Back and forth he went, suckling deeply on one and then the other, while Mary Elizabeth went crazy beneath him.

She bucked against him, her chest heaving. Her head thrashed from side-to-side. Hugh tightened his grip on her hands and suckled more deeply on her breast, until with a scream she came violently beneath him. Damn, that was hot. He loved that he could make her come just by sucking on her breast.

"Again!" He commanded her. "Do it again." He continued playing with her breast until she came again, sobbing beneath him.

As she was deep in the throes of her second orgasm, he released her hands and ripped the underwear from her body. Settling back on his heels, he grasped her beneath her knees and pulled her body forward until her pussy lay open and exposed. Lifting her by her hips, he thrust forward, trying to ram himself all the way home. She was too tight. He only sank a couple of inches before he was forced to stop.

Her orgasm was working against him, tightening muscles that were already tight. He began pumping his hips, working his way in a little bit deeper each time. Mary Elizabeth lay at an angle with his thighs supporting her back, and her shoulders touching the bed. Her arms were spread out to the sides, helping her balance. Had Hugh been a smaller man, in this position her feet would have touched the bed, giving her a little bit of leverage. As it was, her legs dangled in the air behind him.

He hit a spot that caused her breath to catch. Recognizing it for what it was, he adjusted his grip on her body and began working her g-spot, over and over. As he manipulated her body, her hands clawed the bedspread as she tried to gain purchase. She wanted to move, to thrust, to do something, but she was afraid is she did anything she'd cause him to miss that spot, the one that was making her crazy with pleasure.

"Please. Just a little bit more." She could feel the

pressure building. Everything in her began tightening. It was a little bit scary, how intense everything was. She unconsciously began to fight against him.

"Oh, no, you don't." Hugh locked her body against him, preventing her from moving as he worked that one spot mercilessly.

"Stop! Please, Hugh. It's too much. I can't take it. I can't." It would kill her. No one could handle this much pleasure and survive. Already her heart was trying to beat its way out of her chest.

"You can, baby. You will. Come for me." He wasn't about to stop now, not when she was this close. He wouldn't allow her to give into fear and draw back from him. "Come now," he demanded in a growl.

As though his permission were all she needed, she felt her body bear down hard on his cock. Her eyes went wild as she felt something break loose inside and a gush of fluid released. She shook all over, like a person in the midst of a seizure.

Hugh lost it as he felt her ejaculate. His beast broke free as he partially shifted. His eyes changed and began to glow. Claws sprouted from his fingers and he grimaced as his incisors lengthened and sharpened. His cock increased in mass and size as he pounded into her, using every bit of the strength in his body, his balls slapping against her behind with each forward thrust. He was out of control.

Mary Elizabeth closed her eyes, gripped the bed, and hung on for dear life. With each thrust, her breasts bounced. He was so deep it felt like he was at the back of her throat. With each thrust, he butted against her cervix. She couldn't decide if it was pleasure or pain she was feeling, possibly a complicated blend of both. She opened her mouth to tell him to take it easy, to explain that he was hurting her and screamed instead. Another orgasm crashed over her from out of nowhere. She clawed at the bed, her body strung tight as a bow as he continued to hammer.

No more. She couldn't take any more. Her vision darkened as she edged toward unconsciousness. She barely felt it when, with a window rattling roar, Hugh rammed in to the hilt and held himself there as his seed pumped inside to her waiting womb. His back was arched, his head thrown to the ceiling.

Already hovering on the edge of unconsciousness, she shuddered as her body climaxed again, milking the seed from his body. Thank God it was a small one this time. She didn't think her heart could have handled another violent one.

Hugh took a deep, shuddering breath and pulled his beast back inside. This was not the time for his mate to find out what he was. He closed his eyes and willed his claws to retract and waited for his teeth to change back to normal. He'd never lost control like that before. Yes, he liked his sex a little rough. Most shifters did, but he'd never lost control of his beast and partially shifted while making love. He never thought it would happen to him, even though he knew that any strong emotion brought his beast to the surface. In the past, he'd always exerted tremendous control over his emotions, and therefore his beast. Mary Elizabeth blew his control to hell and back.

Once he knew his beast was back in its cage and all signs of it were gone, he looked at his mate. While he had been regaining control, she'd fallen asleep with his cock still embedded inside. His passion had been too much for her. He needed to remember that his mate was human, and therefore fragile.

He was still hard; ready for round two. It appeared, however, that his mate was going to need some time to recover from round one. His moan barely covered the sucking sound her body made as he pulled slowly out of her snug sheath. She fit him to perfection and he hated to give it up, even temporarily. Hugh looked down, wanting to see what he was feeling.

His heart pounded hard in his chest when he saw the blood. It was smeared on his cock. Her inner thighs and pubic hair were full of blood and other body fluids. He gently settled her body onto the bed and went into the bathroom for a washcloth. He did not want Mary Elizabeth seeing this. He wet the cloth and returned to room, cleaning her gently but thoroughly. She barely stirred during the entire process.

Hugh moved her further up on the mattress, and checked to see if there was any blood on the covers. There wasn't. Good. She was sure to freak if there was and she saw it. Returning to the bathroom, he quickly washed off before leaving and turned off the light. He walked through the rest of the apartment, making sure everything was locked and lights off. Noticing the phone was still unplugged, he debated with himself for all of one second before deciding to leave it that way. Last of all, he lowered the heat on the thermostat. With him lying beside her, Mary Elizabeth wouldn't need as much heat.

Coming back into the room, he crossed over to his sleeping mate. She'd rolled to her side and curled into a ball. Lifting her up into his arms, he pulled the covers back before laying her back down. She murmured something that he didn't catch and curled back into a ball. He climbed into bed beside her and pulled her into his arms.

"Hugh," she mumbled sleepily and wrapped herself around him. He reached out and turned off the lamp. As he drifted off to sleep, he made a vow to himself. Never again would he lose control and hurt his mate as he had tonight.

Chapter Thirteen

Shannon prepared for bed, the sleeping pill she ingested making her movements sluggish. Today, she'd accomplished a lot. Home Depot was delivering her supplies tomorrow. She had to pay extra for the Sunday delivery but it was worth it.

In the store, she ran into a human who'd worked for her brother a few years back. He still did the occasional odd job and agreed to be at the house when the supplies arrived. All in all, she couldn't complain about the way that her day went.

Her shower made her even sleepier. She dried off half-heartedly and dropped the towel on the floor. She'd pick it up tomorrow. Yawning so wide that she heard her jaw crack, she cut off the light and dragged herself into bed. She fell into a deep, dreamless sleep the minute her head hit the pillow, unaware of the presence that entered her room and stood watching her.

Nikolai materialized next to the bed of the she-wolf he'd rescued, after scanning first to make sure she was asleep. What started as fascination was quickly becoming an obsession. It was becoming more and more difficult to stay away from his wolf.

Just the mere thought her essence was enough to cause his fangs to throb in his mouth. He wanted to devour her. He wanted to gorge himself in her feminine cream, and then satiate himself with her blood.

With each visit, he pushed the limits of his control. Merging deeply with her mind, he would psychically stroke and caress her body, arousing her mercilessly. He couldn't seem to help himself. Every time she was close to the edge, her wolf took control, she started to shift and he had to leave. While the blood bond he'd formed with her gave him some control over her mind, he couldn't control her beast. It was too strong.

At the end of the bed, Nikolai used his mind to pull down the bed sheet, baring her naked body to his view. Though he'd examined her thoroughly many times before, he still could not determine what it was about her that fascinated him so. She was small, like a red-haired pixie and short like one too. He doubted she'd come to his breastbone when standing.

There was something different about her tonight. Something wrong. He expanded his senses until he found the source of the problem. There was a faint metallic scent of medicine emanating from her body. With their mental link engaged, he searched deep. Whatever she took, it didn't hinder his ability to connect with her subconscious mind, but it rendered her beast defenseless.

Her beast was helpless. A wicked smile crossed Nikolai's face. Her beast sensed him and tried to stir, but the medication was too powerful. It knew he was there but couldn't do a thing about it. Not one to look a gift horse in the mouth, he took advantage of the opportunity she had unknowingly provided him with.

Using phantom fingers, he gently stroked the brow of her eye, gliding his hand down her cheek to finger her lips. Her full lips parted beneath his touch, inviting him to come inside. He ignored her invitation in favor of stroking his fingers elsewhere.

His fingers ghosted down her neck, causing her to arch her neck in response. Goosebumps pebbled her flesh. He continued his exploration to her generously shaped breasts. Her flesh cried out to him, demanding that he cease with the mind games and touch her flesh to flesh.

For a second, he considered giving into the temptation to take her while she was helpless. His code of honor would not allow him to do so. Abandoning the thought, he went back to touching her using nothing more than his eyes and his mind.

He toyed with her breasts, causing her nipples to pucker. Using his mind, he gave her the sensation of mouths suckling on her breasts. Playing her body like a master musician, he touched her simultaneous all over. Mouths suckled on her nipples and between her legs while phantom fingers stroked and caressed all over her body. He kept a firm grip on her mind, having no fear that she would awaken and catch him toying with her.

Her body began to undulate. Her legs spread wider apart as her fingers gripped the sheet. Her heartbeat raced, causing the blood to rush through her veins. The heat of her excitement caused her blood to cry out to him, begging him to taste it.

His beast stirred as blood lust began to rise. His eyes traveled over her, noting every detail. The rapid rise and fall of her chest. Tightly puckered nipples. The rosy flush of her skin as the blood rushed through her veins and arteries. The glistening red curls covering her mound. Her swollen clit, begging to be touched. He could see the clasp and release of vaginal muscles as phantom fingers thrust relentlessly in and out of her foaming pussy.

The more he stared, the more he hungered. *A taste*, temptation whispered, *just a taste. What can it hurt?* Yes, he thought, just one small taste. Maybe if he tasted her just this one time, he could discover what her hold over him was.

He planted a knee on the bed, followed by one hand, and then the other, like a great big cat stalking prey. His eyes were completely focused on his target, the glistening flesh between her legs. A fog of lust covered his mind. One taste. That's all he wanted. One taste and then he could leave and never return.

Bracing himself above her undulating body, he timed his movement just right. Quick as a cat, he swiped at her with his tongue. The taste of her caused his fangs to explode in his mouth as his eyes bled to red and began to glow. Unable to resist, he went back for more, and more, and more until his fangs were pressed tight against her flesh. He lapped at her, trying to get more and more of her essence into his mouth. Pressed as he was against her, it was inevitable that his fangs would nick her flesh, drawing forth a bead of blood.

The taste of her blood caused his beast to break free as blood lust took control. Like a snake he struck, sinking his fangs deep into the femur artery running beneath the skin of her inner thigh. He drew deeply, her rich blood rushing through his body and bringing a surge of power with it.

He was barely aware of her convulsing beneath him as orgasm after orgasm streaked through her body. Her blood was addictive—thick, rich, and powerful. He wanted to gorge. Some small part of his mind that hadn't been swallowed by the blood lust screamed at him to pull back. Too much. He was taking too much.

Using every bit of control in his possession, he closed the wound and yanked himself away from her. He licked away the last bit of blood smeared upon his mouth. His chest fell and rose sharply as he fought against the urge to take her, mark her and claim her as his own for all eternity.

He stood rigidly beside the bed, eyes closed and hands balled into fists as he fought to regain control of his body, fighting his instincts. He broke the link between them, knowing the distance was necessary but hated losing contact with every fiber of his being.

After a period of quiet meditation, he was able to gain control. His fangs retracted and his eyes returned to their natural black color. His hands began loosening from the fist they were in and his breathing even out to a nice, slow and steady rate. When he was ready, he opened his eyes and focused on the woman lying before him. Steely determination entered his gaze. He wanted her and he would have her. No one would be allowed to stand in his way. She was his.

Walking around the bed until he was closer to her head, he once more linked his mind with hers and placed her under compulsion. Bringing his wrist to his mouth, he allowed his fangs to drop and ripped a hole in his skin, causing the blood to flow. Pressing his wrist against her mouth, he compelled her to drink.

When she'd drunk enough of his blood, he commanded her to stop. Bringing his wrist back to his mouth, he licked the wound closed. Instinctively, he started a mating ritual so old it was imprinted on his DNA. Two more blood exchanges and she would be his. Giving her one last lingering look, he dematerialized and left the house. Soon. Very soon, he would claim her.

* * * *

Mary Elizabeth awakened surrounded by delicious warmth. It took her sleep-dulled mind some time to recognize the source of the heat. Hugh lay curled against her back, his arm around her waist the only thing keeping her on the bed. The man was a bed hog, probably due to his size. If they were going to make a habit of this, she would need a larger bed. Her queen size just wasn't big enough.

She pushed back into him, trying to get a more secure position on the bed. She bit back a groan as muscles protested her every move. She was going to pay for last night. She could feel it in her bones. She felt raw and achy, not unlike the time when she lost her virginity. She guessed it was understandable. Her previous experience hadn't prepared her for someone of Hugh's size and strength. A long soak in the tub and a day or two to recuperate and she'd be fine.

Gingerly she lifted Hugh's arm from around her waist, trying not to wake him. His arm tightened briefly in protest before relaxing, allowing her to slide from under it. She froze as he moved, only to relax when all he did was roll onto his back.

Once more on the edge of the bed, she debated her next move. Any move she made was bound to be painful and she wasn't a large fan of pain. Deciding it might be easiest to roll her feet to the floor and sit up, she followed the thought with action. So far, so good. Now came the hard part, standing up.

Taking a deep breath in preparation, she planted her feet on the floor, braced her hands on the mattress and pushed off of it into a standing position. Well, it was more of a crouch. She was hunched over like an old woman with a bad case of osteoarthritis. She took her first step and sucked in a harsh breath at the pain that shot through her pelvis. She could do this. She was a strong woman. She could handle a little pain in light of all of the pleasure she received last night. Telling herself to 'buck up,' she forced herself to stand straight and walk into the bathroom. It didn't matter that a baby could have crawled faster. She was walking and that was the important part. It was at times like these that she wished she had a master bathroom. The bathroom had never seemed further away than it did now.

* * * *

Hugh watched her hobble from the room, cursing himself with every step that she took. He wanted to get up and help her. It hurt him to see her in so much pain, knowing that he was the cause of it all. The only thing stopping him from carrying her was the knowledge that she would be embarrassed by his assistance. She obviously didn't want him knowing she was hurting, or she wouldn't have taken such care not to wake him. She had no way of knowing that he had awakened with her first movements, his entire being focused on her, even in the deepest sleep.

He couldn't kick himself hard enough or far enough for hurting her like he had. He renewed his vow to himself to make sure he never lost control like that again. He couldn't understand what happened. Protecting your mate was a priority with shifters. It was so deeply ingrained that it was instinct. What he did last night went against everything he believed in. Every principle he'd ever been taught. It was a valuable lesson, one he'd be sure not to repeat.

While he'd been castigating himself, his mate had made her way out of the room and into the bathroom. The least he could do was to be useful and get breakfast started. He got out of bed and slipped on his jeans. As he neared the bathroom, he heard the faucet turn on for the tub. Good, she was taking a bath. That ought to help. Knocking lightly on the door, he called out, "I'm making coffee and breakfast. You going to be in there long?"

"I should be out by the time the coffee's done. You need to come in here before I get in the tub?"

"Naw, I'm cool. I can wait until you get out." If necessary, he'd head down to the restaurant rather than make her come out of there. He hoped the hot water would undo some of the damage he'd done.

* * * *

Mary Elizabeth stretched, trying to loosen up tight muscles. Once she got moving, it really wasn't that bad. She was hyperaware of parts of her body that she normally took for granted. Her sex was all swollen and bruised. There was a dull ache deep inside where his cock had hammered against her cervix. Just thinking about it brought back the remembered pleasure, and an echo of the pain.

He was a large man and like most large men, he didn't always know his own strength. She wasn't blaming him. The truth was, she couldn't wait for him to do it again. It did something to her ego to know that he found her so desirable that he'd lost control. When a man who valued control as much as Hugh did lost it, well how could she not be flattered and a little puffed up about it. Made her wonder what would happen if she actually tried to make him lose control. Now there was something worth thinking about.

She eased into the tub, spread her legs and let the heat soothe her. It felt so good. She could feel it right down to her bones. She lay there until the water began to cool. After draining some off, she poured more hot water into the tub until it was as hot as she could stand it. She soaked until it cooled as well. Washing swiftly, she pulled the drain and got out of the tub. She was still a little tender down there but otherwise she felt a whole lot better, ready to face the world.

She came out of the bathroom and dressed in something loose and comfortable before joining Hugh in the kitchen. Due to the sensitivity of her vulva, she'd forgone wearing underwear and chose to wear a loose, flowing skirt that fell below her knees. Teemed with a tunic that came down to her hips, she believed it would totally disguise the fact that she was bare beneath her clothing.

Hugh had made himself right at home in her kitchen, making coffee and scrambling eggs for breakfast. To go with the eggs, there was toast and breakfast sausages. When she entered the kitchen, Hugh kissed her briefly before leaving for his turn in the bathroom.

She poured a cup of coffee and help herself to some eggs and toast, leaving the bulk for Hugh. Judging from the massive amount of food on the stove, he still needed to eat.

While she was sitting at the table listening to the shower come on, she mentally reviewed the morning thus far. Although not sure what she expected to happen, this wasn't the notorious 'morning after' that everyone spoke so much about. It was all so, well, ordinary. It felt as though they'd been waking together a long time, long enough to fall into a routine. There was no worrying about bed hair or morning breath. They'd just gone about preparing for the day as though they'd been doing it together for years. It was kind of unnerving, yet relaxing at the same time.

* * * *

In the shower, Hugh went over his plans for the day. It was a workday and there was just enough time to swing by his place and change clothes before reporting in. The diner was closed on Sunday mornings but opened at eleven for lunch. There was a lot to do between now and then, especially since he'd given his help the day off to make up for calling him in last night. He really hated leaving Mary Elizabeth alone. The last time he left, she had second thoughts about their relationship. He didn't want to chance that happening again. That bridge was crossed and there was no going back.

He returned to the kitchen just as she finished eating. Looking pointedly at all the remaining food, he asked, "That's all you're going to eat?"

"I wasn't sure if you'd eaten. Besides, I've never been a breakfast eater."

"You need to start. You'll need plenty of energy if

you plan to keep up with me." He wagged his eyebrows suggestively, letting her know indirectly exactly what he was referring to.

She blushed engagingly, making him smile. "I'll keep that in mind," she said dryly.

"You do that. Now, what are your plans for today?"

She shrugged and looked around as though an idea would jump out at her. "I hadn't really thought about it. I don't believe I planned on doing anything. Why?"

"I have to leave and I don't want to. Come down to the diner with me. Sit and talk with me while I cook. If you're feeling really generous, you can make some desserts to go with today's dinner. I'll pay you for them."

"Are you going down there now?"

"No, I need to swing by my place first and put on my work clothes. Then I'll come back here to the diner." If he had of been thinking, he would have brought clothes with him last night. He'll make sure in the future to leave enough things here that trips home wouldn't be necessary, at least until he convinced her to live with him. One step at a time.

"Are you sure I won't be in the way?"

"There'll be no one in the kitchen but me."

"You're doing all the cooking yourself, with no help?'

"It won't be the first time. Besides, the menu's planned and the food's all prepped. I've just got to get it going and keep it coming. No big deal."

"If you say so."

His mind already on what needed doing, he headed for the door after extracting one last promise from her to come down. "Think about making those desserts. My customers will really like them. You can make them downstairs in the diner."

"I'd rather do it here, where I know where everything is."

"Nothing too fancy or time-consuming, then. I want you with me."

"I'll keep that in mind and be down as soon as they're done."

"Use the back door. I'll leave it open."

"Alright. Go before you're late."

He glanced at his watched and cursed. "I've got to go. Come down or I'll come and get you. The customers will just have to wait."

"I'll be there."

"You'd better." He grabbed another kiss and left.

Chapter Fourteen

Shannon rolled over sleepily and stretched. What she wanted was another hour or two of sleep, but one look at the clock assured her that she wouldn't get it, at least not today. She rolled out of bed on legs that wobbled before getting her equilibrium. Then she made her way into the bathroom, her mouth stretching in a yawn as she went.

There was a strange taste in her mouth. It was probably from the medicine, but it tasted like blood. She wondered if she bit the inside of her mouth while she slept. As for the medicine, it worked wonders. This was the most rested she'd felt in weeks, even her legs were relaxed. She'd really slept hard last night. Usually she woke several times during the night startled, her wolf agitated. It hadn't happened last night, for which she was grateful. She didn't intend to make the pills a habit, but it was nice knowing she had them to fall back on whenever necessary.

The delivery truck should be here in about an hour. There was enough time to cook breakfast. As she headed into the kitchen, she heard a familiar vehicle in the drive. *What did he want?* She opened the door and stepped onto the porch. Her brother Rory stepped out of the blue crew cab truck he used for business.

"To what do I owe this pleasure?" She was a little wary, considering all the unfinished business between them.

He walked up to the porch like he owned the place, sliding his shades on top of his curly red head. Those curls should have looked feminine but there was nothing remotely feminine about him. He was a big, burly fellow, if a little on the short side. He stood only five-nine, but he loomed much larger, his power emanating from him like an aura.

He nailed her with a hard look. "If you're needing help, why didn't you call me? I'm still your brother, aren't I?"

Oh, hell. Kyle blabbed. "I take it you ran into Kyle?"

"You could say that, but you'd be wrong. Man called, wanting to know why my sister had to hire help when her brother owned a construction company. Same thing I'm wanting to know. Is there any reason why you didn't call me?"

Hell, he was pissed. His accent was showing. *Come on, Shannon. Think fast. You do not want him knowing what's really going on with you. He'd find a way to use it against you.* "This is Raven Pack business. It doesn't concern the Alpha of the Sparrowhawk clan." Maybe that would cause him to back off.

"As long as it affects my baby sister, it affects me. I'm here, not as the Alpha but as your big brother. I ask you again, why didn't you come to me if you needed help?"

Because I didn't know if I could trust you. She thought it, but didn't say it. Despite their differences, he was blood, and she'd never do or say anything to deliberately hurt him. In the heat of an argument? That was different. They both tended to be a little loose with the lips when angry. But to deliberately say words that she knew would cut, that she couldn't do. So now she had to find a reason to give him that wasn't a lie, yet not the full truth. He would smell a lie. It had to be something he would believe.

As much as she loved her brother, this was one thing

she couldn't tell him. There was no telling what he would do, what levels he would sink to 'for her good.' They already disagreed and fought over what was good for her. She wasn't giving him ammunition to use against her.

"I'm building a safe room for the Alpha. The Raven Pack doesn't have one and one will be needed soon. The Alpha's mate is human and hasn't gone through her first Change yet, and the Beta just had a cub. A place will be needed for his first time as well. Since I'm living here rent free, I volunteered to create one for the Pack."

What she said was true to a point. Every Pack has a safe house or a safe room. It was a place where new shifters went for their first couple of Changes until they learned to control their beast. It could also be used by the Alpha as a holding cell for Pack members who got out of line until an appropriate disciplinary action could be determined.

She just hoped he didn't remember that she'd never like the idea of safe rooms. She thought they were nicely decorated jail cells. Not allowing any hint of weakness to show, she silently dared him to disagree with her.

"Then it's a good thing I brought my tools. I'll assume you made all the necessary measurements and you ordered everything that we'll need?"

He was letting it go. Just like that. Either she was getting better at lying or, for whatever twisted reason his mind had concocted, he was letting her get away with it. At least for now. "Yes, I took measurements. The supplies should be arriving in about an hour. Since you're here, and you don't appear to be leaving anytime soon, come on in. I was just about to cook breakfast."

"Sounds like I arrived just in time." He followed her back to the kitchen and helped her to cook. They fell into a routine born over many years of doing the same. There was a strange kind of comfort in it, knowing that no matter what else about their relationship had changed, this remained the same.

As they ate, they spoke of mundane things. Rory updated her on the happenings within the pack since she'd been gone. They hadn't found anyone to replace her, and before she realized it, she was agreeing to continue keeping the books for his business and for the pack, just as she had before. "I won't come to Sparta. You'll have to bring the books to me."

"That's fine. Whatever paperwork we have that can't be transmitted electronically will be hand delivered or mailed."

His ready agreement made her instantly suspicious.

"Show me the room." They'd eaten and the dishes were washed and put away.

"Actually, it's the basement. I think it's perfect for what we've planned."

"I'll let you know how perfect it is after I've seen it." He followed her to the door off of the kitchen that led below. "What are you going to do about this door?"

"I ordered a steel reinforced one to replace it. I actually purchased two. I plan to put one here, and the other one will be installed at the bottom of the stairs."

She opened the door and led the way down. "Right now this is open, but I intend to close in this stairway and put the second door right here for extra security."

"So if someone gets past the first door, they still have to get past the second one."

"Yes, that's exactly what I was thinking."

He walked around the basement, looking around. "There's a bathroom down here. That's good. It looks like someone started remodeling this area and then stopped midway. The walls need finishing. What about these windows?"

"They're relatively small. I bought some steel netting to cover the windows. I don't think they are big enough for anything to get through, but you never know."

"The netting won't keep anything in unless you spray it with silver. It's not sturdy enough. A shifter's claws will go right through it. You need to install bars on the outside."

"Wouldn't anything trying to get in simply pull the bars off of the window?" She silently cursed herself. She'd told him they were trying to keep something from getting out. If that were the case, she shouldn't be worried about something getting in.

He gave her a look that spoke volumes, but didn't comment on her slip. "We'll put the netting on first, then put the bars over the netting. We'll spray both down with silver paint. The smell of the silver alone should be enough to deter any shifter from using the window as a means of getting out, or in. By putting everything on the outside, you'll still be able to open the windows. You don't want to cut off your air supply."

Grateful yet worried that he hadn't commented on her slip of the tongue, she gave the windows another look. She hadn't thought about the window as a source of fresh air. She was more concerned about security risk they posed.

"Have you located the breaker box?"

"Yes, it's over by the washer and dryer. The shut off valve for the water is down here, too, along with the furnace."

"Good. This would be a good location to put a panic room. It can also work as a safe room but it will function better at keeping people out."

She looked at him sharply. He stared at her knowingly. She neither confirmed nor denied his suspicion and he didn't push the issue. He knew what she doing, just not why she was doing it.

His sharp ears picked up the sound of an approaching vehicle. "Your supplies are here."

"I hear them. Did Kyle say if he was still coming?"

"Yes, he'll be here. I changed the time of his arrival. When he gets here, he'll be working for me. I've already set up payment arrangements."

Shannon didn't bother arguing. This was one of the reasons she and Rory usually fought. He was manipulative, controlling, and domineering. It wasn't just the alpha in him; it was his nature. He had to be in charge, things had to go his way and he was always right. Add to that a quick temper and it was a wonder they didn't fight more often than they did.

Kyle showed up just in time to help with the truck. They unloaded it, piling everything in the basement for easy access. Under Rory's direction, they removed the basement door and framed the stairway first. Once that was finished, Rory and Kyle dry walled the interior wall, a tedious and time consuming process due to all the varying levels. When that was done, they broke for lunch, which Shannon prepared.

After lunch, Shannon prepped the wall for painting while the guys installed the first steel door. Rory worked like a man possessed. By the time he left late that night, both doors were installed, the walls had dry wall on them, and the windows were secured. He was coming back to install motion sensors and a video camera that could be controlled from the basement. By the time her brother was finished, the basement would be tougher to get into than Fort Knox.

* * * *

Mary Elizabeth kept Hugh company while he worked. She didn't offer to help and he didn't ask. She would have only been in the way. The man had his routine down to a science. He was quick and competent. It was evident that he'd done this hundreds, if not thousands of times.

The man was a master at multi-tasking. He kept up

with the food, kept track of the diners and servers, all while maintaining a steady stream of conversation with her. He didn't say much about himself, preferring instead to talk about her. He asked so many questions, she felt like she was being interviewed.

He wanted to know everything. He asked about her childhood, her relationship with her parents, and her sister. He asked about previous relationships, her years at college and everything and anything between. His questions were insightful, forcing her to think hard and reach deep for answers. It was easy to be open with him, revealing things about herself that she'd never spoken to another soul. It helped that although she knew his mind was completely focused on what she was saying, his eyes were focused on what he was doing. It gave her a feeling of anonymity; the illusive safety of shared confessions in the dark. She stayed talking with him through lunch and into dinner, which he served to her personally.

Her cakes were a big hit. They received so much praise that she let Hugh talk her into making at least one dessert of her choice for each Sunday. Hugh made sure everyone knew who baked the delicious lemon cake on the menu. Even though she was uncomfortable with all of the attentions, there was a dry place in her soul that soaked it up, knowing she'd pleased so many people.

Around six she excused herself and returned home to prepare for tomorrow. She was ready to return to work, excited even. She was in a new town, a new facility, and her co-workers would all be new. She would be the one selecting the majority of them. Hiring employees to man the store was one of her new responsibilities as General Manager. There was merchandise to select for the new store and who knew what else needed to be done. The next few months would be challenging and she was looking forward to it.

Feeling a little stiff, she pulled out her yoga tape and

exercised. Then she took another long soak in the tub, locked up, and turned in for the night.

Chapter Fifteen

She snuck away to her private place. The ranch was hustling with the business of spring, but she lay there decadently in all her natural splendor. Whenever she got the chance, she would slip away from the house and endless chores, and climb up to the hayloft above the barn. There she kept a special quilt, made with her own hands. On days like today when the loft doors were open, she would spread out her quilt on the bales of hay and lay there, sometimes reading, sometimes daydreaming.

Today she felt particularly naughty. Despite the chill in the air, the sun felt so good that she'd stripped down to her skin. She laid spread eagle, like a pagan sacrificial offering to the warmth of the sun. As the cool breeze caressed her naked flesh, she allowed her mind to drift, never noticing when her musings turned into dreams.

It was the touch of a hand on her body that awakened her. Her eyes opened slowly to see Jake, one of her father's many ranch hands, standing over her. He stood there, his lean muscular chest bare and his jeans ridding low on his hips. Most of the ranch hands gave Jake a wide berth and part of it was due to his size. He was a veritable giant of a man. The other part of it was due to his obvious Indian heritage. No one would dare say it to his face, but behind his back they referred to him as that 'damned half-breed.'

He made no bones about who or what he was. You took him as he was or not at all. His midnight hair flowed to his shoulders, emphasizing his native blood. Normally he kept it tied back out of his way, but today it was flowing loose, blowing in the gentle breeze that came through the open doors. Jake was a good man who was good with his hands. He had two areas of expertise: horses and knives. The first one guaranteed him a job on any ranch in the state. The second one guaranteed that no matter how negatively a man felt about him, they would keep it to themselves.

She'd had her eye on him for a while now. Oh, she would never pursue anything with him. Not because she was too good for him. No, never that. She was too big and too plain to ever be noticed by him. He could have his pick of any woman he wanted. While many of them wouldn't be seen with him in public, they would spread their thighs for him in an instant in the secret dark of the night if he but asked.

She had no hopes that he would ever notice one such as she. Even if he did, there was no future in it. Her father would have a conniption fit. There was no way his lily-white daughter was marrying some damn half-breed. She had to content herself with her virginal fantasies, knowing that's all she'd ever have of him.

The hand that held her foot slowly glided up her leg, reminding her that she lay naked before him. A blush painted her body pink but she did nothing to cover herself. This was her fantasy come to life and she was going to enjoy it. This man that she wanted above all others was looking at her with desire in his eyes. He could do with her as he willed.

His hand slid up the inside of her thigh all the way to the apex of her legs, which he bypassed and drifted over her stomach to her breasts. He circled his finger around the base of one, through the space between and then around the base of the other. His circling finger eased higher and higher until finally, he touched her nipple. It felt so good that she bit back a moan. A part of her was afraid that this was really a dream and that any sound on her part would cause him to vanish.

He knelt on the quilt beside her and lowered his mouth to her breast. She'd played with her breasts in the privacy of her room, wondering how it would feel to have a man's mouth on them, but never could she have imagined this. She'd heard some of the faster girls talking, telling about some of the things they secretly allowed boys to do to them and how good it felt. She'd been skeptical but now she was a firm believer.

His mouth traveled down over her belly and he used his knee to part her legs, making a place for himself between them. She watched, unable to believe this was really happening to her. It had to be a dream. There was no other explanation.

His mouth drifted lower and she caught her breath at the direction in which he was heading. Surely he wouldn't kiss her there. He did! Stars alive! She'd never in her wildest dreams imagined a man would put his mouth on a woman there. It felt so strange, forbidden. She barely touched herself there, even when bathing. The things he was doing with his mouth amazed her. She bit her lower lip, trying valiantly to keep quiet. She didn't want to distract him or do anything to cause him to stop.

She gripped the quilt beneath her so tightly, her knuckles showed white. Completely beyond her control, her legs opened wider and her hips began to move, thrusting upward to get closer to his mouth. Something strange was happening in her body. There was a pressure, a tension that was growing inside of her. The feelings scared her but it felt too good to stop.

She began to silently whimper, her eyes closed to better capture the feelings he was creating inside of her. Finally, like a rubber band stretched too tight, she snapped. The feeling caused her back to arch off of the bed as she shuddered and groaned.

Jake pulled off his jeans and moved up between her openly splayed thighs. His rod was thick and heavy with desire. He leaned on one elbow and used his hand to guide himself to her opening. She felt his rod as it nudged against her a heartbeat before it plunged inside.

Mary Elizabeth's eyes snapped wide open as she hissed in pain, her nails digging into the muscles of Hugh's back so hard that she drew blood. He stopped immediately and held still over her, recognizing the sound as one of intense pain, not pleasure. Leaning to the side, he reached out and flicked on the bedside lamp. His movement caused her to grip him tighter and suck in a sharp breath as swollen, tender vaginal tissues attempted to adjust to his presence.

After one look at the pain on her face, Hugh braced on his forearms above her and began to gently withdraw. Knowing instinctively what he was about to do, she locked her legs about his hips and used her strong leg muscles to keep him locked inside. "No, it's alright. Don't stop. I'll be fine in a minute."

"It's not alright. Look at you. You're in pain. Hell, I knew better than to do this. You're still sore from last night." He began cursing himself under his breath for allowing his lust to get the better of him.

"Hugh, I'll be fine. If we take it slow and easy, it'll be okay." She gripped him tighter with her legs. She was tender, but it was nothing she couldn't handle. Already her body was starting to loosen and relax around him. She wanted him. She was not going to let a little tenderness prevent her from enjoying his touch.

"I'm not willing to take that chance. I will not be responsible for hurting you. Once was enough. You think I didn't see you hobbling around this morning? I saw. What's more is that I expected it. I'm the one who cleaned the blood from your body last night while you slept. Until you are totally healed, I won't be touching you and that's final."

Thrown for a minute by the knowledge that she'd bled, she opened her mouth to argue. Hugh cut off the argument she was about to make by dropping his upper body down on her. The weight of his chest knocked the breath out of her, preventing her from speaking. Reaching behind him, he pried open her legs and freed himself.

As Hugh rolled to sit on the side of the bed, her alarm clock went off. She reached out angrily and slapped the thing off. Hugh took advantage of her brief distraction to slip on his pants and leave the room. As he walked out of the door, he called over his shoulder, "I'll get the coffee started while you get ready for work."

The words that flowed from her mouth would have shocked her mother. She stomped into the bathroom and slammed the door. She was horny and frustrated. It didn't matter that Hugh had brought her to climax only moments ago. She'd been sleep and thought she was dreaming. Who the hell told him he could spend the night with her anyway? Didn't he have a home?

She washed and went back into the room to dress, still calling Hugh every name she could think of under her breath. When she was dressed, she stalked into the kitchen to get some coffee to drink, anger in every line of her body.

"Hardheaded, stubborn man. Like I don't know my own body." She ignored the little voice of reason telling her that Hugh had done the right thing. She ignored him as well until he went into the bathroom to prepare for the day.

She slammed cabinets, looking for something to eat. "Screw it. I'm too angry. I don't even like breakfast."

Hugh entered the kitchen dressed differently from the night before. He must have packed a bag yesterday, which meant he'd planned on staying here last night. "Yes, Hugh. I'd *love* for you to spend the night. So good of you to ask," she muttered under her breath. Yet another thing to be pissed about.

"You need more than coffee this morning. You need to eat. You don't know what's in store for you today and your brain will function better if you eat a little something. It doesn't have to be much. Why don't I make you some toast?"

She finished her coffee and walked around him to put her cup in the sink. After retrieving her lunch from the refrigerator, she walked out of the kitchen and went to get her purse so she could leave. She had nothing to say. Didn't even want to look at him. Purse and lunch in hand, she walked to the door and opened it.

"Oh, no, you don't. You're not walking out of here angry. We'll settle this thing here and now, before you leave."

The door shut with a bang as he spun her around. Knocking her things out of her hands, he caught her by the thighs and lifted her up, pressing her back against the door. The move startled her into grabbing his shoulders. "I know what your problem is and I'm going to fix it. Right here, right now."

Lining his cock up with the notch in her thighs, he held her open as he pressed his erection against her throbbing clit. He rubbed against her in a motion that quickly had her squirming in his arms. When she was sufficiently aroused, he lowered his mouth and kissed her. She was so on edge that it didn't take long to make her explode in his arms. He continued to rub against her, drawing out every last drop of pleasure.

With her body still shuddering, he broke their kiss and slid to his knees. He reached under her skirt and removed her underwear. Then he draped a leg over his shoulder and lowered his mouth to her pussy, which glistened with honey. He licked her slit, before concentrating on her clit. He took a single finger and stroked it in and out of her sheath, until she came apart in his arms.

When she lay panting against the door, he licked his mouth and fingers clean. "Better?"

Mary Elizabeth buried her face in her hands. "God, I acted like such a brat. I'm sorry I got so mad."

"Sexual frustration will do that to a person."

"What about you?" She cupped his erection. "You didn't come."

"You don't have time to take care of me. You've got a job to get to. Go get cleaned up so you can leave before you're late."

She went in the room and straightened up. When she returned, he handed her things to her. He kissed her lightly on the lips and opened the door. "Have a good day at work. Come to the diner tonight when you get home, after you've had a chance to unwind. I'll feed you. I hope your lunch is okay."

"Even if it's not, it won't change the taste and that's all that matters." She reached up for one, last lingering kiss before walking out the door. At the bottom of the stairs, she turned and waved when she spotted him still standing there watching.

Hugh stood there until she got in her truck and drove away. As soon as she was gone, he headed straight for the bathroom, undoing his pants as he went. He dropped his pants and stood over the toilet. His cock was so hard that he could hammer nails, and just as painful. Three to four strokes later he was shooting his load into the bowl.

Pulling out had been one of the hardest things he'd ever had to do. As her mate, her needs came before his own, not that she'd thanked him. The little hellion had quite a temper on her. A wicked grin crossed his face before he laughed. Fortunately, he was man enough to handle her. Damn, the next couple of days waiting for her to heal were going to be rough.

* * * *

Kiesha pounced as soon as she walked in the door. "Where the hell have you been all weekend? I've been calling since Saturday and you never answered. The phone just rang and rang."

"Well, hello to you, too. And for your information, my phone never rang. I would have heard it if it had. I've been home all weekend." Except for the time she spent with Hugh, but she wasn't ready to talk about that just yet.

"I was really worried about you. I know Hugh told Alex that you were fine but I needed to know for sure."

"I'm fine. It got a little rough Friday night but everything turned out okay. I can guarantee that I won't be drinking any more Shifter Surprises, no matter how good they taste. My one experience with their potency was enough."

"Alex said you were sick but that Hugh stayed long enough to make sure you were alright. He was really worried about you when you left the party. Are you sure the two of you don't have something going?"

Mary Elizabeth had forgotten their conversation about Hugh. It seemed a lifetime ago. So much had happened since then. "I'm sure I'm not ready for a serious relationship with anyone right now. I might be persuaded to fool around and have a little fun, but he would have to agree to keep things light." Then she laughed, thinking to herself, Hugh was definitely fun.

Kiesha laughed with her. "Well, I'm glad you're okay. I'd hate for you to have come all this way and have something serious happen. Your mother would kill me."

"I doubt it." There was only a hint of bitterness in her tone. She'd learned a long time ago to accept things the way they were. Changing the subject, she looked around at the construction site that was her new place of employment. "Okay, now that I'm here, where do I start?"

Kiesha showed her where everything was going to be when the work was finished. She explained in greater detail what Mary Elizabeth's duties would be and showed her the office that was hers alone. There was an office for Kiesha and one for Shannon, which probably wouldn't be used.

Kiesha gave Mary Elizabeth a budget, put her in charge of hiring and turned her loose. She spent the morning posting job notices and setting up her office. The rest of the afternoon was spent in conference calls with the other store managers going over potential merchandise for the new store. Kiesha was still studying the feasibility of relocating the on-line store to Refuge. It was a move that would require a lot more personnel than what they were currently planning on hiring and/or relocation for some of the current staff. There was a lot to consider before a final decision could be made.

Mary Elizabeth left the store at the end of the day, tired but invigorated, and looking forward to tomorrow. Remembering what Kiesha said about calling reminded her that she planned to buy a new phone. She went to the local drugstore and found one with caller ID and a built-in answering machine. While hooking it up, she noticed the phone cord was unplugged from the wall jack. That was strange. She didn't remember the cord being loose. She plugged it back in and spent a few minutes setting up the phone before she was completely satisfied. Then she changed clothes and went to join Hugh in the diner, hungry and ready to eat.

It was Monday and business was slow. Hugh called out as she entered the diner, "Come on back and wait in my office."

She did as instructed. She'd barely glanced around when Hugh entered the office with two plates piled high with food. "I am so hungry."

"Good, I fixed plenty." He sat the plates on his desk and motioned for her to eat.

"How was your first day of work?"

"Good. I spent most of the day setting up my office and reviewing the budget Kiesha gave me. I also posted job announcements in the paper."

"How many people are you looking to hire?"

"For now, until we get a better idea of the volume, only two or three full-timers. Later we may add some part-timers as well."

The conversation transitioned from discussing their day to how they each ended up in their current careers. Hugh told her about his career in the military and his decision to open the diner upon retirement. With each conversation they shared, she was coming to know and like him better.

Before it could get too late, she excused herself to go home. Hugh walked her to the door, kissed her goodnight and kept watch as she climbed the stairs until she entered the apartment. Thirsty again, she threw her keys on the table, and went to the refrigerator to get something to drink. "What the hell?"

The refrigerator was full of food. Food she didn't buy. She closed the fridge and started opening cabinets. The story was the same. Her cabinets, even the pantry, were all full of food items she hadn't bought. Some items were familiar favorites while others were things Hugh must have a preference for. "Why would he...?"

She left the kitchen and stood in the living room staring into space, trying to understand what would make him do such a thing. Finally, it occurred to her to see what else he'd done while she was at work.

In the bathroom, the toothbrush he used this morning was still there. Inside the mirror, a can of shaving cream and a razor sat on the shelf. *This isn't so bad,* she thought. In her room, everything appeared to be the same until she opened the closet. Several of his pants and shirts, enough to last at least a week, hung beside her clothes. On the floor sat a bag containing several changes of socks and underwear.

She backed up slowly and sank onto the bed that still smelt like him. He was doing too much—way too much—too fast. More than she was comfortable with. They'd only been a couple for three days and the man had virtually moved in with her.

She tried to give him the benefit of the doubt. Maybe he wasn't trying to move in. Maybe he was just leaving a few items here for convenience sake; the same way women like to leave things at their lover's homes where they spent a lot of time. After all, a few outfits did not a wardrobe make. She tried to make herself believe it through her entire yoga routine, shower and as she prepared for bed. It didn't work.

Part of her was shocked and offended that he'd dared to invade her space in this manner. Since being on her own, she'd always lived alone, even in college. She wasn't used to sharing her space, and was a very private person, rarely inviting people to visit. She enjoyed her privacy too much.

Another part of her, the more animalistic side of her nature, recognized his actions for what they were and was deeply disturbed. The man was claiming her space even as he'd claimed her body. It was too much for her to handle, so she did what she always did, buried it to deal with later. She pulled out her CD of the sounds of the ocean that she played whenever she needed to relax. With the sounds of nature all around her, she climbed into bed and was immediately engulfed by Hugh's scent, which did more to calm her nerves than anything else.

Chapter Sixteen

When her alarm sounded, she woke surrounded by Hugh. His arm was around her waist, his leg was thrown over hers, and he was curled against her back. At least time she wasn't hanging off the edge of the bed. She wasn't a heavy sleeper, but once again Hugh managed to come into the apartment and slip into bed, undetected by her.

As she reached out to turn off the alarm, Hugh muzzled her neck. "Good morning."

She growled in reply and shrugged him off.

He untangled himself, rolled out of bed, and pulled on his jeans while she was still trying to force herself to sit up. "I'll make coffee while you get dressed."

By the time she came out of the room dressed for work, not only was the coffee done but he'd made breakfast as well and it was sitting on the table.

He kissed her lightly on the cheek as he passed by, headed for the bathroom. "Eat. You'll feel better. I want to see an empty plate on the table when I come back."

"Eat, you'll feel better." She mimicked him lightly under her breath. God, she hated mornings. She poured a cup of coffee and sat to the table to eat as he commanded. The sad thing was, he was absolutely right. She did feel better. More alert and ready to face the day.

Over the next couple of days, they fell into a routine. She'd awaken with Hugh in bed beside her. He'd fix coffee and breakfast while she prepared for work. They would eat breakfast together and then she'd gather her things and head for the door. Hugh would stop her at the door, kiss the breath out of her and give her mind-blowing orgasms. Then he would shove her outside and on her way to the office before her heartbeat had a chance to settle. He never touched her at any other time or removed any more clothes than necessary, meaning what he'd said about giving her body time to heal.

After work, she would unwind by puttering around the apartment before heading downstairs to spend time with Hugh. He'd stop working long enough to eat with her and then they'd talk while he worked. About nine, she would go home and prepare for the next day. Once in bed, she'd fall asleep knowing that at some time during the night, Hugh would join her.

Between work and the time she spent with Hugh, she was rarely home. Even so it occurred to her, now that she had her new phone, it was strangely quiet on the home-front. She'd really expected Charles to call back after she hung up on him like she did. He'd called everyday prior to that last time. That he hadn't called again was a cause for concern.

He'd been acting a little off lately. When he called she would encourage him to speak to a grief counselor. He had some serious issues that he needed to deal with. The next time she called home, she'd ask her father to speak to Charles about seeking professional help. She wouldn't call Charles herself. He'd see it as a sign of weakening on her part and the last thing she wanted to do was encourage him.

* * * *

As her body healed, she became hungrier and hornier. The orgasms Hugh gave her, while satisfying for the moment, only served to increase her overall hunger for him. She had to do something to get through to him. She didn't want to be treated like some fragile blossom. She was a woman with a woman's passions and she wanted all of him—his passion *and* his strength. He was holding back on her. While she was healing it was fine, but now she needed more. She tried to convince the stubborn man that she was healed and it was okay to have intercourse, but he wouldn't listen. He refused her at every turn.

She needed to feel him pounding in her, thrusting mercilessly until all she could feel was him. She wanted him deep and she wanted him hard. Umm, yes, just like that. Deep, hard, and fast. She wanted him to power into her until her world exploded and he was the only thing left to hold onto.

She planned her attack carefully. Thursdays were slow. He'd be retreating to his office soon. She took a shower and shaved, leaving her skin silky smooth. Into her skin she rubbed essential oils until it glowed with health and vitality.

In her room, she pulled on a pair of black, lace-top, thigh high stockings that ended high on her legs, framing her pussy. One side of her mound was shaved bald, the skin soft and gleaming. The other side was trimmed very low, presenting an intriguing contrast.

Over the stockings she wore a very conservative skirt that gathered at the waist and flowed to her ankles. On her feet was a pair of black ankle boots with "fuck-me" stiletto heels. Dipping her fingers between her legs, she drew the moisture she found there and dabbed it between her breasts, behind her ears, and in the hollow at the base of her throat like it was the most expensive perfume. Last of all, she put on a silky, black wrap shirt that tied at the waist. She played with her nipples until they stood up straight and tall, drawing attention to her braless state. One last toss of her hair, which she left loose and tousled looking just the way he liked it, and she was ready to go.

Leaving everything behind, including her keys, she

locked the door and walked down to the diner. Hugh would unlock the door for her later. She did not intend to return home alone.

She entered the diner via the back door, which Hugh left unlocked just for her. She caught his attention as she walked by on the way to his office. She pointed, indicating that she'd be waiting for him in there. He nodded to show he understood and went back to giving instructions to his staff.

She didn't have long. He would follow shortly. She moved the heavy armchairs from in front of his desk and pushed them to the side. Their previous position would block his view of what she wanted him to see. Next she cleared his desk of anything that looked important or that might be painful to lie upon. With any luck, he'd have her flat on her back on the desk shortly, driving into her.

Hopping on top, she arranged herself in a way that was sure to get his attention. With her hips on the very edge, she spread her legs as wide as they would go. Then planted her feet on the desk pointing in an outward direction. If she were less flexible, she wouldn't have been able to hold the position. Thank God for yoga. She straightened her back and rested her elbows on her upraised knees while making sure her skirt covered her completely.

She was so excited about what she was doing that she could feel her feminine juices leaking from between the lips of her vagina to wet the fabric of her skirt underneath. Her nipples were tight little stubs pressing against the silk of her shirt, betraying her arousal. She finished arranging herself not a moment too soon.

As Hugh approached the office, he threw on last comment over his shoulder before opening the door with one hand. As soon as he stepped through the door, the scent of her arousal hit him like a hammer between the eyes. He could smell it over the food he was carrying in his hands. His cock immediately sprang to life, and he swallowed and prayed for control. It had been excruciatingly difficult holding back these last few days. His beast demanded that he claim her fully, as he had the night he'd caused her to bleed. The mating fever was riding both of them hard, and only his fear of hurting her pain enabled him to hold back.

It looked like she was taking matters into her own hands. He closed the door and leaned against it, holding onto the plates like a drowning person held onto a life preserver. He didn't trust himself to come any closer, because the minute his hands were empty, he would be all over her. Yes, it was better for him to stay right where he was. His control was already razor thin. Any little thing was liable to push him right over the edge.

"Lock the door, Hugh." Her voice was husky with arousal.

Balancing both plates on one arm, he reached blindly behind him to do as she said. He took in the way she was seated on his desk and knew he was in trouble.

"I want your honest opinion, okay?"

He swallowed to clear his throat, which had closed up, and took a firmer grip on the plates. "Sure. I'll be honest." He watched as she began to ease up her skirt. His eyes were glued to what was slowly being revealed.

"I couldn't decide which was better, so I decided to leave the final decision to you." Her skirt was up to her knees now. His eyes took in the shoes and the stockings, but it was what waited between her legs that caused his heart to stutter.

Using a finger to illustrate, she pointed out to him what she'd done. Drawing her index finger up the side of her sex that was baby smooth, she asked, "Do you prefer totally bare? Or," sliding her finger slowly down the other side she continued, "barely there?"

When she reached the end, she slid her finger deep

into her dripping hole and spread the moisture on her distended clit. Rubbing her finger in a circular motion, she masturbated while he hungrily watched. "This feels so much better now that there's not all of that hair in the way."

He came toward her like a man hypnotized, his eyes never once leaving the motion of her fingers. The plates in his hands dipped alarmingly, the food slid to the edge, then dropped unnoticed to the floor. She shivered delicately as the pleasure from what she was doing raced up and down her spine.

"You know what feels even better than this?" She continued before he could answer, her words coming out choppy as her orgasm approached. "Your big, thick cock pounding into my wet pussy the way you did last Saturday night. Mmm, it felt soooo good. I love the way you fucked me. Deep and hard. Pounding into my pussy until I could hardly catch my breath. You made me want to scream, scratch, and bite. You brought out the wild woman in me."

She was panting now. She was so close. She could smell his arousal, see the war he was waging to remain in control and not fall on and devour her as he wanted to. Just a little bit more and she would have him right where she wanted him. She sped up the motion of her hand, her finger pressing firmer. Her hips were making little thrusting motions, following the movements of her hand.

"At work I think of you taking me. Fucking me hard. The fantasy is so vivid, so real that I cream my panties as I come." She was so in tuned with her body that her attention strayed from him, focusing inward.

She never noticed his eyes changing as his beast began rising to the surface. His nostrils flared as he breathed in deeply of her scent. The plates dropped to the floor with a crash. His hands clenched into fists. He was fighting a losing battle to remain in control. His hand crept to his cock, stroking its rigid length through his pants. The pressure was so great that he undid the zipper and released his cock to give it some relief.

Her finger picked up speed. She brought her other hand up to squeeze her aching nipple, until with a keening cry, she threw back her head and came. Her cry shattered the last fragment of his control. He leaped forward and grabbed her hips with his hands, stabilizing her as he rammed home, sliding in to the hilt in one stroke.

Pushing her down onto the desk, he locked his teeth onto her shoulder and gave his beast full control. He hammered into her, each thrust bringing forth a grunt from her mouth. Her nails clawed his back. Her feet dug into the desk as she braced herself to counter each thrust with one of her own. Her heels were probably leaving score marks on his desk, but she didn't care. THIS was what she'd wanted. This is what she'd been craving.

"Yes! Fuck me. Fuck me *hard*. Just like that."

He growled and pumped into her even harder, pounding against her cervix. She slid her fingers down his back and dug her nails into his ass, gripping him tightly. She wanted him in her so deep that she couldn't tell where he began and she left off.

The sensations bombarding her body were so intense, she couldn't catch her breath. She wanted more. She wanted all he had, everything in him. She urged him on with her words, her mouth right by his ear. "You feel so good. You're so big and hard. I love the way you fill me. I need you. Harder! Faster! Give it to me! Don't hold back. Give it all to me!"

He growled low and long as he began to shift. His fingernails lengthened into claws. His incisors became fangs that cut into her shoulder drawing forth blood. The little bit of pain was all she needed to fall over the edge.

With no breath left to scream, instead she reared up and bit him on the tendon where his neck and shoulder joined, her jaw locking down so hard that she drew blood. He gave a mighty roar and pulled out of her. He flipped her over onto her stomach and was back, pounding into her before her mind could fully comprehend the change in position. Her breasts were squashed against the desk. The pistoning motion of his hips caused them to rub back and forth across the smooth surface of the desk, abrading the nipples and sending streaks of fire to her womb.

Her hands had automatically slapped down on the desk to break her fall when he flipped her over. Hugh had one arm under her hips, lifting her and holding her steady for his thrusts. The other hand held her by her thigh, holding it up and keeping her open, allowing him maximum thrusting potential.

"Oh God, yes. Right there, Hugh. Just like that. Oooooh!" This position hit all of her hot spots, which triggered another orgasm and kept her at a high peak. One orgasm bled into another until with a mighty thrust and a powerful roar, Hugh came, spurting his seed deep into her waiting womb. He continued to thrust as he came, filling her to the point where sperm began flowing out of her body, coating her thighs. When he released the last of it, he slumped down on top of her breathing heavy.

The heavy musk of sex filled the office. He lay there while his fangs retreated and his claws retracted. His mind was mush. Her pussy gave one last spasm and his cock twitched but stayed soft. He was totally spent. When his mind began to function again, he realized he was crushing Mary Elizabeth. He gathered his strength, pulled his arm from under her and lifted off of her, balancing on unsteady feet.

He reached back and pulled the chair closer before toppling into it. He became concerned when Mary Elizabeth didn't move. He jumped up and grabbed her off of the desk, before sitting back down with her on his lap.

"Honey, are you okay? Was I too rough?" He tipped

her head back so that he could see her face.

She gave him a dreamy smile and looked at him with eyes that were unfocused. "Ummm," she purred, "That was great. As soon as the feeling comes back in my legs, I want to do it again. But next time, let's do it in bed. That desk is a little hard."

Her words startled a laugh out of him and caused his cock to harden. He was deeply satisfied. His mate was a match for him in every way. He should have known she'd be able to handle his passion. He looked around at the mess they'd made. He wondered if Mary Elizabeth realized that everyone knew what they were doing in here. They were so loud, he was sure even the customers in the dining area heard.

He gave a small chuckle. He was seated in the chair with his shirt on and his pants down around his ankles. Mary Elizabeth's blouse was ripped, something he had no memory of doing, and her skirt was around her waist. One of her stockings had fallen and now sagged around her ankle.

Papers were scattered on the floor. There was food on the carpet as well as shards of pottery from the broken plates. If he had taken her on the floor, she'd be covered in food right now. Good thing she positioned herself on the desk.

"You never did answer my question."

"What question was that?" He had a vague memory of her talking, but he couldn't recall a word she'd said.

Taking his hand in hers, she spread her legs and used his hand to rub over the wet mound of her sex. "Which side do you prefer?" She released his hand and he continued to pet her, rubbing one side and then the other.

"I'm not certain. I think I need a closer look."

He stood with her in his arms, and then turned and sat her in the chair, arranging her legs so that they hung over the arms of the chair. He pulled her hips to the edge of the seat and flipped her skirt to the side.

Then he kicked off his shoes and pants and tossed them into the other chair before dropping to his knees. He dropped back until he rested on his heels, his hands rested on his outspread knees. His cock stood up straight and proud as his balls dangled to the ground.

"Hold up your skirt up so that I can see you better."

She did as she was told, her belly clenching in response to his intense gaze on her most intimate parts.

"I've touched it, and looked at it, and I still can't decide. I don't have any choice. I'm going to have to use the tongue test. It's the only way," he informed her solemnly.

Her eyes widened as his meaning sank in, her nipples tightening in response. She clutched her skirt tighter and braced herself for what he was about to do. He placed his hands on her thighs and leaned forward from the waist. She watched as his dark head descended toward her pussy, anticipation riding her hard.

He began by delicately running his tongue up one side and then the other. "This side is really smooth. My tongue just glides along the surface with no problems, especially with you being as wet as you are now." He licked her again to demonstrate what he was talking about.

"Now this side, it's a little rough, a little prickly. It feels good to my tongue. It tastes good, too. The stubs of hair are actually catching your honey and holding it captive for me. Watch." He dragged his tongue along the side with the hair, his tongue laving the moisture clinging there, causing it to tickle. "See what I mean?"

He gazed at her seriously when he was finished. "I still can't decide. This is going to call for further study." He looked at her pussy like it was the results of a particularly puzzling scientific experiment he was struggling to decipher. Lord, give her strength!

He ran his tongue down the crease in one thigh, and

then the other, pausing for a moment to verbally compare the contrast. Then he ran the flat of one tongue down the outer lip of one side, and then once again on the other. After he compared the two, he pinched her inner lips together and ran the point of his tongue down the crease one side, and then the other. From there he gently suckled both lips together in his mouth before spreading them wide to run his tongue down the slit in between.

By this time Mary Elizabeth was squirming. He'd never paid such close attention to her sex before and it was driving her crazy the way he kept stopping and starting, taking time to offer scientific observations between each and every swipe of his tongue.

"Let me see how it feels when I rub my tongue against your clit." He gave her clit a few licks, stopping when her hips began to pump, betraying her excitement.

"That's nice but it doesn't help me decide. Let's see what difference it makes here." He spread her lips apart and plunged his tongue inside her hole, flicking it in and out as he fucked her. He brought her right to the edge of release and then stopped.

With an angry growl of frustration, she lunged out of the chair and shoved Hugh onto his back. Following him down, she grabbed his cock with one hand and impaled herself on it. Hands on his chest to balance, she rode him like he was a wild bronco, humping and bucking on him until she came in a gush of fluid. Spent, she sagged upon him until she lay on his chest, his pulsing cock still embedded deep inside.

He stroked her back languidly. "Satisfied now?"

She gave a contented little murmur. "Oh, yeah."

He allowed her to relax for a few moments before sitting up and bringing her with him. "My turn." He reached out and dragged his pants closer. "Pull my pants onto my legs and put my shoes on my feet." He stopped her when she went to rise off of him.

"No, don't get up. Spin around." When she didn't understand what he wanted her to do, he guided her hips with his hands. He rotated her slowly around on his cock until her back was flush with his chest. In this position, she balanced on her knees and leaned forward until she could reach his feet and pull his pants on his legs.

Hugh made her task more difficult. He leaned back on his elbows and contracted the cheeks of his butt, causing his cock to flex inside of her. When she moaned and fumbled with his pants, he laughed. "You aren't finished? What's taking you so long?"

"Hugh, you're not being fair. I can't concentrate with you doing that."

"What? This?" He flexed again and his cock rubbed against the inner walls of her sheath.

Trying to ignore him, she stretched forward to grab his shoe. As she did, she lifted a few inches off of his pelvis until only the tip of his cock remained buried inside. Once she had the shoe on his foot, she sank back down, giving him an excellent view of her vagina swallowing his cock.

He reached forward and spread the cheeks of her ass, guiding her hips into a slow, up and down motion as he lifted her up a few inches, then pulled her back down. The sight of his shiny cock entranced him, disappearing and then reappearing, in and out of her wet sheath.

She bit her lip and struggled to stay on task. He wasn't making it easy for her and several times she got distracted from what she was doing. When she finished, she rested her head on his legs and just enjoyed the sensations he was creating in her body.

"Are you finished?"

"Huh? What? Oh, yeah, I'm done." His pants were on his legs down around his knees and his shoes were on his feet with the laces tied.

"Good. Turn back around." He sat still and leaned

back out of the way and she slowly rotated back around until she was facing him.

"Brace yourself." That was all the warning he gave as he planted his feet, lifted his butt and pulled his pants up around his hips. Then he pushed up into a squatting position. The sudden move had her wrapping her arms around his neck and gripping him tightly with her thighs to keep from falling.

"Wrap your legs around my waist and hold on tight." When she'd done as he'd said, he used his powerful leg muscles to push up into a standing position while holding his pants in place. He lifted her bottom with one hand, still keeping his cock embedded inside and adjusted his pants so that he didn't have to worry about them falling down. He made sure her skirt covered her and gripped her bottom with both hands to hold it and her in place.

"Hugh, what are you doing?" she asked in alarm as he began walking toward the door.

"I'm taking you some place more comfortable." He took a few more steps and then spun around. "Forgot the keys." He picked up the keys and slipped them in his pocket; then walked back to the door, side stepping the mess on the floor.

As soon as he opened the door, Mary Elizabeth buried her face against his shoulder. "Don't be embarrassed now," he told her, deeply amused.

He called to Ralph, "I'm going home. Do me a favor and have someone clean up the mess in my office. You're in charge. Make sure you lock up."

When he walked out of the back door, she looked up at him. "I can't believe you just did that."

He grunted in response and gritted his teeth, fighting the urge to finish this here and now. The stairs just about did him in. With each step he took, her internal muscles clenched and released around him, caressing his cock and pushing him closer to the edge. By the time he got to the door, he was sweating, his control hanging by a thread. "Got to make it to the bed," he muttered. "Just a few more steps and you'll be on a nice, comfortable bed."

Mary Elizabeth licked his neck and then bit down, giving him a love bite. When she pulled the meat between her teeth and sucked it hard, his control snapped. "Oh fuck, screw the bed."

By this time they were in the apartment. He slammed the door shut and fell with her against it, bracing her back against the door as he drove into her, riding her vigorously. Mary Elizabeth hung there in his arms as he pounded into her, unable to move and loving every minute of it.

The force of his thrusts was violent, causing her head to hit against the door with each impalement. She'd have a headache in the morning but it would be worth it. It didn't take long before Hugh locked his knees and came with a load roar. Good thing she didn't have any neighbors sharing her walls or they'd be banging on them right about now at the racket they were making.

Hugh rested against her for a minute before reaching down to lock the door. "I can't believe I just did that." He'd lost it, coming in seconds like an untried youth.

He carried her into the room and flipped her back to tumble onto the mattress. He stood over her and began taking off his clothes. "I hope you're not tired because we're just getting started. I have several days of abstinence to make up for. That was just an appetizer."

She gaped in amazement when she saw that he was still hard. "If you like those clothes I suggest you take them off. Otherwise I'll rip them off of you." She gulped and struggled to remove her clothes quickly.

Hugh placed one knee on the bed and then a hand, crouching over her. "Are you hungry?"

She shook her head no.

"Thirsty?"

Again she shook her head.

"Need to use the bathroom?"

She thought about it for a moment. "No."

"Is there anything you need to do or want to get? Do you have any final words?"

Her eyes got large and she slowly shook her head, signaling no.

"Good." He grinned, right before he pounced.

Chapter Seventeen

The next morning, Mary Elizabeth lay in a tub of scented bubbles. She was deliciously sore and pleasantly tired, having gotten little, if any sleep last night. When Hugh said he had days' worth of abstinence to make up for, he hadn't been joking. He'd been insatiable, his passion causing hers to rise over and over again, far beyond anything she ever believed her body capable of sustaining before.

He truly brought out the wild woman in her, reducing her to her most animalistic nature. She became a creature of sensation, all thought and reasoning swept away. He touched and she responded. He demanded and she gave. She'd bitten, clawed, scratched, and screamed. Hugh's body looked as if he'd been in a war, and he had, one of the most sensuous kinds. He'd brought out the feral part of her nature and then tamed the beast he created.

She looked up as the door opened and Hugh walked into the bathroom naked, carrying a cup of coffee. His cock jutted from his body proudly. After the excess of last night, he shouldn't have been hard. One thing she learned last night was to never underestimate this man's ability to achieve and maintain an erection. Granted she was a novice, but whatever the normal parameters were for men, Hugh fell way outside of the norm.

He came over to the tub and squatted, holding the coffee out to her. She reached out, bypassing the coffee and grabbed his cock instead. Just the mere sight of his desire for her raised an answering desire within her. She stroked her hand up and down and he gave a hiss of pleasure.

"Woman, we don't have time for this. You have to be to work in an hour."

Ignoring him, she rose up out of the tub and replaced her hand with her mouth. She made slurping sounds as she sucked on him for all she was worth.

He sighed. "I tried to warn you. Don't blame me if you're late." Having said that, he gripped her under her arms and pulled her off of him. As he stood, he lifted her dripping, slippery body out of the tub.

"Wrap your legs around me."

She immediately obeyed. He cupped her hips with his hands and buried himself inside, driving in to the hilt. After a night of intense loving, her body was so sensitized that she immediately came. He rocked her through her first orgasm and straight into another. He loved the way she responded to him. Knowing they didn't have time to linger, he braced her against the wall and took her hard and fast, growling as he came.

Once their breathing settled, he carried her to the tub and lowered her into the water. Kissing her lingering on the mouth, he stepped away as she lay back down, her body sated for the moment. He handed her the coffee and called over his shoulder as he left, "Breakfast will be ready in ten minutes. Hurry and finish. I will not be the cause of you being late."

She smiled wickedly in satisfaction as he left. There was something to be said to having all of that potent masculinity at her beck and call. She would hate the way she responded to him if she didn't know that his reaction to her was just as strong, if not stronger.

Because she'd never desired any man before Hugh, she'd secretly feared that she was frigid. Because of Hugh, she now knew she was as warm-blooded as any other woman. *Umm, imagine having all of that in your bed for the rest of your life?* The minute the question crossed her mind, she shied away from it. This was an affair and she would enjoy it while it lasted. She wouldn't ruin things by allowing thoughts of the future to intrude.

Although Hugh seemed to be her perfect match in every way, what did she really know about him? She'd known Charles a lot longer and a lot better and look how that relationship ended. Since she didn't expect anything from Hugh, she wouldn't be disappointed when the relationship ended, which it would. It was better this way. There was less chance of being hurt.

She finished washing and got out of the tub, her body offering only a twinge of protest. Knowing Hugh would come and get her if she dawdled any longer, she dressed in a loose outfit that was also concealing. She pulled her still wet hair up into a knot at the nape of her neck after making sure that her neck was sufficiently covered. She didn't want to answer any embarrassing questions about the love marks on her body.

Her stomach growled reminding her it was time to eat. Because of Hugh's spoiling, her appetite was changing. Where before she disdained breakfast, now she needed it, and not the coffee and toast she was used to eating. Eggs, bacon, sausage, and more. She wanted it all, and heavy on the protein, which was surprising since she'd never been much of a meat eater. Lately she craved the stuff, which she guessed was a good thing since Hugh did most of the cooking and he ate a lot of meat.

She poured another cup of coffee before sitting down to eat. She was so hungry, manners went flying out the window as she wolfed down everything in sight, going so far as to snatch the last piece of bacon off of Hugh's plate. He just sat and watched, amused.

Finally, once she'd eaten her fill and all the food was gone.

"I told you that you would have to eat more if you

wanted to keep up with me."

She leaned back in her seat, cradling her coffee in her hands before replying. "After last night, I'd say I keep up with you just fine."

Heat flared in his eyes as the memory of the night before lingered in the air between them. With a low growl, he got to his feet and reached for her. Laughing, she slipped out of the chair and darted out of reach. "No, no, no. You wouldn't want me to be late for work, would you?"

"Kiesha will understand." He unbuttoned his jeans and pulled down the zipper, allowing his heavy cock to spring forward. The sight of it stopped her for a minute as lust surged to the surface, causing her to lose her train of thought. Fortunately, the phone chose that moment to ring, snapping her out of it and allowing her to dance gracefully out of the way of his reaching hands. She ran to the phone to answer it.

Looking at the Caller ID, she felt her desire die when she recognized the name. She picked up the receiver.

"Hello, Mother."

"Mary Elizabeth, you need to come home." Her mother's voice was as commanding as always.

"I'm not coming home. We have this conversation every time you call. This is my home now. I like it here and I'm staying."

When Hugh realized who was on the phone, he zipped his pants back up and came closer to her, silently offering support.

"That is not your home. It's time you gave up this foolishness and came home where you belong."

"Mom, this is not foolishness. This is my life, my career. I explained all of this to you before. I'm not moving back."

"Well, since you refuse to move back here to be with your father and me, when are you coming for a visit?

You've been gone a long time and your father misses you."

The comment about her father got to her, weakened her resolve. "It's only been three weeks. I just started working. It's too soon for me to ask for time off and the distance is too far to come down for just the weekend."

"Mary Elizabeth, you're our only child now that your poor sister is gone. It's only natural that we would want to spend time with you, no matter how short a timeframe. So, when can we expect you?"

Feeling harassed, her eyes unconsciously sought Hugh's for support. He must have understood, for he wrapped his arms around her. His presence gave her the strength she needed. "Mom, I can't come home for a visit right now. I'll come when things are more settled on the job."

"I can't believe the selfishness I'm hearing. Fine, we'll wait until *the job* is more settled. Imagine, putting a job before your aging parents. Since we have to wait for you to find time to visit, at least tell me where you're living. All I have is this phone number and your email address. I don't even know your mailing address. What am I suppose to tell my friends when they ask about you?"

Mary Elizabeth immediately felt guilty. She hadn't told her family where she was living. All they knew was that she lived in a small town in North Carolina. She hadn't even told them the name of the town. She meant to give them more information once she arrived, but it had slipped her mind. "You're right. Forgive me. I should have given you my address. If you have a pen, I'll give it to you now."

When her mother was ready, she rattled off the address to her. Looking at the time, she said, "Listen Mom, I've got to go or else I'll be late for work. I promise I'll get home for a visit to see you and Dad as soon as I can."

"Okay, dear. You go to work. I'll speak with you later."

"Bye, Mom. Give Dad my regards." Mary Elizabeth hung up the phone, grabbed her things and headed for the door, with Hugh trailing behind her.

"Everything alright at home?"

"Everything's fine. I've got to run or I really will be late." She buzzed him on the lips before heading out of the door.

* * * *

At the other end of the line, Susan Brown hung up the phone and turned to the man seated next to her. "How was that?"

Charles smiled at her and said, "You did just fine, Mom. I couldn't have done better myself."

"And you'll do what you said?" Her eyes were full of hope as she handed him the sheet of paper with the address on it.

"I'll bring your little girl home. I promise." No matter what it took, Mary Elizabeth was coming home where she belonged.

* * * *

In spite of everything, Mary Elizabeth was only a few minutes late. Both Kiesha and Shannon were waiting for her. She called out as the breezed in the door, "Sorry I'm late. Things were crazy this morning. Hey, Shannon. I'm surprised to see you here. I thought Kiesha said you preferred to work at home?"

Shannon rolled her eyes. "I do, but my brother's there right now. I came here for some peace and quiet."

Kiesha turned to her in surprise. "From the little Alex said, I got the impression you and your brother weren't on speaking terms."

"It's a long and complicated story. I'd rather hear about Mary Elizabeth. I gather you changed your mind about Hugh? You're positively glowing."

Mary Elizabeth sputtered in surprise, causing Kiesha to turn and examine her closely. "You know, now that you mention it, there is something different about her." She sniffed the air around Mary Elizabeth. "You even smell different. Are you wearing a different perfume?"

"Would you quit smelling me! That's just freaky, the way you people do that."

Shannon shook her head. "That's not perfume you're smelling. That's Hugh. His scent is all over her."

Kiesha looked at Mary Elizabeth and smiled as she began to fidget under the weight of their combined stare. "Do tell," she smiled wickedly. "You have anything you want to tell us?"

Mary Elizabeth shoved her bangs out of her face and wondered if she could get past them and into her office. Knowing them, they'd follow her and then she'd be trapped. Damn, they were nosey. Couldn't a woman satisfy a few needs without everyone knowing about it? Damned wolf senses!

"If you must know, Hugh and I have been seeing each other a bit."

Shannon snorted in disbelief. "Yeah, try telling that to someone who doesn't know any better. You've been doing more than seeing him 'a bit.' The man put his mark on you."

Kiesha squealed and hugged Mary Elizabeth. "Oh, I'm so happy for you. Now I know you'll be staying. Wait until I tell Alex."

Mary Elizabeth pushed Kiesha away. "Tell Alex what? And what do you mean, 'now you know I'll be staying'? I had no intentions of leaving." Turning to Shannon, she said, "And what the hell are you talking about, 'he put his mark on me'? Hugh's not a werewolf. I haven't been *marked* by anyone."

Kiesha immediately sobered. She and Shannon exchanged a look that spoke volumes, before turning back to Mary Elizabeth. "Sweetie, he's not a werewolf, but he is a shifter. Didn't he tell you?"

"What do you mean he's a shifter? If he's not a werewolf, what else is there that he could be?"

Shannon piped in. "I don't really know the man, but from his scent, I'd say he was a were-bear."

"*A bear! There are bears?* No one said anything about bears."

Kiesha frowned at her, obviously thinking back. "Well, no. But I did tell you there were other shifters here besides Alex."

"I thought you meant there were other werewolves! No one said ANYTHING about there being other types of shifters. Just how many others are there?"

Shannon started counting them off. "Well, there's Rome, the sheriff. He's some type of cat. Fatima, the woman who owns the health food store, she's a fox. And of course, there's Hugh. He's a bear. That's all I personally know about, but then I'm new. If you really want to know, you'd have to ask somebody like Alex, or Hugh."

Kiesha brought the conversation back to the main issue. "I take it Hugh didn't tell you what he was before he mated you?"

"Stop saying that! I am *not* mated. This is just an affair. We agreed. I won't allow it to be more." Mary Elizabeth was ready to pull her hair out.

Shannon said under her breath, "Damned sneaky bear."

Kiesha nodded in agreement. "So he hasn't bitten you on the tendon where your neck and shoulder join?"

Mary Elizabeth's hand flew to that spot instinctively,

as though trying to hide the evidence, forgetting that her shirt covered the mark on her neck. Her movement only gave her away and she knew it.

Kiesha patted her on the shoulder sympathetically. "Don't worry. There's still hope. According to Alex, the mating bond isn't complete until you mark him in return. As long as you didn't bite him like he bit you, it should be okay. If you really don't want him, though, you'll have to stay away from him from now on."

Mary Elizabeth looked at Kiesha in despair as memories of last night exploded in her mind. She'd marked Hugh. Not once, but several times. What the hell was she going to do now?

Correctly interpreting the look on her face, Shannon asked, "I take it by the look on your face that it's too late? You've already marked him?"

Mary Elizabeth nodded. "Last night, but I didn't know what I was doing, I swear. What am I going to do?"

Kiesha turned to Shannon. "I'm new to this whole mating business. Does it count if she didn't know what she was doing? Is there any way out of it? Any kind of loophole?"

Shannon shook her head, and Mary Elizabeth knew she was not going to be happy with what she was about to say. "They are well and truly mated now. If this was just a regular mating there might be a way, but I've got a feeling from the way they react toward each other that she's his One. Even if there were a way, he'd never let her go now. They are as good as married. There's no divorce in our world. Mates stay mates until the day they die."

Chapter Eighteen

Mary Elizabeth's gaze bounced from object to object, instinctively looking for a way of escape. "I've got to get out of here. I need to think. I only met the man three weeks ago and now you're telling me I'm married to him?" She began to pace, too agitated to stand still.

Kiesha reached out and caught her by the arm. "Mary Elizabeth, calm down. Don't do anything rash. If there's one thing I've learned, it's that the Creator doesn't make any mistakes when it comes to true mates. I think if you just give yourself some time to get used to the idea, you'll find out that everything is okay. Believe me, I know how you feel. I wasn't any more accepting of this when Alex told me about it than you are right now. I think when you have a chance to get over the shock, you'll find that Hugh really is the perfect man for you—your soul mate. That's how it was for me with Alex. You just need time to adjust your thinking."

She pulled her arm away and went back to pacing, throwing her hands up in the air in frustration. "And when am I supposed to find time to do that? The man is practically living in my apartment. He knew I only wanted an affair. I was very clear about that. I told the man I couldn't handle anything more serious."

"He's just waiting you out. Bears are very intelligent and cunning creatures. He knew if he hung around long enough, the mating fever would take over and before you knew it, the mate bond would have you both. Once the mating fever kicks in, the only way to stop things is for one of you to die before the bond can be completed." Shannon continued, "I could tell at the party that the two of you were in the grip of the mating fever. I didn't know at the time that you had no idea what Hugh was. He should have at least told you that much about himself."

"He probably thought that at best she wouldn't believe him or at the worst, the information would scare her away. I'm sure neither option appealed to him. He still should have told Mary Elizabeth. That's men for you. There's a lot I wouldn't have known until it was too late if Carol hadn't told me about it first. People in love do some strange things when that love is threatened."

Mary Elizabeth held her hands up protectively in front of herself. "Whoa, back the horse up. No one said anything about love."

Shannon and Kiesha both looked at her like she was stupid. "What do you think we've been talking about? The mate bond is synonymous with love. It's love in its highest form. He may not have said the words to you but you can't tell me he hasn't been showing you how he feels about you. Based on my experience with Alex, I have no doubt that it's love, and not sex that's motivating everything that Hugh does for you."

Mary Elizabeth thought over everything Hugh had done. The way he fed her and took care of her. The way he was concerned about her safety and did what was best for her, even when it meant denying himself something he really wanted. She'd been in denial. The man was in love with her. His love showed through every word he said and every action he took.

Suddenly she was overwhelmed. This was just one truth too many for her mind to handle. She needed to get out of her. Shoulders hunched protectively, she told Kiesha, "I've got to go. I need to think. My mind's about to burst. I know this is short notice but I need to take off a few days. Go somewhere where I can get my head together. I need space. I'm suffocating." She turned to walk out of the door, breathing like someone having an asthma attack.

Kiesha grabbed her by the shoulders. "Wait! Don't leave. At least, not yet. I agree that you need time to think and you won't be able to do that here with Hugh, but you can't just run off willy-nilly. You need a plan. Where will you go?"

"Go? I don't know. Just away. I need to get away from here."

"I understand. Listen to me. I have an idea. You can get the space you need and take care of business at the same time. This is something I was going to have you to do anyway, so you might as well do it now. Go around to all the neighboring towns and check out their thrift stores. Find out what's selling and what's not. We need an idea of what the people around here like so we don't stock the store with a bunch of useless merchandise. I'll give you the business credit card and you can charge your gas, lodging and meals on me. This way you can kill two birds with one stone. Get a jump on business while taking time to get your head together, okay?"

Mary Elizabeth didn't hesitate. She took the lifeline Kiesha offered her with both hands. "Deal. I'll leave as soon as you give me the card. I won't even go home to pack. I'll buy what I need while I'm out. I can't face Hugh right now."

"I understand. Do what you have to do. I'll go get the card. You wouldn't have been able to do much here anyway. Now that the computers have arrived, there isn't much we can do with them until Shayla comes to set up the systems. This is the perfect time for you to be away." She turned to go and get the card.

While she was gone, Shannon said to Mary Elizabeth, "I can't say I know how you feel, but I've heard about true mates all of my life. One thing I know, no matter how things start, they always end up being the most dedicated, committed, and loving relationships anyone has ever seen. It's what all shifters pray for, that they might find their One—the only one they can truly be happy with. You take this time you need to think about things but know this, now that Hugh has found you, he'll never let you go. He can't. You hold his heart in your hands. Be careful what you do with it."

Mary Elizabeth nodded, indicating that she understood. Kiesha returned and handed her the card. "Be careful and stay safe. What do you want me to tell Hugh when he comes looking for you?"

"Just tell him that I needed time to think, and not to call my cell phone. I'll have it off unless I need to make a call."

"Okay, I'll do that. You make sure you check in every day with me or I'll tell him how to track you down."

Mary Elizabeth shuddered, knowing Kiesha meant what she said. He'd do it, too, and drag her back to Refuge, kicking and screaming. "I will. I'll call and tell you where I am and what I've found." She gave Kiesha a hug and turned and walked out of the store.

Watching her drive off, Kiesha asked Shannon, "What do you think?"

"I think Hugh is going to have a shit fit when he finds out she's gone. I wouldn't want to be around when that happens. Although, it's no less than he deserves for not being honest with her."

Kiesha agreed. "That's exactly how I feel about it."

They shared a look that women have shared throughout the ages. One of sisterhood and camaraderie, steeped in the knowledge that sometimes women had to stand together just to be able to hold their own against the men in their lives.

* * * *

Hugh was feeling great, as great as only a night of mind-blowing sex with the woman he loved could leave him feeling. The mate bond was working. Each time they joined as one, the cords binding their souls together became stronger. Soon, his mate would be totally his. Right now, she was actively resisting the idea that they might be more to each other than just a temporary amusement. Somewhere in his mate's past she'd learned to be leery of love; probably the fault of her messed up childhood and her screwed up mother and sister. She didn't have a high opinion of love, something that her brief relationship with Charles had reinforced.

If it hadn't been for her getting sick that night, she would never have let him close enough for a relationship to develop. She'd spent the last couple of years keeping men at arm's length. She knew exactly what to do to keep men away. This last week had been a delicate dance of pushing inside her boundaries yet giving her space to be free. Although he was living with her, he allowed her to believe that he was simply a nightly visitor.

Unnoticed by her, they'd already fallen into a routine. Each morning they ate breakfast together before she left for work. After work, she had time to herself to unwind and enjoy her privacy. He'd noticed that his mate was a very private person and needed plenty of personal space. His working evenings allowed her the time she needed alone to recharge her batteries.

When she was ready for company, she came down to the diner and sought him out. He gave her the excuse she needed by providing food for her to eat. In reality, she came down because she wanted to be with him as much as he wanted to be with her, and not for the free meal. He knew it was the truth because any woman that loved to cook as much as Mary Elizabeth did would never have turned over all the cooking to him. That she had was simply her mind's way of giving her a valid reason to do what her heart wanted to do. She wasn't ready to admit to herself that she loved him.

She definitely wasn't ready to hear that he loved her. In her mind, love had to be earned. She didn't consider herself worthy of being loved. It's a lesson she learned from her parents when she'd had to earn her place in their affections. She wasn't taught that she was lovable just as she was. The message she drilled into her since early childhood was that the beautiful people were given love, everyone else had to earn theirs. She didn't see her own beauty. Not only was she beautiful on the outside, more importantly, she was beautiful on the inside. Her inner beauty radiated out of her like sunshine, visible for all to see.

There was so much he needed to tell her that she wasn't ready to hear. She still had no idea that he was a shifter. She had no inkling that they were mated, which in his world was more binding than marriage and more permanent than death. She thought she was involved in an affair, something that could be ended at any moment.

Somehow he was going to have to find a way to force her to face her feelings. She needed to know that what they had was forever, but he had to get the timing just right. If he confronted her before she was ready, she'd run. He'd rather face her temper than have her run from him in a panic.

"Hey, Hugh. Where's your lady? Shouldn't she be here by now?"

Hugh looked at the clock. It was way past the time when Mary Elizabeth usually joined him. "Yeah, she should. Maybe she took a nap. I'll give it another hour before I call her," he told Ralph, his other cook.

Business picked up in the diner and before he knew it, another two hours had passed. Realizing she still hadn't arrived, he fixed a "to go" dinner to take to her. "I'm taking a break. I'll be back in an hour."

"Okay, boss."

He went out the back door and started up the stairs. He was halfway to the door before he realized her truck wasn't in the parking lot.

Stopping, he turned and started back down the stairs. Surely she wasn't still at work. It was after eight o'clock. She should have been home hours ago. He crossed over to the Hummer, put her food on the passenger seat and drove the few short blocks to the store. Mary Elizabeth usually parked in front. There was no sign of her vehicle and the store was locked up tight. All of the lights were off inside.

He sat in the vehicle, trying to think of where she could be. She was still new in town and didn't know too many people. That left Kiesha, Mary Elizabeth's best friend and the reason she was here. He backed out of the parking space and made a U-turn in the middle of the street. He was going to find the one person who would know where his mate was.

* * * *

Kiesha was jumpier than a long tailed cat in a room full of rocking chairs. Every time the phone rang, she expected it to be Hugh, demanding to know Mary Elizabeth's whereabouts. Alex informed her that no one was allowed to interfere in the bonding process between mates, not even Alphas, a rule she'd forgotten. Those who did ran the risk of being ostracized by the Pack. When Hugh did come calling, and she had no doubt that he would, she would have two angry males on her hands.

They both looked up at the sound of a vehicle in the drive.

Alex said, "That sounds like Hugh. Wonder what's so important that he had to drive all the way out here instead of picking up the phone and calling." He headed to the door.

Kiesha got off of the couch and began to ease up the stairs. She knew it was useless to run but she had to try any way. There was no way she could just sit there, knowing what was coming. She was halfway up the stairs by the time Alex opened the door for Hugh.

"Come in and tell me what's wrong."

"Alex, sorry to disturb you but I need to speak to your mate. It's extremely important."

Alex gestured toward the living room. "Sure, she's right in here. Where did that woman go? She was right here a minute ago."

Kiesha flinched when one of the stairs creaked under her foot, knowing they'd heard.

"Kiesha, there you are. Hugh is here to see you."

Kiesha slowly turned around, knowing the look on her face screamed her guilt.

Seeing her expression, Alex asked, "Kiesha, what have you done?"

She straightened up her shoulders and held her head up high, deciding to brazen it out. "I didn't do anything. I was simply heading for the bathroom."

"Then why do you look guilty?"

Hugh butted in. "Kiesha, do you know where Mary Elizabeth is? She's not at home, nor is she at the store. I was hoping she was here."

Kiesha began to fidget. The moment she dreaded was at hand.

Alex got a suspicious look on his face. "Kiesha, you know where Mary Elizabeth is, don't you?"

"Well, technically I don't, not really." She wasn't lying. Mary Elizabeth hadn't checked in yet, so she didn't know where she was. She just knew where she wasn't, and that was in Refuge.

Hugh, obviously holding onto his patience, asked, "Why don't you tell us what you do know?" His voice was strained, like he was trying not to yell.

"Watch how you're speaking to my mate," Alex said with a hard look.

Hugh returned his look with one of his own. "As soon as your mate tells me where mine has disappeared to, I'll leave and be out of your hair."

"Your mate? Mary Elizabeth is your One? Damn, that's great news. I was hoping this would happen." Alex grinned from ear-to-ear and slapped Hugh on the arm, congratulating him.

"It would be fantastic news except for the fact that she seems to have disappeared, and your mate is the only one who knows what happened," Hugh said dryly.

At this, they both directed their attention to Kiesha, who had managed to climb up two more steps. "Love, don't you move, not one more step, you hear? Otherwise I might be forced to come and get you. Where's Mary Elizabeth?"

Kiesha stopped, knowing he wouldn't hesitate to do exactly as he had said. She could occasionally push Alex, but she'd learned not to cross him. She took a deep breath and blurted, "She left town." Her hand gripped the rail and her body was tensed to run. If they came after her, she wouldn't have much of a head start.

"What do you mean, she left town?" The question came from Alex. Hugh was too busy growling, not a good sign. She had no desire to see an angry bear. Shannon's words came back to her.

"Well, she sort of found out by accident that she was mated to a shifter, a fact she didn't know," she turned to glare at Hugh and quickly turned back to Alex when she saw how furious Hugh was. "She freaked out and needed time to think, so I sent her on a business trip." Seeing the looks on both men's faces, she spoke faster. "She was just going to run but I slowed her down and gave her something constructive to do while she was gone. She'll be back once she's had time to settle down."

Hugh was so furious his eyes shifted and his jaw elongated, making his face look funny.

Alex was in Alpha mode. "And how did she, as you put it, 'accidentally' find out that she was mated to Hugh?"

"Well ... she came into the store and Shannon was there. I asked her if she was wearing new perfume because she smelled different but Shannon recognized Hugh's scent. Mary Elizabeth mentioned that she and Hugh were seeing each other and well, you know how it is. One thing lead to another and before it was all over, it came out that Mary Elizabeth and Hugh had done the whole bonding thing only she didn't know about it and when she found out about it she freaked." Kiesha dragged in a huge breath of air. She'd gotten all of that out without stopping to breathe, wanting this over and done with.

Hugh closed his eyes and looked a little hopeless. "Do you know where she went?"

Seeing the anguish on his face, Kiesha felt her heart melt. This man really loved her friend. She was sure he had a good reason for keeping what he was a secret. "No, I'm sorry Hugh. She's supposed to be going around to the neighboring towns to check out the area thrift stores, seeing which items really sell so we know how to stock our store. I made her promise to call each night and check in or I told her I would send you after her. For what it's worth, I think she really does love you. She just needs time to get her head straight and think things through. She would never have allowed you this close to her if she didn't care."

Hugh's shoulders dropped in defeat. "Promise me you'll call as soon as you hear from her."

"I will, Hugh. I'm sure she won't be gone long," Kiesha tried to reassure him as he walked out the door.

Once Hugh was gone, Alex turned to her with a look on his face she didn't like. "I see we need to have a little talk about staying out of other people's business." He locked the door and started up the steps toward her.

Kiesha turned and ran, knowing he'd catch her but doing it any way. Alex would never hurt her, but the man had a way of getting his point across that left a deep impression, one to be avoided at all cost. She'd barely made it to the door of their room when she felt him behind her. He scooped her up in his arms and carried her into the bedroom, slamming the door shut behind them.

"Let me give you a refresher course on how we do not interfere in the lives of mates and see if I can make it stick this time."

He did, and it was a lesson she wouldn't soon be forgetting.

Chapter Nineteen

Charles went through his mental checklist to make sure he had everything he needed for his trip. A one-way plane ticket to Knoxville was in his pocket. The confirmation paperwork for the cargo van he rented was in his briefcase. Being familiar with small towns, he knew the quickest way to be noticed would be to be seen driving around town in an unfamiliar luxury car. He didn't want to chance drawing any attention to himself while he was there.

Also in his briefcase was a bottle of quick dissolve tranquilizers, just in case his fiancée proved a bit reluctant. He'd humored her minor rebellion thus far, but his patience was coming to an end. Yes, he'd made a mistake in marrying The Whore and his true love was entitled to her pound of flesh—a woman scorned and all that bull— but enough was enough. It was time to end this foolishness and bring her home where she belonged.

Neither one of them were getting any younger. They needed to get to work producing his heirs as soon as possible. He had to have someone to leave his empire to, and it would be one of his own. He'd make sure Mary Elizabeth was properly taken care of, as well. He'd already made provisions for her future financial security in his will, as any good husband would.

She'd discover that he was an excellent provider. He'd already settled a generous monthly allowance on her that would began next month, so she could give up that ridiculous job of hers. As if he'd allow any wife of his to work, especially after what happened the last time. No, she could spend her time taking care of him and the children. If that wasn't enough to keep her busy, there were always charitable organizations. They always needed dedicated workers. Not only would it give her a chance to use the business skills she'd acquired in college, it would make him look good as well.

He'd found a boutique with a good reputation and had them create a wardrobe just for his love. Although they'd done an excellent job in clothing The Whore, he'd chosen not to use the same retailer that The Whore used when she was alive. He didn't think his fiancée would appreciate any more comparisons being made with that of her sister. A few of the items he'd ordered had already been delivered; the rest should arrive shortly. When Mary Elizabeth came home, she'd discover a closet full of clothes waiting just for her.

They'd be leaving that clunker she called a truck behind in North Carolina. She'd have her choice of vehicles and if there was nothing she wanted to drive already parked in the six-bay garage, then he'd just take her out and buy her the vehicle of her choice. He could easily purchase it under his business name and use it as a tax write-off.

It shouldn't take more than a couple of days to retrieve his bride. He already had the minister booked and the marriage announcements ready to go. He figured something private but tasteful would be appropriate this time around since he was still a grieving widower. His business associates would understand his hasty remarriage. After all, he was marrying his wife's sister, keeping it in the family as they say. He already knew her background was impeccable and the practice was common among his set.

He informed his staff that he would be bringing his fiancée back with him and to have everything prepared.

Everything that he could think of that needed doing was done. Oh yes, his insurance policy. His bride could, on occasion, be extremely stubborn. Going to the safe, he pulled out his secret weapon, something no southern gentleman worth his salt would be without. He doubted he would need it. He was sure she would see the error of her ways once they'd had a chance to talk face-to-face. If not, well there nothing like a nine millimeter to help push matters along.

Opening the safe, he pulled out the gun case and ammunition. He wasn't worried about security at the airport. His case would be checked in with his luggage and as long as he had all the appropriate documentation, there should be no problem. If not, well, that's why he had money. What good was it if it couldn't be used to occasionally pave the way?

* * * *

The first day, sheer panic kept her moving. She ran from everything, but mostly she ran from herself, and from Hugh. Not, surprisingly enough, from what he was. She had no problems with his being a shifter. It was his feelings for her that scared her.

She had no experience with love. She knew how to give it, but she had no practice in receiving it. In her experience, love came with strings. It was only given when you did something to earn it. She'd done nothing to earn Hugh's love. He gave and she received. That was the basis of their relationship. The only thing she gave to him was her body, and she didn't see how that counted for anything because he always made sure she received more pleasure than she ever gave.

It puzzled her and she couldn't trust what she didn't understand. She didn't realize that love wasn't supposed to make sense, that it wasn't logical. It astounded her that

Hugh could really love her. After all, no one else in her life did.

The next day, the panic receded and she could think clearly, but she wasn't ready to return home. Going home meant facing Hugh, and she wasn't quite ready. She still wasn't sure how she felt about everything. It was difficult for her to comprehend that what she thought of as an affair was something more, something permanent. Just the idea of it made her head hurt.

By day three, she acknowledged that for whatever reason, Hugh really did love her. It showed in his actions, and in every word he spoke to her. It was apparent in the way he cared for her. She'd soaked up his attention like a sponge, not being used to it. She was the caretaker in all of her relationships. No one *ever* took care of her. She hadn't examined his actions too closely, because if she had, her innate sense of fair play wouldn't have allowed her to enjoy his attention, knowing that he wanted more from her than she was willing to give.

But she still couldn't go home. Not until she figured out what she wanted. It wouldn't be fair to Hugh for their relationship to continue when she didn't know her own heart and mind. She wasn't a user.

On day four, loneliness kicked in. She kept wanting to share the things she'd seen with Hugh. Somewhere in the last two weeks, he'd become her best friend. She missed sharing her day with him, the amusing and sometimes troubling things that happened. She'd find herself thinking, 'Oh, I can't wait to tell Hugh about this,' or 'Hugh would love that.'

The nights were the worst. She tossed and turned, seeking the heat of his body. She missed the sound of his breathing in the still of the night. She missed his scent filling her nostrils. It went far deeper than sex, though she missed that, too. She didn't just miss the sex. She missed Hugh.

While she wasn't looking, he'd imprinted himself on her soul. She felt incomplete without him. He'd subtly made himself such a large part of her life that she hadn't realized how big until he was gone, even if it was by her own doing. Did she really want to spend the rest of her life like this? No, she didn't. She wanted him in her life, totally and completely.

One thing she knew for sure, Hugh was not Charles. With him, she'd never have to worry about infidelity. Maybe she didn't know how to deal with his love and maybe she didn't completely trust it to last, but according to Kiesha and Shannon, she could trust in the mate bond. According to them, it was more permanent than marriage, and more binding in love. Yes, she could put her faith in something like that.

By day five, only sheer stubbornness was keeping her going. She was way past ready to go home. She missed her bed, her apartment, and she missed Hugh's cooking, but most of all, she missed Hugh. She had an assignment to complete and she was determined to get it done. Once she got home, she didn't plan on leaving again unless Hugh went with her, and with his schedule at the diner, she didn't see that happening any time soon.

That was one of the things they needed to discuss, the time he spent at the diner. It was fine for now, but when the kids started coming things were going to have to change. With the way they'd been going at it like bunnies, it wouldn't be long before there was a little one on the way.

Another thing they needed to talk about was the living arrangements. While the apartment was nice and convenient to both of their places of employment, she wanted a house. She'd planned for half of her life to build her dream home and she wasn't giving up the dream now. She was sure Hugh wouldn't mind. Before her, he'd been living in an efficiency apartment. He said he didn't need more than a bed to sleep in since he spent most of his time at the diner. It was a wonder he didn't sleep in his office.

It was after three o'clock before she finished with the last store. She had the information Kiesha needed and she was ready to go home. It was a four-hour drive back to Refuge. She'd checked out of the hotel, was packed, and ready to go. A quick stop through the drive-thru to get something to eat and she'd be on her way. Next stop, Hugh and home.

* * * *

Where was she? He'd been in this rinky-dink little town for two days now and hadn't seen a sign of her. She wasn't at her apartment, although he'd seen some guy coming and going from the place as though he lived there. Her truck was never home and never at the store where she worked. It wasn't like he could just walk into the store and ask for her, not after he'd gone through so much trouble to keep his presence here a secret.

He was reduced to driving by her place, and then only at night, hoping for a glimpse of her truck. He couldn't risk being seen driving around too much or people would get suspicious. There were no tourist for him to blend in with and as a result, he stuck out like a sore thumb.

He was beginning to realize taking Mary Elizabeth was going to be more difficult than he'd planned on. Susan didn't tell him that she lived in the center of town over a diner. The self-centered bitch probably didn't even know. After all, Mary Elizabeth wasn't her precious Babs. If Mary Elizabeth wouldn't come willingly, then it was going to be tricky getting her out of there. The only good thing about her location was that the entrance to her apartment was at the rear of the building. Since he'd been checking, only one other vehicle had parked back there, a massive Hummer that must belong to the guy who owned the diner.

Taking a big risk, he went into the diner the third night he was there. If asked, he'd pretend to be lost and in need of direction. He sat down at the counter with some of the other men and picked up the menu. Fortunately, he'd bought clothes that were not his usual style of dress. With the jeans and flannel button down shirt he purchased at one of the local thrift stores, he blended right in.

An hour and a half later, he was back out on the street and in possession of some much needed information. It seemed Mary Elizabeth was out of town on a business trip. No one knew for sure when she'd return, but it wasn't expected to be longer than a week. She and the big guy who owned the diner were going at it hot and heavy, but it seemed that Mary Elizabeth was trying to put an end to things. She must have come to her senses. She hadn't even told the big guy she was leaving. Just took off. His time spent in the diner was well worth the risk.

He pulled away from the building and then found an out of the way place to park. Thankful he was dressed in dark colors, he walked back to the diner, sticking to the alleys and back streets. Once there, he found a place to sit and watch. He was so focused that he never even noticed the cold. He watched, waited, and planned. He had the next few days to learn everyone's schedule and determine the best way to successfully complete his plan.

* * * *

Mary Elizabeth phoned Kiesha. "I'm done and on my way home."

"That's great. Have you told Hugh?" This was news he would definitely want to know. He had been calling every day to check up on her progress.

"No, I want to surprise him. We have a lot to discuss and I'd rather not get into it over the phone."

"I understand. To be honest with you, I surprised you managed to stay away from him this long." Kiesha paced while she talked.

"I was ready to come home two days ago. I just wanted to make sure I had all the information we needed while I was out. Once I finally get home, I won't be leaving again anytime soon."

"As if Hugh would let you," she chuckled. "Well, I know business-wise the trip was a success from talking to you during your daily check-ins. What about emotionally? Are you okay with everything that's happened now?"

"It scares me how much I missed him while I've been gone. He's such a big part of my life and I didn't even realize it. Yes, I'm okay with being mated to him, because I have to be okay with it. The alternative is living without him and that's no longer an option for me."

Kiesha sighed, understanding totally where she was coming from. "It's a little scary at times, how intense everything is, but you won't regret it. I was scared to let go with Alex, to trust in my feelings for him but I'm glad I took a chance on a future with him. Things have only gotten better as time goes by. When will you be home?"

"Probably in another two hours, if I don't get lost. I'm following the directions they gave me at the hotel. Barring any unforeseen complications, I should definitely be home in time for dinner."

"Well, I for one am glad you're on your way home. I missed you, and that big lug of yours misses you, too. Call me when you get in, that is if Hugh lets you out of bed long enough to get to a phone. He's going to be one happy man." Kiesha could feel her mouth stretching in a grin too large to contain. Mary Elizabeth was coming home and everything was all right.

"Remember, don't tell him I'm on the way home."

"I won't. Be careful and drive safely."

"I will. Bye."

Alex walked up behind his mate. "Was that Mary Elizabeth?"

Kiesha turned to him and leaned back against the counter where she'd been standing, happy with the world. "Yes, she's on her way home. Everything's going to be okay. She's had time to adjust to the idea of being Hugh's mate and she's fine with it. I would call Hugh and tell him but I promised not to. She wants to surprise him."

Alex kissed her lightly on the mouth and then went to the fridge to get the things he needed for their dinner tonight. "Good. I'm glad things worked out. You look a little tired. Why don't you go relax in the tub while I get started on dinner?"

Her eyes lit up, as he'd known they would. She loved their tub. "Are you sure you don't want me to help with dinner?"

"I'm sure. You go ahead and relax. I'll call you when dinner's ready." He waited until she was in the bathroom with the water running to pick up the phone. He called the diner and asked to speak to Hugh. When Hugh came to the phone, he said briefly, "Your mate's on her way home. She just spoke to Kiesha. She should be there in about two hours."

"Thanks Alex for the heads-up. I owe you one," he said and then hung up the phone. Alex disconnected the call on his end as well. Hugh didn't owe him anything. They were men and men had to stick together or get taken over by the women in their lives.

Hugh made a few phone calls and called in some workers to replace him. Then he adjusted the schedule to allow him to be free for the next few days. Once his workers arrived, he left and went back to his place. He'd run out of clothes at Mary Elizabeth's and needed to change. He was also packing the rest of his things. Now that she knew the truth, there was no need to be cautious and play it safe. They were living together and she'd just have to adjust to the reality of it. They were going to have a long talk when she got home, once he got rid of a little of his pent up frustration, that is.

* * * *

Charles watched the big guy get into the Hummer and leave. That was strange. His vehicle hadn't moved in the five days that Charles had been there. Maybe his luck was finally changing. He took advantage of the Hummer being gone to move his van closer to the diner. He'd found the perfect spot that allowed him to still keep an eye on the apartment without easily being seen.

Chapter Twenty

Mary Elizabeth pulled up to her apartment with a sigh of relief. She was home, finally. The drive seemed to take forever, much longer than the three-and-a-half hours it actually lasted. The Hummer was missing from its spot, so that meant Hugh wasn't at the diner. It wasn't like him not to be there on a Saturday night. For a minute, she wondered if Kiesha broke her word and called him anyway. On second thought, if Kiesha told Hugh she on her way home, he would be planted right here at the apartment, waiting for her.

Time to quit lollygagging. No telling how much time she had, but hopefully it was enough to take a shower and refresh herself. She grabbed her purse and the bags of clothing she'd purchased while she was gone. Her arms loaded down with the bags, she wondered if maybe she should have bought a suitcase like she started to. She didn't need more luggage but if she had, she would only be making one trip upstairs instead of the two it was going to take to get everything inside.

She took her things into the bedroom, taking the time to put things away rather than doing it later. Hugh could walk in the door any minute, so she'd better do this while she could. She'd bought a bit more than the little she'd needed to wear while she was gone. Who knew shopping could be so therapeutic? Besides, she'd run across some deals that she just couldn't pass up. With Kiesha paying her travel expenses, she'd been well able to afford her little shopping spree.

After hanging the new outfits up and throwing the dirty clothes in the hamper where they belonged, she went to go back out to the truck to get the rest of her belongings only to pull up short. "What are you doing here?"

* * * *

Charles couldn't believe his good fortune. He'd only been in position for a few minutes when Mary Elizabeth arrived. She never once looked in his direction. Not only was she back, she'd conveniently left the front door open for him. He wouldn't get a better opportunity than this.

He reached back and got his briefcase. Everything was prepared and waiting. Once he had her, he could be on his way and leave this little hellhole behind. Checking to make sure no one was around, he got out of the van and quietly closed the door. He climbed the stairs rapidly, wanting to catch her while she was still inside. He made it inside and was pushing the door closed when Mary Elizabeth came out of one of the rooms in the back.

"What are you doing here?"

Surprisingly enough, his future bride didn't seem all that pleased to see him. Oh well, that would change soon enough. "Gee, Mary Elizabeth. I came all this way to visit you and you don't appear happy to see me. Is that any way to treat family?"

She responded just as he knew that she would. "I'm sorry, Charles. You took me by surprise. Of course I'm happy to see you. Why didn't you call first and tell me you were coming?"

"Then it wouldn't have been a surprise. I've been here several days, waiting for you to arrive. Your friend Kiesha told me you were out of town on business."

"Yes, I was," she said slowly. "As a matter of fact, I just arrived home not five minutes ago. That's strange. I just spoke to Kiesha and she didn't mention…"

"Aren't you going to ask me to sit down?" He interrupted quickly, not giving her time to finish that thought.

"Oh, where are my manners? Come in. Have a seat. Can I get you anything? I'm not sure what I have but you're more than welcome."

"No, I'm fine. Come, sit beside me and let's talk."

She came and sat, but she kept looking at the door expectantly. "Are you expecting someone?"

"My landlord. Kiesha said he was looking for me."

So the big guy was her landlord. Makes sense. Maybe the folks in the diner had it all wrong.

"Charles, why are you here?"

"I came to take you home. Your parents miss you and asked me to bring you home."

Mary Elizabeth closed her eyes and sighed. "Charles, I wish you hadn't come. I've told you and mother countless times that I like it here. I'm not coming home. Refuge is my home now."

"Mary Elizabeth, I think this foolishness has gone on long enough and your mother agrees. I've told you how I feel about you. Yes, I've made mistakes but it's time we moved past that. You've had your revenge, moving away, making me chase you and even playing around with that yokel. Now it's time to stop playing hard to get and come home so we can marry the way we should have all those years ago."

She looked at him as though he wasn't quite sane. "Charles, I'm not playing hard to get. This is my home and I'm not marrying you. I told you that before I left and again on the phone when we last spoke. Your insistence on referring to me as your fiancée has me concerned. I don't think you've dealt with Babs' death like you should. Maybe you should get some professional help."

"I AM NOT CRAZY!" He screamed at her, causing her to flinch away from him and slid to the edge of the couch, ready to jump to her feet, watching him warily. He took a deep breath to calm himself and held out a hand in silent appeal. "I'm sorry, dear. I didn't mean to frighten you. It's just that your sister used to say things of that nature to me all the time. That's why I had to do it, you see?"

* * * *

"Had to do what, Charles?" She didn't get up but she eased further away from him, still unsettled by the way he'd lost it a minute ago. She'd never seen Charles act like this.

"Why, had to get rid of her, of course. She wanted to leave me. She was going to tell everyone who would listen that I was crazy, not that anyone would have believed her. Still, the scandal would have been horrendous. Couldn't have that, now could we? Can't have any taint associated with the Remington name." He laughed, a horrible maniacal sound that raised the hairs on the nape of her neck.

Mary Elizabeth looked at him in dawning horror. There was something seriously wrong with Charles. She was beginning to believe his mind had snapped. "Charles, Babs' death was an accident, remember? She was hit by a drunk driver."

He smiled at her as though amused by her naivety. "Actually, it was a hit and run. Don't *you* remember? Presumed to be caused by a driver who'd been drinking and fled the scene to avoid detection. It really wasn't that difficult to plant that idea in the mind of the investigating officer. Happens all the time. No witnesses to contradict the supporting circumstantial evidence and case closed. Now come along. We've wasted enough time. Let's go before your friend with the Hummer decides to return." He rose to his feet and held out his hand to her in expectation.

She shook her head in denial. "Charles, do you realize what you're saying? You're saying you killed Babs."

"Really, dear. She needed killing. I don't see what the problem is."

She looked at him, really seeing him for the first time. "You *are* crazy. You stand there and confess to killing Babs and think I'd go anywhere with you?"

She stood and began backing toward the door. Charles moved to intercept, blocking the path to the door. "Get out of my house. I never want to see you again."

"Don't be foolish. Of course you want to see me. You *love* me. We're getting married, remember? Now come along, we don't have time for this. We need to leave before your landlord arrives."

He really is insane. She needed to get him out of here. He stood between the door and the bedroom. That left the phone. "Charles, if you won't leave on your own, I'll call the police."

He took a step toward her and she backed away, stepping closer to the phone. He stopped and a puzzled expression crossed his face. "Mary Elizabeth, are you *afraid* of me? I love you. I would never hurt you." He took another step forward.

Mary Elizabeth put her hand on the phone. "Just leave, Charles. Don't make me call the police."

He stood there, looking hurt and confused. "You obviously need a little time to yourself. I forgot you just returned from a trip. You're tired and not thinking straight. Let me grab my briefcase and I'll go. We can finish talking later."

He came closer to her and she tightened her grip on the phone, until she realized he was just getting the briefcase he'd laid on the coffee table near where she stood.

"I know you left because of your mother. She's never given you the love or appreciation you deserve. All of that

224

will change once we're married." He turned and started walking to the door, one hand holding the briefcase, the other playing with something in his pocket. Mary Elizabeth followed behind, careful not to get too close. She wanted to lock the door as soon as he was safely on the other side.

"I wish you could have seen her face when I told her we were marrying. She was so happy, especially when I promised to give her plenty of grandchildren to spoil."

Mary Elizabeth bit her tongue, trying to keep from commenting. He was almost to the door. Just a few steps more.

"Tears came to her eyes when I told her we'd name one of our daughters Anne, in Babs' honor."

Just then, the phone rang. She automatically looked in its direction. Charles swung the briefcase at her head and it connected with the side of her face. The force of the blow spun her around in a semi-circle and she dropped like a rock. Pain exploded in her head, so intense, she almost threw up.

She lay there crumpled on the floor, struggling to get to her hands and knees. She shook her head, trying to clear her mind. As the buzzing in her ears stopped, she could hear Charles droning in the background.

"Look what you made me do. I knew you were going to be difficult about this. You can be so stubborn, Mary Elizabeth. No matter, I came prepared." He set his briefcase on the table and opened it.

"Since you can't be reasonable about this, I'll just have to tie you up. I brought plenty of tape and insurance, for just in case." He held the gun up where she could see it, then placed it on the table. Then he reached back inside of the briefcase and came out with a roll of duct tape.

Mary Elizabeth made it to her knees and drunkenly tried to crawl away, heading for the door.

Charles tsked at her. "And where do you think you're

going? I would really hate to put a bullet in that lovely body of yours...but...if that's what it takes. I brought tranquilizers so you won't feel any pain on the long ride home if I have to shoot you. I realize you're angry, but once we're married all will be forgiven. I really am a superb catch. I intend to take good care of you. Leave all of this trash behind. I've already purchased you a wardrobe befitting your position as my wife and it's waiting at the house for you. And you can forget this silly little job of yours. As my wife, your only responsibility will be to take care of me, and our children, of course. Come along now. I've already spent more time here than I planned."

Each word he spoke caused the anger building inside her to grow stronger. Anger was good. It cleared her head and strengthened her resolve to get out of this alive, no matter what it took. Charles wouldn't get away with his attempt to kidnap her, for that's what this was.

"We'll have to drive all night to make it back in time for our wedding. Let me get you tied up. Then I'll carry you down to the van, which won't be easy. You *are* a little on the heavy side. That's something we'll have to work on once we're married."

Mary Elizabeth was so angry, she was literally seeing red. There was a strange tingling in her arms and legs which she ignored, her attention wholly centered on Charles.

"You ought to appreciate the trouble I'm going through for you." The sound of ripping filled the air as Charles tore off several strips of tape and hung them on the briefcase for ease of use. "Now let's get you all bundled up. I really wish this wasn't necessary, but I can't have you flailing around distracting me while I drive."

He put the tape back in the briefcase and accidentally knocked the gun off of the table. Seeing her opportunity, with a mighty roar, she rose up in a rush and lunged at him.

Her roar made him jump and jerk in her direction. His eyes opened wide in shock and the color left his face. *"What the hell?"*

It was all he managed to get out before she struck. The hand groping for the gun never connected as with another roar of pure fury, she hit him with all the strength in her body. He flew across the room and slammed into the wall before dropping to the floor like a limp, rag doll; eyes rolled up into the back of his head.

The door burst open a seconds later and Hugh came rushing in. He took in the scene in a glance, his eyes widening when he saw her before he turned and saw Charles crumpled on the floor. Hugh checked Charles's pulse while she paced back and forth, cursing under her breath.

Mary Elizabeth wanted to hit him again. She didn't care if he was crazy. He'd hit her! She'd never been struck in her life. Who did he think he was? First, he calmly announced that he killed her sister. Then, despite how many times she told him she wouldn't marry him, the man goes and arranges their wedding, and was willing to kidnap her to make sure she fell in line. Then, he hit her, after calling her fat! The woman he supposedly loved. She wanted to kill him. It was all she could do to keep herself from going over there and kicking him until she broke a few ribs while he lay there unconscious. It was the least that he deserved.

Hugh walked over to the phone and made a call. "Rome, this is Hugh. I've got a situation over here. Attempted kidnapping. Perp's unconscious right now. I'll tie him up before he comes around." He listened for a moment and then said, "Right. The apartment above the diner. Door's open." He made short work of tying Charles up and then turned to his furious mate.

"Mary Elizabeth, I need for you to calm down."

She growled in reply.

"Honey, I know you're angry right now and you have every right to be, but I really need for you to get a hold of your temper and calm down."

She shook her head so hard she wobbled as she paced back and forth, citing all the things she'd been through. She wasn't calming down anytime in the foreseeable future.

Hugh took a deep breath, placed his hands on his hips and shook his head. "I want you to remember that I tried doing this the easy way. Mary Elizabeth, look at your hands."

Of all the stupidest things she'd ever heard in her life, this was the worst. Look at her hands! She knew what her hands looked like. The man hadn't seen her in days. He walked in on an attempted kidnapping and all he could say was calm down and look at your hands? She gave him a look that showed how stupid she thought his command was.

"I mean it, honey. Trust me. You need to look at your hands."

Giving a huff of aggravation, she did as he'd said and screamed in surprise. Her hands were gone. In their place were some big, hairy paws with lethal looking claws on the end. She followed the line of her paw up her arm as far as she could see.

Her arms were also covered in fur. Everything that she could see had thick, brown fur on it. Now that she was calmer, she realized she was still on all fours. She looked between her front legs at the rest of her body and saw that she had two in the back just like the front. She tried to get a good look at the rest of her body, only to give up when she spun around uselessly in circles.

She looked at Hugh with fear in her eyes. Unless she was mistaken, she was a bear. She didn't know how she got this way. More importantly, she didn't know how to change back.

"Take it easy. As soon as you calm down, you'll change back. It's strong emotion that brings on the Change. Take some deep breaths. Practice your yoga breathing."

He looked up as Rome and one of his deputies, a man by the name of Harris, walked through the door. Rome looked around at the evidence, and then gazed at Mary Elizabeth with interest. "I take it that's your mate? First Change?"

"Yeah, I'm trying to get her to calm down long enough to change back. She's got a hell of a temper and I'm sure that's what triggered the Change."

Mary Elizabeth sat down on her haunches abruptly. Now that the crisis was over, the adrenaline was leaving her body. Suddenly, she was too tired to be angry any more. She just wanted this whole day to be over. She felt a tingling in her spine and looked down to see her body changing. In a matter of seconds, she was back in her own skin. Her very bare, very naked skin. Where were her clothes?

Hugh stripped off his shirt and put it around her, before scooping her up in his arms. "We'll be in here when you need us," he said as he headed toward the bedroom.

Mary Elizabeth looked over his shoulder and saw shredded pieces of material on the floor of the living room. That explained the missing clothes.

Rome nodded as he directed Harris to put the unconscious prisoner in the patrol car. Then he pulled out a camera and began taking pictures while another deputy began collecting evidence. Having taken all the pictures he needed, he went to the room to get Mary Elizabeth's statement.

* * * *

Hugh laid her down on the bed gently and removed his shirt, running his hands over her body, checking for damage. She had a knot on the side of her head near her temple that was slowly healing before his eyes.

"Did that bastard touch you? If he did, he's a dead man."

"No, he hit me with the briefcase when I wouldn't go with him willingly."

"What!"

Right then, Rome knocked on the door. Hugh grabbed the covers and wrapped Mary Elizabeth in them before calling out for him to enter.

Rome came into the room with a small notebook in his hand. Mary Elizabeth looked him over with interest. This was the first time she'd seen a police force in the month she'd been living in Refuge. He was Latino, and a very handsome one at that. Instead of the usual police uniform, he was dressed in a pair of faded blue jeans and a black polo shirt with Refuge County Police Department monogrammed on the pocket in red. He pulled the police issued baseball cap off of his head and ran his hand through his mane of shiny, dark curls before sliding the cap back on his head.

"Are you okay to answer some questions? If not, you can come down to the station tomorrow and answer them. I know you've been through an ordeal."

"I'm fine. Let's just get this over with." She straightened up her drooping shoulders and wrapped the cover around her more securely, uncomfortably aware of her nakedness. Hugh sat down on the bed beside her and wrapped a comforting arm around her shoulders, silently offering his strength. She leaned into his warmth as she turned to Rome and asked, "What do you need to know?"

"Everything you can tell me, starting with who the unconscious gentleman in the front is. Just start from the beginning. Then, if I have any questions or need any clarification, I'll stop you and ask, okay? Be as detailed as possible."

She took a deep breath before starting. This was going to take awhile. "His name is Charles Remington and he's my brother-in-law." She felt Hugh tense beside her at the information, but he said nothing. "He was married to my sister Babs, who we buried a few weeks ago. Up until tonight, I thought she'd died as a result of a drunk driving accident."

Rome interrupted. "What happened tonight to make you think differently?"

"Charles confessed to killing her. I'm not sure how he managed it but he said that he was responsible for her death." Hugh's hands gripped tightened until she winced in pain. "Hugh, please, you're hurting me."

"Sorry." He loosed his grip.

"Okay, we'll come back to that later. So Charles is your brother-in-law. What's he doing here?"

This was the part she hated. It all sounded so sordid. "After the funeral, Charles came to see me. He was making noise about how he should have married me and how, now that Babs was dead, this was his opportunity to make things right. I figured it was the grief talking. I had already been offered the job here but hadn't decided yet. The incident with Charles, along with a few other things I won't go into, pushed me to say yes."

"That one piece of news just saved his life," Hugh said with a growl.

"Hugh," Rome said warningly. "Law present, in the room?"

Rome asked Mary Elizabeth to clarify. "Why did he say he should have married you? What made him think that you would be interested?"

"Charles and I were engaged when he met my sister." Mary Elizabeth thought that the less said on that subject, the better. Seeing how crazy Charles was, she realized she'd had a lucky escape. Instead of being angry with Babs when it happened, she should have been down on her knees, thanking her instead.

"So he married your sister instead, and now feels he made a mistake."

Mary Elizabeth nodded. "Babs was cheating on him. I didn't think he knew about it but I found out after her funeral that he did. That's why I think he's so fixated on me. He figured if he married me, I wouldn't have strayed. I told him he was seven years too late and I was no longer interested. Anyway, I came here. Charles used to call daily, asking me to come home. The last time he called, about two weeks ago, he referred to me as his fiancée." Turning to Hugh, she said, "That was the night of the party. I told him again that I wasn't marrying him, and that I was here to stay. That was the last I heard from him until he showed up tonight." Then she told him everything that happened from the time she walked in the door until Hugh arrived.

Hugh bristled and vibrated beside her during the telling, his anger a tangible thing. Once she was finished, Rome turned to Hugh and asked, "Do you have anything to add to this?"

"Yeah, Charles called again, only this time I answered the phone. He introduced himself as my mate's fiancé. I didn't tell him who I was but I did tell him she belonged to me. Then I hung up on him and disconnected the phone to keep him from calling back and disturbing Mary Elizabeth."

"So he was aware that there was a man in her life. It's probably what pushed him over the edge."

Mary Elizabeth shook her head. "I don't think it would have mattered. I thought he was just going through a difficult grieving process. I knew that my saying no to his proposal made him more determined to have me, but after tonight, I realized that the man's nuttier than my grandma's fruitcakes."

Hugh thought Mary Elizabeth was right. Charles was insane and from the sound of it, he had plenty of money to cover the signs of his illness. He could afford good legal representation. The kind that didn't care about guilt or innocence and did the job they were paid to do—get their client off. He and Rome shared a look that showed they were thinking the same thing. With a small nod, Rome indicated he would handle it.

Mary Elizabeth didn't notice. She was slumped against Hugh. Reaction was finally setting in. All she wanted to do was wrap herself around Hugh and celebrate being alive and with the man she loved. Things could have turned out so differently tonight. She was ready for everyone to leave so that they could be alone. This was so not the homecoming she'd envisioned.

Rome closed his notebook. "That's all I need for now. We'll be here a little longer gathering evidence, but from the looks of things, it collaborates with what you've told me. Charles has already been taken to the station. Hugh, bring Mary Elizabeth to the station tomorrow so she can sign her statement and press charges."

"What about Babs? Can you charge him with murder?" She really didn't want him to get away with killing her sister, but she knew things like that happened all the time, especially if you had enough money.

"I forgot about the sister. What can you tell me about the accident?"

"It was listed as a hit and run. Babs' car was totaled. The driver of the second vehicle was never found. The vehicle was listed as stolen and there were open containers and the strong smell of alcohol inside. Babs bled out on the way to the hospital, never having gained consciousness."

"It sounds like your brother-in-law covered his tracks well. Even if he confessed, there's probably not enough evidence to get a conviction."

"Yeah, that's what I figured. So he'll get away with it after all." The thought was depressing, and a little frightening. She hoped they could make these charges stick. She didn't want to be looking over her shoulder for the rest of her life. Right now Charles was obsessed with her. What happens if he decided that if he couldn't have her, nobody would?

Rome told Hugh he'd talk to him later and then left Hugh to comfort his mate. As soon as the door closed, Mary Elizabeth came out of the covers and climbed into Hugh's lap. She wrapped her arms around him and held him tight. "I missed you so much. When I first saw Charles, I was so mad at him for messing up my surprise. That's before I realized how crazy he was."

"Don't you ever leave me again," he said sternly.

She ran her fingers through his hair before cradling his face with her hands. "I'm sorry. It won't happen again. I just needed time to get my head straight. To figure out what I wanted."

"And have you figured things out?" His look was very intent, as though he could see right into her soul. Maybe he could.

"Yes, I want you. Whatever that means. Whatever it takes. You've crawled into my soul and now I can't imagine my life without you in it."

"It's called love and I feel the same way about you." He went to say more but she kissed him to silence.

"Later. I have several days of abstinence to make up for."

His eyes glowed as he recognized his words from earlier being spoken back to him. He lowered his mouth to hers. She was right. They could talk later. Much, much later.

From the sounds coming from the room, it didn't take any investigative skills on his part to know what was going on in there. Rome ushered his deputy out of the apartment. Anything they needed and didn't already have would have to wait until later.

He walked out of the apartment and locked the door behind him with a sad smile on his face. He was glad Hugh's mate was safe and sound, in his arms where she belonged. It was his job to make sure she stayed that way. He'd give anything to be able to hold his mate in his arms again. Now that he'd finally found her, he was working on a plan to bring her back to Refuge where she belonged. Once she was here, he'd never let her go again.

Chapter Twenty-One

In the station's only questioning room, Rome looked at the man seated across from him in disgust. Mr. Charles Remington the Third was as arrogant as his name sounded. It was evident from his behavior that the man considered them to be nothing more than a backward bunch of hillbillies. For now, it suited his purpose to play down to his image of them.

He looked down at the paperwork in front of him and straightened it slightly on the table, in pretended nervousness. "There are some discrepancies between your statement and those of the other two, but since Ms. Brown is unwilling to press charges, I have no choice but to let you go, on the condition that you leave town immediately. Ms. Brown has expressed her desire to be left alone. Any further attempt on your part to see or contact her in any way will be seen by this department as harassment, and a restraining order will be issued against you, with or without her consent. Since both you and Ms. Brown are sporting bruises, this will officially go on record as a domestic dispute." Rome glanced up, then quickly looked down at the table again.

"Once your statement has been signed, your belongings will be released to you. I strongly advise you to leave town now. Do not stop for any reason. To make sure you don't run into any problems, one of my deputies will follow you to the county line." Rome slid the paperwork across the table.

Charles smiled triumphantly as he signed his

236

statement, not bothering to read it to make sure it was correct. He now knew for sure that Mary Elizabeth loved him. She'd refused to press charges against him, not that it would have mattered if she did. They both knew that he'd done nothing wrong. Had these yokels tried to detain him, he'd have had his team of lawyers swarming all over them before they knew what hit them.

As for Mary Elizabeth, he still wasn't clear on what happened. He'd been told that the big guy had come in after Mary Elizabeth ran into his briefcase. He'd thought that she was being attacked and had done what any man would do under the circumstances—protected her by striking back.

He packed a hell of a punch. Charles's last clear memory was of standing over Mary Elizabeth informing her of their wedding. Which reminded him, he still had a bride to collect. He'd play along for now. Leave as they instructed, but double back. Nothing and no one was going to keep him from the woman he loved.

Later at the front desk, when the sheriff handed him his keys, he gave a friendly warning. "We found your van and parked it in the side parking lot. If I were you, I'd take it to a mechanic and get it checked out. It seemed to pull a little to the right while I was driving it. Oh, and be careful of the wildlife, especially on the roads at night. They tend to come out of nowhere with all of the woods around here. With the curves in the road, sometimes you're on one before you realize it. Drive carefully. We wouldn't want you to have to return for any reason. Stay within the posted speed limits and you should be okay. Deputy Harris here will make sure you make it to the county line in one piece." Deputy Harris tipped his hat to Charles, and then went out to his cruiser to wait.

Charles gave the sheriff a look of scorn as he took his belongings. Checking to make sure everything was there, he noticed his gun was missing. "Where is my gun?"

"Deputy Harris has it. He'll return it to you once you reach the county line."

Knowing there was nothing he could do about it at the moment, Charles took his things and left. They hadn't heard the last from him. As soon as he had Mary Elizabeth safely home, he'd slap a lawsuit on this town so large he'd own it. Smiling at the thought, he walked out and got in the van.

As instructed, he checked it out carefully. Everything appeared to be just as he left it. Starting the van, he strapped on his seatbelt. He wouldn't put it past them to give him a ticket for not wearing one. He turned onto the main road leading out of town. As promised, Deputy Harris was right behind him.

Once he cleared the main part of town, he picked up speed as the posted speed limit increased. The mountainous road was dark and curvy, downhill all the way. Several times he tapped his breaks to slow his speed, as the grade of the road caused his vehicle to roll faster and faster.

Steering became harder and harder as the power steering seemed to fail. He was using more and more muscle to steer into and out of the sharp curves. His brakes felt funny, too. They'd been fine at first, but the longer he drove, the mushier the pedal felt and it was taking the van longer and longer to slow in response to his foot on the brake pedal.

The suspicion that someone tampered with his brakes had just crossed his mind when something large and furry darted out into the road in front of him. Thinking it was a deer, he instinctively jerked hard on the wheel to avoid hitting it. The last thought to cross his mind right before the world went topsy-turvy was, 'That was the biggest damn wolf I've ever seen.'

Because he'd been heading into a sharp curve at the time, his action caused the van to overbalance and flip.

His seatbelt popped loose as the van flipped several times before slamming into the trunk of a huge oak tree. The impact of the crash caused the van to crumple like an accordion.

Deputy Harris, who was several feet behind him when the accident occurred, slowed the police cruiser before coming to a stop beside the wolf sitting on his haunches in the middle of the road. As he opened the door and got out, the wolf shape-shifted to reveal Deputy Wilson standing there in all his naked glory. He casually walked over to the cruiser to collect his clothes from the passenger side of the car while Deputy Harris went to check on the accident victim.

After looking things over carefully, he radioed back to headquarters. "Boss, you'd better send the coroner. Mr. Remington done had himself an accident. Seems he was driving too fast down the mountain and swerved to avoid the local wildlife. Saw the whole thing with my own eyes."

"Some people just don't listen. I warned him to be careful, drive slow and watch out for the wildlife. Oh well, I'll wait until morning to inform the next of kin. No sense waking up any more people than we have to at this hour of the night." Rome signed off the radio with a smile of satisfaction on his face. *Yes, siree, some folks just don't listen.*

* * * *

Hugh told Mary Elizabeth about Charles's death late the next morning, when she finally awakened. She thought it highly suspicious but inside was deeply relieved that the threat of Charles was effectively removed from her life. It was poetic justice, Charles dying in a manner similar to the method he used to take Babs' life. She decided to wait before calling her parents to give them the bad news. She was cowardly, hoping that someone else would tell them first.

Somewhere in between all the loving, she and Hugh had talked, working out all the kinks in their relationship and making plans for their future together. They'd held nothing back, each of them secure in the strength of their bond and growing love for one another.

It was going to take some time before she adjusted to being loved by Hugh. Hugh said he was okay with that. To him it just meant that she'd never take his love for her for granted. He also said he'd be thanking the Creator every day of his life for blessing him by giving him Mary Elizabeth for a mate. And, she thought to herself, she really couldn't ask for more than that. Life, after all this time, was finally good.

Epilogue

Nikolai Taranosky stood at the edge of the ridge overlooking the river, his dark hair blowing in the wind, the light of a half-moon shining down around him. In a few more days, the moon would be full, and then it would be time to claim his mate. He'd been unable to get close to her since the night of their initial blood exchange. Soon, he wouldn't have to sneak into her dwelling at night. She would come to him. He had a few more days to prepare. Then nothing, and no one would stand in his way.

About the Author

Zena Wynn is a multi-published author of erotic romance, and the author of *Illicit Attraction* and *The Contract*, also with Phaze Books.

LaVergne, TN USA
12 January 2010
169797LV00001B/23/P